The Tell-Tale Heart

THE TELL-TALE HEART

Jill Dawson

SCEPTRE

First published in Great Britain in 2014 by Sceptre
An imprint of Hodder & Stoughton
An Hachette UK company

1

Copyright © Jill Dawson 2014

A CIP catalogue record for this title is available from the British Library

Hardback ISBN 9781444731064

Typeset by Hewer Text UK Ltd, Edinburgh
Printed and bound by Clays Ltd, St Ives plc

Hodder & Stoughton policy is to use papers that are natural, renewable
and recyclable products and made from wood grown in sustainable
forests. The logging and manufacturing processes are expected to
conform to the environmental regulations of the country of origin.

Hodder & Stoughton Ltd
338 Euston Road
London NW1 3BH

www.sceptrebooks.com

for Meredith

simply the best

I sleep, but my heart waketh.

Song of Solomon 5:2

Part One

Helen looms into view as I come round. It might be days since the operation. I'm no longer in ICU but somewhere else, who knows, perhaps a private room. Helen, in all her loveliness, sailing towards me. It takes me a moment to realise that she is fifty years old and no longer my wife. The room is grey and deathly. I could be in the mortuary but no, dear God, here's Helen gliding in – what a trouper! – Helen in a glorious splash of colour, cheeks glowing. It's almost unbearable, the aliveness, the brightness, the sweetness of Helen – the shining chestnut of her hair, the eye-pricking green of her jumper. She is holding something out to me and moving her mouth; perhaps she's talking.

When I make no reply she pulls things out of her bag. I can't easily turn my head so I try to indicate interest – gratitude – with my eyes. I'm hooked up to an IV. They told me that when I woke up I would find an endotracheal breathing tube taped to my windpipe and that I would not be able to speak. The tube is connected to a respirator, doing my breathing for me; Helen is doing my talking. Oh and now, just to complete the arrangement, someone else's heart is pumping the blood through my veins. Story of your life, Helen would no doubt say.

Helen shows me the gifts – a welter of colours. A can of Lilt and a packet of flower seeds. And a hospital leaflet: *Your Recovery After Beating-Heart Surgery. Looking after Your New Heart: A Guide for Patients and Carers.*

Ha. We both know that'll go in the bin.

'Sorry about the Lilt,' she says. 'Hospital gift shop. Unless you want a ghastly sweatshirt with a Papworth Hospital Trust logo. And these—'

'These': a packet of seeds called heartsease. *Giant Fancy Mix. Pansy seeds to brighten your garden.*

Helen gazes at the small red packet, presumably looking for the apostrophe.

'Ah. I've just read the packet. You have to sow them Feb to April. Next year. But that's nice, isn't it? You know. Next year.'

She puts them on top of the grey cabinet next to the bed.

Helen. Bloody good of her to come. Hadn't seen her for a few months, before all of this. And yes, I get the implication. Now I have a *next year*. I put my hand up and touch my throat as if I'd like to say something. Perhaps there are tears in my eyes. Helen glances around. Seems to be wondering whether a nurse will come and tell her what to say next. As one doesn't, she sits down anyway beside the bed, turns her gaze towards me: a headlamp flashing onto full beam. I close my eyes and squeeze hard; I don't want to seem rude, Helen, but you're almost too much for me. Too alive. Too sparkly.

'Bit like a golf club, this hospital somehow, isn't it?' she says, as if in answer to a comment of mine. 'All those lawns.'

She is fidgety. Gets up, shifts *Transplant News* magazine from the bottom of the bed to beside the leaflet at the top of my metal bedside cabinet. Sits down again.

'Glorious weather for October, though. Glorious. It's like *The Truman Show* or something, you know? There are fires. Smoke in the sky. On the way here, I mean. Something on the news about fires near Ely. Stacks of straw. There's black smoke over the roads. I don't know, maybe it's the weather. Too hot for autumn really, isn't it? It's not right. There was even an old couple on the grass picnicking. You know, deckchairs and a flask and everything.'

Between her pauses the room is deathly quiet. Soundproofed perhaps. Muffled. I could indeed be in my coffin, lying in padded grey silk. Perhaps I hear a TV murmuring some-where. Hushed voices. Trolley wheels, the soft hum of machinery. I have a sudden tiny image of myself, lying in the operating theatre, my chest sprung open like a birdcage, with the door wide and the bird flown. Robbed. Like Thomas Hardy; wasn't he, horribly, buried without his heart? Some dim memory of a story about a biscuit tin. The dog eating the heart, which had been kept in a biscuit tin, and Hardy's friends having to bury someone else's heart. Body and soul separated.

'How long do you have to be here for?' she asks. Her eyes stray towards my throat, to the tube there and somehow down to my chest, the grey, sprig-patterned hospital gown, as if reading my mind.

I daren't put my hand there. *Like a letter lifted from an envelope, something else slipped in its place.* I haven't yet checked the wound. I try not to look when they come to dress it. So many wires and bindings; I feel like a mummy. I swallow, trying to wet my throat; a searing dry pain is there. Helen shakes her head gently as if to say: no, don't struggle, it's fine. I'll do it. I'll talk, make everything OK for both of us, isn't that what I'm good at?

'Nice to have a private room. You're lucky. We have a perfectly *wonderful* NHS, but then again . . . At least you're not taking up space in the general ward, stealing a place away from somebody else. This nice chap let me off with the park-ing. It was two pounds fifty and I only had two pound coins and he said, oh well, tell me which is your car and I'll cut you some slack! You wouldn't get that in London, eh?'

We're interrupted then. Helen falls silent while the male nurse comes to take my blood pressure and ask if I want the bed raising. I can't shake my head so I shake my hand and he takes this as a no. Nurse Adam. He looks awkward. He glances at Helen and puts his hand to his own throat and says:

'You know about infection, of course. That's the main thing. He's on very heavy immunosuppressants. Even a cold, a common cold . . .'

Helen gives him such a brilliantly withering look that, if I could, I'd chuckle.

'I know that,' she says. 'I don't have a cold.'

Nurse Adam nods and leaves. Helen waits pointedly for the door to close again and then leans in close. She bites her lip and puts a hand out, patting the sheet where my arm must be.

'I got a bit lost coming here. You know me. And I saw the sign. Mortuary. Chapel of Rest. I thought: That must be where *he* is. If it is a he. I suppose it could be a woman. Did they tell you? Is it all a bit hush-hush?'

I want to lick my lips, crackly with lack of moisture, but my tongue won't move.

'When you're up and about you could go there, you know, Patrick. Pay your respects.'

I don't know what my eyes convey but Helen registers it.

'No, you're right. He – whoever's probably long gone. They'll be planning the funeral by now.' She pushes a curl of hair behind her ear. 'I wonder if the family knows. About you, I mean.'

She glances out through the glass in the door to the ward beyond, as if the family might be waiting there, ghouls all, ready to pounce and snatch back their gift. Nosy as ever, she darts forward to peer into the little cupboard next to the bed where folded trousers and shirt, my toothbrush and paste lie side by side in lonely bachelorhood. She shuts the cupboard door and smiles apologetically.

'It's odd, isn't it – no flowers. I thought hospitals were full of flowers. On the way here, there was this funny place called, I think it was, St Ives, like in Cornwall and there were these buckets of flowers, I can't remember what they are, must flower quite late, pinks, is it? – anyway, they were outside a house. And pumpkins for Halloween. Carrots. Just 60p a bunch for the pinks. Isn't that nice? That they still do that round here? Money in a little tin and not worrying about getting it nicked. And I bet you'll never plant these.'

She flaps the heartsease disdainfully.

'It was sudden, wasn't it?'

The word 'harvest' floats into my head. They used to say that they *harvest* the organs; I don't know why. And it's October, it's harvest time. Safely gathered in.

'All those tests. I thought you'd be on the waiting list for ages. That's what Alice said. Poor Alice. She was so worried about you. And then – well, she rang me Monday night in hysterics, said you'd gone in, you'd got the call, all so suddenly, an ambulance, you were at Papworth.'

She's biting her lip. 'Some people wait for years, Patrick. Some people never find a – they must have rung you Monday, yes? That must be when he – when they heard. . . . He, she, they must have carried a card. You're lucky, you know.'

God knows what drugs are coming through that IV. Though I see her mouth is moving I can hardly concentrate on Helen's words. The most powerful hallucinations are forming and fading in front of me, random words floating, and pictures. Roadkill. Squirrels squashed on the side of the road. Blood, a fox's tail, mostly flattened. A heart bouncing alone, like a yo-yo with no string, into a river.

'I asked him. The doctor. The Scottish one. The ugly one with the beer gut? Yeah. He said it all went well. That it's only the third time they've done it that way. Beating-heart surgery, it's called. Weird, isn't it? You'll be here for a while. Don't worry, we'll visit . . .'

Don't go. Don't go yet. Keep talking.

'Alice will come tomorrow. I'm taking her stuff up to Cambridge this weekend but she'll come tomorrow and maybe Friday too. I don't know about Ben. Might be a bit much to ask of Ben. Is there anything you want Alice to bring you? You know, more cans of Lilt?'

Oh, Helen. What's wrong with me? 'Thy hyacinth hair, thy classic face.' You look so lovely to me, so lovely with your freckles and your habit of fiddling with that necklace and your eyebrows that almost knit in the middle and make you look like you're frowning when only I know you're not, you're not frowning at all! You're *concentrating*. Any minute now, no matter how serious your face might look to others, to colleagues perhaps or those you meet in court, no matter what they might think, *only I know* that any minute you could burst into loud giggles, that giggling is never far away for you, is it, such ease, the way you bubble up sometimes, how irrepressible you turned out to be . . . Helen. Oh my God. I feel an ache in my chest, a pain so severe it's like something is thrashing there, like a wire when you accidentally step on one end of it, whipping up at the other end. My hand wants to fly to the pad of bandages at my chest, but I refuse to let it. Is it a real feeling? Is it a physical one?

'You have a fully functioning, healthy heart now. Look after it.' Did some consultant doing his rounds actually say that to me, or am I imagining it? Patronising git. Like my old one was . . . Well, I suppose I was ill, OK, he has a point, but I don't like his phrase: fully functioning. It's damning, somehow. Like the bastard is saying I wasn't *fully functioning* before.

'It's sort of creepy, though, isn't it,' Helen says, not meeting my eyes.

She's twiddling the buttons on her black jacket, the smart professional woman's jacket she took off earlier and draped over the back of her chair. Now she has it across her lap and is fiddling, one by one, with each button; twirling it. Her fidgets always irritated me. Now I'm transfixed.

'The beating-heartness of it all, I mean, like a live animal or something? I can see the point, of course, can't you? That they can keep it viable, you know, that if there's no need to pack it in ice you get a bit longer, allow them time to transport it . . .'

Her voice trails off.

'I hope the roads are cleared by now. Those fire engines. I have to be in court by three.'

She stops fiddling with the buttons and decides to put the jacket back on.

'Well, I hope you feel better soon. So they didn't – did they – do they – you know, tell you anything about the donor?'

I give a tiny shake of my head. She smiles then; that shake was my first proper reply. She nods and stands up.

'Patrick. I do have to go now. I'm so sorry, love. I'm due back in court.'

Love. The Yorkshire term of endearment she can never quite stop herself using, even when she most patently doesn't mean it. I watch her, watch the way her breasts jut out as she slips her arms into the black jacket. I think for the first time of what is under there. Under the black linen, the green jumper. Under her bra, under the lace and flesh of her, under the white freckled skin, the fine curved ribs. When you peel it all back. I see it for the first and only time and it's a shock. What is it like? I know very well: I saw mine here on a screen. From a distance it looked like a baby alien, a sort of ET with a giant, all-seeing eye, moving, pumping, grimacing at me. The colours

9

were all wrong too: livid purple and gold. That was before they explained it. The superior vena cava. The right atrium. The large aorta. The pulmonary artery, the mitral valve. I know, I know. I was married to her for sixteen years. It's beautiful. It's red in tooth and claw. It's alive.

She closes the door behind her. Through the glass I watch her move into the ward beyond. Her upright shape, the backs of her heels, her splendid posture: all those years of wrenching her shoulders back manfully, putting up with me, *shouldering*. She pulls and pushes the ward door before managing to figure out the huge button on the wall that releases it, and looks back through the window at me to give a rueful smile over her shoulder, as if we both expected this.

A drumming starts up in my temples: tears threatening. For God's sake, what on earth is wrong with me? I rub my eyes, hard. I don't think I've cried since 1984. Just my luck: must have been a weeper, my donor.

A ridiculous thought. Everything tumbles and crowds me: a sick feeling sweeps through me. My back prickles cold with sweat. God, I hope I'm not about to throw up.

Helen didn't kiss me when she left. There was only one, very small moment when I wanted to tell her about my unseemly, unmanly outburst of the night of the operation, how I wasn't calm or prepared; fuck, I wasn't even barely competent or adult. I wanted to ask her if any of the staff had mentioned it to her – that Scottish doctor, he must have mentioned it, surely? I wanted to be honest to someone, to fess up, be reassured. I was shit-scared. That's what I was. Practically blubbing. The space between being told: *your heart failure is now so advanced that you won't live another six months* and *yes, we've found a donor, we can go ahead and operate* – barely the space of eight weeks, hardly time to function, let alone ready myself. And in the middle of that, at

10

work, came the letter, the accusation and the pending investigation . . . Then, as if that wasn't enough, beating-heart surgery is new, there is an increased risk. Only the third time it's been done that way.

In the middle of all this – I mean, in the middle of the operation – I suddenly saw a bird. In the hospital. Fluttering above my bed, wings outspread, beating heroically to master a strong wind. A kestrel. Only it wasn't in the hospital and neither was I. I was on a long grey road, flat as a ribbon laid along a landscape, a road like a runway, leading directly to the sky. And in that white sky, a lone kestrel.

And if it's not a hallucination then it's a memory: the green masks of the operating theatre, the scrub-nurse just before, shaving my chest; the strange underwater lighting, their eyes all peering at me, above the masks, the soft swish of green curtains sweeping closed around my bed. Going under, deeper.

There was a moment when I was cracked open on that bed, emptied. Rigged up, machines doing my living for me. Awaiting. My heart lifted out and somewhere else. I shouldn't be alive; I must be monstrous, or magical. No human being can have their heart scooped out of their ribcage, be without it, while they await another, and live, can they? It's inconceivable.

Nurse Adam, the morning of the operation: *This will be your life now. Four different pills to take.* The itch of the stubble on my chest, wanting to return. The staples in my chest.

And then that other moment: in the green watery theatre, that object they wheeled in, smouldering like a witches' cauldron, with something steaming and sputtering inside it. I didn't see it, of course, I was anaesthetised by then. But in another way, I remember it perfectly. That cauldron held my donor's organ. Littleport, I heard the scrub-nurse say earlier in ICU. That's all I knew. The ambulance was bringing my heart from Littleport.

This is my only clue. Later, on my BlackBerry, I Google it. *Littleport: the largest village in East Cambridgeshire, six miles north of Ely. Probably takes its name from the Latin word portus, meaning a landing place. Was once an island, before the Fens were drained, surrounded on all sides by fens (fields), meres (lakes) and marshes. Famous for the Littleport riots of 1816.*

No man is an island. Littleport was. I am now. A strange man, unlike any other. I'm a burglar, carrying off the heart of someone else, one that doesn't belong to me. I'd like to go back to my old self, to my old life, but I have a curious, powerful certainty: my old self won't have me.

This morning I had my first heart biopsy: the best way to detect rejection, I'm told. Snipping a little piece of the new organ *so soon*? Then a chest X-ray. Then an ECG. I get to see my new heart on the monitor. That freaks me. There it is. The right ventricle and the left ventricle are pointed out to me. 'Look how pretty your new heart is,' says Dr Burns. He's grinning like a madman. It's been champagne and newspaper reporters for him since the surgery, and Helen's right: he is an ugly bastard. I'm scratchy with lack of sleep but exhausted with a weariness beyond anything I've ever felt. Dr Burns tells me that two journalists from the local newspaper are here again and whenever I'm ready they'd love to talk to 'Papworth Hospital's Third Successful Beating-Heart Transplant Survivor'. I ask Burns for a Zopiclone and he says he doesn't believe in sleeping tablets.

'I don't believe in heart transplants!' I shout after his departing back. My voice barely rises above a croak.

A different nurse, a young Asian woman with a lisp, comes to tell me that a 'deep dithspair' is very normal after major

12

heart surgery. Indeed, after any major operation or 'near-death exthperience'. I stare at the little mouth while she's speaking and ponder that strange phrase and how readily people use it. *Near-death experience*. She's not the one whose diseased heart is lying lonesome and abandoned in a hospital bin somewhere.

She's taken pity on me and got another doctor to prescribe Valium. I want to sleep, but, I tell her, I need it to be dreamless.

My second visitor is the transplant co-ordinator. Cheery, cute little woman I've already had far too many dealings with, called Maureen. She sits beside me, knitting. She has the hair texture of a Jack Russell terrier and she's small for a grown woman, more the size of a leprechaun. Maureen says I can write to the 'donor family' if I want. My throat doesn't feel as bad today. I grunt. I can form words again but I see no point in wasting effort on talking to a midget. She's not allowed to reveal details of the family, she says, unless they permit it, and we must respect their privacy at this 'tragic time', but I could write to them and she would forward the letter, without revealing to me their address.

'I could show you a sample letter, if you like,' she continues, undeterred. 'You know, an example of what kind of thing to write.'

'I'm on the AHRC Research Council for American Studies. I think I could write a short letter without help, thank you.'

She giggles. After a pause she looks up from her knitting.

'Remember those forms you filled out – psychiatric evaluations to see how you would fare after surgery on this scale? I remember you came out feisty enough!'

'Feisty. That's a woman's word.'

'Yes, it's funny, that. How we say it about women more than men.'

13

'It's from the German. A little dog. Touchy and quarrel-some, over-sensitive. It's hardly a compliment.'

'Is that so?' The needles clack while her diminutive brain seems to contemplate this. 'Overly sensitive? Men. That's right. They're easy to wound, in my experience. Needy. I think women are stronger, emotionally.'

I'm about to reply to this ridiculous generalisation but I spy the glorious figure of Alice through the glass door to my room and Maureen follows my eyes and hastily stands up, stuffing the knitting into her bag.

'That must be your daughter. What a lovely-looking girl!' Maureen reminds me to take my pills and sweeps out, nodding to Alice as their paths cross in the doorway.

I think at first that Alice is simply standing there, wringing her hands in an old-fashioned way; then I realise that there's some obligatory hand-washing lotion for visitors and Alice is obediently disinfecting herself. She bursts into my room, tries to hug me, stands back in horror at the sight of me and then starts blubbing. I immediately find my own eyes filling with tears. Then we laugh, glancing at each other, and she offers me a tissue.

She looks beautiful: her usual get-up of some girly kind of skirt or dress and clod-hopping Doc Marten boots, masses of black eye make-up (now all over her face) and bouffant blonde hair, like a young Brigitte Bardot. The pain on staring at her – pain, did I say? But it's joy surely – the pleasure, the delight, it's like a pinching, a twisting in my chest: it does actually hurt. My heart seems to be responding, racing, it's definitely beating faster as I gaze at her. It's working, then? Such a strange, delirious thought: the new organ responding to *my* feelings.

'Oh, Dad!' Alice says, plonking herself into the chair beside my bed and succumbing to another bout of weeping and sniffing. 'You look really young and pathetic in that nightie!' she adds.

'Marvellous. I must wear a fetching hospital gown more often.'

Unlike Helen, she's brought useful things. She's been to my flat in Highgate and got my laptop. She's bought me pyjamas and a nice pair, too, with a T-shirt instead of a shirt, not the old-man, button-up kind. Socks: warm, cashmere, the right size.

'Come on now, poppet, what's all this crying about?' I say, when she doesn't seem to be able to stop. 'Look, I'm fine! I'm here. It's all been fine.'

'Did you know I was here, all the while they did it? I slept in the waiting room. They kept giving me updates but I never knew if they told you I was there. I had to go back to Cambridge afterwards so I didn't get to see you when you first woke up.'

This takes a minute to sink in. Alice, who once accused me of being the World's Most Self-Centred Dad and having No Fucking Interest Whatsoever in her life, and failing to keep *one single* appointment that Helen organised with the school about her GCSEs, A levels or university choices . . . Alice, bothering to come to the hospital and keep me company – though I didn't know it – while I was having the operation. I don't know what to say. I can't even meet her eyes.

After a while, minutes perhaps, I stretch out my arms to indicate to Alice that she's to hug me carefully, not to touch my chest, to mind the IV and the wires. We manage an awkward embrace and she pulls away, smiling at last. Her little-girl face with her big blackened eyes and her upturned nose.

'I did think . . .' She's dabbing at her eyes with a shredded tissue but not making much impact on the huge smudges of war-paint. 'Well, you'd been so ill. And then there was – you know. The strain. All that trouble. And the doctors told me it was – well, you know. Not everyone . . . some people reject it.'

'So far so good, poppet.'

I tap my chest, trying to sound upbeat; trying to sound like a confident, reassuring father.

'Mum said . . . she said you looked terrible.'

'Charming! She looked very pretty, I thought. Has she lost weight?'

'Dad! I don't think so. She's probably been worried about you. We all thought – God, I really thought . . .'

She bursts into tears again and the sobbing is long, and goes on some time. I tell her to find my clean handkerchief in my folded trouser pocket, in my locker, which she does, and starts to calm down.

The discovery that Helen has been worrying about me is equally astonishing. We've had telephone conversations, yes, and I suppose I had told her about the deterioration of my heart and that the chances of a transplant coming along were slim, but she had simply told me that my self-pitying was getting tiresome and now that we were no longer married she didn't have to listen to it, and I'd taken her at her word.

'Who was that woman?' Alice asks, once she's composed.

'What, the knitting one? The woman with the haircut like an eighties feminist?'

She smiles; nods. 'Yes. Is she a friend of yours?'

'Jeez, Maureen? I don't think she's my type, do you?'

Alice grins. 'Well, she's pretty! Petite. But, I guess: no. Your type is more – you know. You like them to look like – an achievement.'

'Cheeky! Anyway. Maureen. The teeny tiny transplant co-ordinator. She'd come to tell me about the donor family.'

Alice's eyes widen. There's a big blob of black eye-stuff on her cheek that I'd like to wipe away for her.

'What about them? Who was it, do you know?'

'No. She can't tell me that. Confidentiality, I suppose. But . . . I have a hunch. I think it must have been a woman.'

'Can that happen? I mean, does – the sex of the donor matter?'

'Apparently not. You can have a woman's heart. Or a woman can be transplanted with the heart of a man. The heart is an organ with no gender.'

'Amazeballs.'

'Quite.'

'Why do you think that, then, what makes you sure your donor is a woman?'

'Well, I fear my IQ has dropped.'

'Dad! Seriously.' Alice laughs and the black blob of make-up falls from her cheek.

'Now I have the heart of a weak and feeble woman . . .'

'Isn't it, "I may have the *body* of a weak and feeble woman but I have the heart of a *King*"?'

'So it is. It's just that—'

I stop and consider. I find I can't continue.

Alice leans forward: 'Do you feel, like, really weird? Having it inside you?'

'No. No, of course not. I feel – fine.'

'You don't look *fine*.'

'Well, I know I could do with a shave.'

'No, it's not that. You look weird. Odd to me. Different.'

'Well, poppet. You haven't seen me in a while. And I have just had major surgery. I expect I'm not looking my best.'

I smile but close my eyes. The effort, the unaccustomed effort of talking like this to my daughter, leaves me breathless. I lean back onto the pillow.

'Dad, am I tiring you out? Is it too much? I can come back early next week—'

I try to sit up properly; I'm slumping. Some backbone would help me.

'You know how I used to joke that your mother had three thousand six hundred and twenty-two feelings and I had the requisite five basic ones which have an evolutionary purpose? Because, quite frankly, most of the time I didn't know what the bloody hell she was on about? Well, since coming round from surgery I'm finding myself having others, another . . . perhaps the sixth emotion.'

'What's the sixth?'

'Surprise.'

'Surprise? Is that an emotion then? Separate from these five basic ones you're on about?'

'Yes. Happiness, anxiety, sadness, anger and disgust. It's none of those. So it might be . . . wonder. Perhaps wonder. Which is, arguably, an aspect of happiness, so not in fact new.'

'Yes. That's OK then. Phew. Not a new one at all, just a variation on a theme?'

'Still. It's irksome. I don't know what to do with this new feeling. Or feelings.'

'But Dad. There's nothing to *do* with feelings, is there? You just feel them.'

This sentence sits between us.

'Ah,' I say, eventually. 'And there's me thinking I had to intellectualise about them.'

She smiles. 'Maybe it was a brain transplant you needed after all?'

I sit up, trying to shift the mood back to the familiar one, the old one. Me joking and batting away, Alice expressing things in Technicolor, rich enough for both of us. 'I am on heavy medication of course,' I say. 'Might account for my new-found eloquence on the subject of emotions.'

'You're funny.' She tries to ruffle my hair and goes instead for a kiss on the cheek. Both are painful, but not unwelcome.

I'm exhausted. My hand strays to my chest and I see Alice notice this.

'Does it hurt then? Do you feel, like, weird there?'

'You've asked me that. No, no, honestly, it's fine.'

I tap the bandages through the hospital gown. I know that I have a scar on my chest, described by Burns as 'single longitudinal sternal splitting' but I haven't examined it. With the various wires and drains in me, I think again of aliens. Yes, an alien creature is right, because who on this earth who is human carries a heart inside him that belongs to someone else?

I try a different tack. 'You know when I was about nine I went on this big trip to London, went to the Science Museum, my mother took me. And they had this giant pumping model heart. Bright red and blue. A plastic model. Do they still have that? Have you seen it?'

Alice shakes her head.

'Jeez, I hated it. It was bigger than a shark and suspended, I think, loud and booming, this amplified beat. It was probably demonstrating Harvey's principles of circulation or something but I remember turning on my heel and running out, feeling sick. Cushie, my mother, was completely bewildered. What on earth was wrong with me? Scared by a *giant booming heart.*'

Alice grins at me. She's looking hugely reassured now that I'm talking nonsense and sitting up properly again.

'Why did your mum take you if it was scary?'

'Oh, I don't know. Part of her educational drive for me, I suppose. She wanted me to have a more rounded education, she said. She thought my school, my father too, I suppose she meant, was obsessed with my just passing exams and winning cups and *achieving* things.'

'Did you? Win things all the time?'

'Of course.'

'You never talk about your mum. I've never even seen a photo of her.'

'No? Cushie. *A big lass and a bonny lass and she likes her beer.* That was the song. Her real name was Constance, I don't know why she was always Cushie. You're lucky you didn't get it – Helen hated the name.'

I change the subject then, remembering to ask Alice about Cambridge. The joys and horrors of having to read Edmund Spenser's *The Faerie Queene.* Why it is that envy and other emotions are always depicted as female? Girton, and how it's more relaxed than the other colleges. Punting and the price of wine and whether you can get Weil's disease from swimming in the River Cam. The strange warm weather we're having.

At one point she flicks through *Transplant News* and asks breezily: 'So, when do you think you'll be back at uni, Dad?'

'Didn't your mum say? I've got a sabbatical. After that business – well, I don't have to face the hearing now. I don't have to go back until the autumn semester next year. I was so ill.'

Her eyes are on the magazine. I watch her for a moment and then find myself saying:

'Maybe I won't go back. Ever.'

The thought is delicious. An absolute shock, but thrilling.

'Huh?'

Alice's equally shocked expression gives me pause. Did I really just say that?

'Well, I just mean, I don't *have* to go back. There is the possibility of doing – other things.'

Alice stops flicking through *Transplant News* and darts me a look.

'What other things? What the – what would you *do* with yourself?'

'I don't know. You're right. Yes, of course. Though . . . maybe I could take early retirement. I don't know. It's just occurred to me.'

Alice puts the magazine down and gives me a frown exactly like one of Helen's.

'Maybe not a good idea to make, like, major decisions when you're in this – you know. Stage,' she says.

'When I'm not in control of all my faculties, you mean?'

She grins. 'OK, I'm not bossing you around! I just think it's a bit sudden, that's all. You *love* that job. You're like – obsessed with it. It's always been *everything* to you. That's all.'

'Right. I know. It just popped into my head. That I could, that's all I mean. Nothing's stopping me. And there's my book. I could work on my book.'

'Your book. What is it again?'

She stops talking, aware that a nurse has opened the door to my room and is hovering. It's Nurse Adam again, back on shift: powerful smell of Lynx aftershave and a florid spot on his forehead. He beams me a big smile; must have bad news. Alice stands up and picks up her denim jacket, which clanks noisily with its clash of brooches and badges and metal buttons.

'No, don't get up, Missy, a quick word with your father.'

She sits back down.

'I asked Dr Burns,' Nurse Adam says, in a confiding tone. 'Apparently the cavity around your heart is still big. The new heart has lots of space around it so the chest drains will have to do more work than usual. Sorry. So that means the big one has to stay. I'll take the small ICD drain out, that should make you more comfortable.'

21

Alice is biting her bottom lip, her eyes huge. I pat her hand. 'Don't worry, lots of space around my heart. I don't think that's bad.'

The nurse nods, busying himself around me and then turning slowly to give my daughter only a glancing look. (He must be gay.)

'Is that why you want your laptop? Looking for another job?' Alice asks, nodding towards it.

'Oh, I don't know. Just emails. Looking up stuff. Jeez, it's just boring here.'

'Read a book!'

She laughs. Touché. The times Helen said that to her, over many years, catching her on Facebook when she should be doing her homework, or was lying in bed texting on her mobile.

'Dad!'

Alice is staring at me, making me wonder what my face is doing.

'Mum said she'd come tomorrow. Visiting time is over, sorry.'

'I know. Marvellous! I'll be fine.' I hesitate, while a hive of bees inside my head hums incessantly.

'Is it just me or is that extractor really noisy?'

Alice agrees that it's noisy.

'And, you know, people keep talking to me and I can't quite hear them with that sound going on.'

She seems disappointed; was she expecting me to say something else?

She takes my hand before she leaves and kisses my cheek with a waft of some light girlish perfume: the exact smell of a wooden lolly stick, warm from the sun. That damned snake inside my chest uncoils and leaps as she does so; I feel it struggle inside its basket as her breath touches my cheek. Blackberry bushes. Sherbert pips, the smell of grass on school fields. I'm just so glad of you, I want to say. Or, what did I do to deserve you? Or, look at you, all grown up, the strength of you, the solid, sunlit, living thing that you are with all that hair and those big eyes and crashing noise and daft boots. Thank you. Thank God for you. And then an obvious thought, one I'm surprised I never had before. If only my mother could have met you and seen what I produced. Look, Cushie, see how I did something right: look at good and solid Alice.

And my eyelids are heavy and Alice is right, I'm very, *very* tired. I don't know when she leaves. I don't remember her going. Maybe I took a sleeping tablet.

And then, in the middle of the night, I suddenly wake up coughing. The ward is lit with a peculiar blue light and there's a high whine everywhere, like they are trying to scare off youngsters, or bats, with their sound warfare. And I see a couple of black dots on my hospital gown and wonder what they are, are they specks of blood? Alarm – there is a button on the wall by my hand. I reach for it, and then stop.

Is this it, then? Is this the moment my new organ fails and all that work, all those efforts, prove to be for nothing? I didn't choose to be here – who does? (I didn't *ask* to be born, I remember Alice screaming once in one of those flaming teen-age outbursts, and Helen standing her ground and shouting back: *you!* Don't give me that, you were kicking me from the day your first cell formed! You were *begging* to be born!)

I've made a cock-up for sure, an almighty cock-up, I'm fifty years old with one ex-wife and one ex-mistress and one daughter and one son I hardly see and one crappy job I no longer want and a case hanging over me and, God knows, nothing much to show for myself.

I am barely breathing, I stare into the room, willing my eyes to accustom to the strangeness of the light: the pale blue wall opposite, the square light switch, the pimpled vent above me on the ceiling with its collection of dusty fluff clinging to it. Do human ears prick up, like dogs'? My breath ruffles the sheets and seems to tear round the room in a sudden draught. Is there someone else here with me?

'Who's there?' I ask. Really, my heart – his heart – the damn organ is going ballistic. Racing, pounding. The hospital room emits its terrible whine.

I cough again, a great wrench at my throat and lungs. 'I know you're there,' I whisper. Show yourself.

When I was about ten, I had a religious phase when I prayed incessantly and under my breath in all situations. Dear God, please let me do well in the exam. Dear God, please let me score a goal. Dear God, please make me a good boy and help me to stop doing this. Dear God, please don't let Mam die. That was the point I stopped, of course. When I realised He wasn't listening to the mutterings of a boy in County Durham whose father was snoring on the sofa, still in his suit with the *Telegraph* over his face, and whose mother had suffered a car accident and lay on a life-support machine. I remember it now, though: prayer. The sense of quietly talking to myself and how comforting it was. Did I believe even back then that I was really talking directly to God, I wonder now?

I remember it like this: I knew that there were different parts of me. There were conscious thoughts like 'Twelve times ten is one hundred and twenty' and deeper, inchoate thoughts that I couldn't reach. And in praying I briefly heard these different selves quietly chatting to one another.

Another consciousness inside me. When Lucy was pregnant with Ben I went with her, one time and one time only, for an antenatal visit, and I watched them put that green slime on her belly and slide the sonar over her and we listened together to the baby's heartbeat, strong and loud in that room with us, amplified and strange in its watery home, marching inexplicably into my life. I thought of breathing, and deep-ocean sonar, and whales. I tried not to think of how I would keep the news from Helen, and of the impact of another baby, with another woman, on my life with my new wife.

'I knew weeks ago,' Lucy said, in the car as I drove her home, 'because I just had a feeling of another consciousness inside me.' That was the exact phrase she used. I had forgotten it until now.

I cup my hands over my ears. I reach for the switch on the lamp beside my bed, but I knock over a plastic cup on the table and feel the cold trickle of water under my palm. 'Are you trying to escape?' I whisper. Damn fool. The lamp casts a yellow glow and the room changes, reshapes.

I breathe in, quietly, softly, then more forcefully. I watch my chest rise and fall. It was a dream. That's right. That's all. I had a nightmare. That's why I woke up.

I'd been looking up Littleport on my laptop after Alice had gone, and the detail I remember was that five people in this village in Cambridgeshire were hanged in 1816 for rioting – it seems the only fact about Littleport worth noting in Wikipedia. A bad idea to read that just before falling asleep. The drugs make dreams loom with hallucinogenic vividness once I'm awake again.

And suddenly I am staring at a stage, but I know it isn't Graduation Day, that instead some terrible moment is poised to happen. Five nooses dangle. I know exactly who the nooses are for, know their names. *Say something*, a voice cries out. *Comfort them.* 'See you later!' I croak, peering into the shadowy stage, searching for a glimpse of the people waiting to be hanged. There is no one there. I am already too late. Only five nooses, swinging. Black shadows. My last words, the last thing they hear from me, the sum total of my offering: that one feeble phrase. See you later.

I put my hand up to the TV screen, angled on its movable metal arm above my bed, hoping to distract myself with that. Then I think better of it. A nurse slides past the glass door to my room; I see her shadow. I think of Alice again and the surprise discovery of her kindness in sleeping here at the hospital while my operation took place, and Helen's too, in visiting me. I picture both of them walking away down the ward. I always seem to be calling out something, some forgotten request. I hate to see women walking away from me. People I love. I want to see them turn around, force them to twist their chins over their shoulders, glance one last time at me. Not see you later, but goodbye. Kiss me again. *Come back early or never come.*

'I've brought you the *Cambridge Evening News*. It's a – it shouldn't happen. But I thought you'd better see it.'

Maureen's agitated. She takes the folded newspaper from her bag, and sighs. She seems reluctant to hand it over but she does; she has carefully marked the relevant page with a yellow sticker. Marked the page! What kind of person would do that? This Maureen must have time on her hands.

'The local press,' she says, crossly. 'There are protocols. It must have been that young journalist. It's really annoying, though.'

Doctors at Papworth have carried out another successful beating-heart transplant.

The recipient, a fifty-year-old Professor of American History from North London, who received his new heart three weeks ago at Papworth Hospital in Cambridgeshire, is said to be doing 'extremely well'.

The technique, used successfully twice before in the UK since 2006, involves keeping a donated heart warm and beating throughout the procedure, rather than packing it in ice for transport. The process gives doctors more time to get hearts to the recipient.

Donor hearts are normally given a high dose of potassium to stop them beating and are packed in ice, which helps to keep them in a state of 'suspended animation'.

But there is only a four-to-six-hour window for the organ to be transplanted into the recipient, which could be a problem if a heart becomes available in a remote area – many organs in the UK are transported by road. Under the new system, doctors hook the heart up to a machine that keeps it beating with warm oxygenated blood flowing through it.

This gives doctors time to examine the heart for any damage and the chance to better match the organ with a recipient.

The heart can be kept outside the body longer and reaches the transplant patient in much better condition. In this recent case, the donor was a sixteen-year-old youth, Andrew Beamish of Littleport. He died in a motorcycle accident, in a remote and rural part of the Fens.

'Ah.'

For a few moments I say nothing else. Then, 'Ah' again.

A sixteen-year-old youth. Andrew Beamish of Littleport. A motorcycle accident. A remote and rural part of the Fens. A buzz goes through me: a tiny electric shock.

'It's disastrous,' Maureen says, breathlessly. 'I don't know how they found out, the hospital doesn't release names, and there is usually an understanding in the media too. I've had to – I've been on the phone all morning. But I think it's fine for you to know now. It can't be avoided. And since it wasn't me who told you.'

A young boy. Younger than Alice. Younger than my son Ben.

I am very silent. Maureen puts the newspaper back in her bag and sits tentatively on the edge of the bed, careful to avoid my legs.

'It's American Studies actually,' I mutter, for something to say.

'Sorry?' Maureen says.

'My subject. Not just American History. Literature as well. Though it's the history bit that interests me. Custer.'

'Sorry?'

'General Custer and his last stand? The Battle of Little Bighorn?'

'Oh yes. I think I saw that. Was it a film?'

'Yes. There have been various – films.'

'Your wife not been in to see you today?'

'Helen?'

Can't be arsed to tell her we're divorced. Maureen wouldn't even tell me whose fucking organ is nestling in my chest. I sit up.

'So,' I mutter. 'A boy. Strange that I was convinced it was a woman's heart. And I did somehow know he was from the Fens – from Littleport. Is it near here then?'

'About an hour away. So you're very lucky. The family was able to make the decision quickly – Drew carried a donor card. Which was when you got the phone call—'

'Drew? You called him Drew?'

'A slip! Obviously I'm not supposed to tell you anything more. That's really – I'm sorry.'

'But can a sixteen-year-old carry a donor card? How is that legal?'

28

'Yes, any child can register with the Organ Donor Register. But a parent has to give consent of course, at the moment . . . when they're deciding.'

A remote and rural part of the Fens. A sixteen-year-old boy. *Drew.* A memory of Ben pops into my head; it must have been the last time I saw him, round at Lucy's flat in Stoke Newington. About fifteen, I guess. He was wearing a horrible oversized navy dressing gown that clearly belonged to a man, one of Lucy's boyfriends, no doubt. He'd just come out of the shower with his wet hair sticking up in tufts, and it was his long white legs, nearly six foot he was, already; it was his skinny ankles, the memory of those now, that make me want to cry. The bones fierce and fine like a delicate white cuttlefish.

'I have a son about that age,' I tell Maureen. She's watching my face closely. She takes her knitting out of her bag. New wool – yellow.

She nods. 'I saw his sister, remember, the other day.'

'Half-sister. Different mothers. I don't see Ben much.'

Maureen nods again, a polite nod, she's clearly uninterested. Two children by different women is hardly remarkable. Trying to give a stranger even the briefest glimpse of the *carnage* that this simple fact of my two children, two women, concurrently, contains.

Lucy told me Ben has a serious dope-smoking habit these days. He didn't stay on to the sixth form, though it was obvious he was clever enough. He wanted to get a job and save up for a car but in fact that didn't happen. She was hinting, as she always bloody was. Could I help with driving lessons? I said that I couldn't. Then Ben had had some small troubles this past summer. He was arrested during the riots – not for looting, luckily, but for lobbing a bottle at the police. He spent the night in a cell but was one of those lucky ones released the next day with no charge. I didn't go down there to see him. It

29

was Graduation Day at UCL. I had to sit on a bench with the American Studies department gazing solemnly out at students for hours and hours of annual hand-clapping.

Lucy had to collect Ben from the station. Couldn't I have come with her, she whined down the phone, just this once? How important was *another* graduation day; did she have to do every single fucking parenting thing, every time, on her *own*? She said it was upsetting, seeing him shuffling out of the cell in paper trousers; being handed back his clothes and watching him have a cotton bud pressed inside his mouth. Then she said, her mood veering into hysteria, as it always did: Oh well, much use you would have been. You would probably have laughed. All those years of gangster trousers nearly falling off his arse and finally Ben gets to experience the real thing – give up his belt! – and he looks like an idiot.

'If you're planning to write and express your thanks to the donor family, do let me know,' Maureen says. I guess she thinks that now that I know it was a youth, a lad of sixteen, I'll feel guilty and long to express my appreciation. It's her job to liaise between me and the bereaved family: I suppose you can't blame her for trying. She has her coat on ready to leave and the huge knitting bag strapped across her, like a postman. Albeit a tiny pixie postman. From Tiny Town.

Dear Donor Family, I am finding it very difficult to know what to say to you. A terrible truth: your good son's heart is probably wasted on a man like me.

Helen visits again. She must have asked Alice's advice because the presents are a little better: a large new T-shirt, from Marks and Spencer, in my size and white. A sort of golf-jumper, in grey wool, that isn't very me, but it's the thought. Giant box of grapes and a bag of Doritos, which she thinks are probably a Banned Substance for Transplant Patients and puts back in her bag. And she agrees to go to my flat tomorrow and pick up a few other bits and bobs for me, my post and stuff, and better still, next week, she'll drive up here in my car, and leave it for me while she takes a taxi and train back to London, so that I have it here at Papworth for when I get out.

'Wow, Helen, that's very – that's beyond—'

'Don't worry about it. Who else would do it, if not me?'

Silence then for this little grenade to explode. She's right. Not one text from Lucy. Nothing from Daisy. (Daisy! Why would there be?) Nothing from Ben. Nothing from the department. Well, I know this sounds self-pitying but I'm going to think it anyway: Who in the world except my ex-wife and daughter cares about me?

Helen crosses her legs in her – rather flattering, I've just noticed – skinny jeans, and coughs.

'It's all looking good,' she says, after a longish pause. 'I asked Dr Burns – each day the threat of infection gets less. That's the main thing, isn't it, apart from rejecting it? Infection. Yes, that's it. When you leave here they want to progress you to a flat near by where they can keep an eye on you.'

'Progress me?' Am I in an episode of *Scrubs* then?

'Well. They do tell you things, Patrick. I get the feeling you – do you keep rolling over when they're talking to you? Closing your eyes? Making rude breathing sounds?'

'Rude breathing sounds?'

'They're only trying to help you. That woman, that lovely transplant co-ordinator, or is she a counsellor of some sort, anyway, the one with the Mia Farrow haircut? She said . . .'

Ha!

'The thing is, Helen,' and as I struggle to say this, suddenly I have the most horrible, disgusting, terrifying feeling: that the thing inside me just leaped into my throat and is beating there, is trying to get out, it's like a trapped bird or something—

'Fucking hell! Help me! Fuck, Jeez! It's trying to get out! It's escaping!'

Dr Burns happens to be doing ward rounds and appears instantly at the door of my room. A ponytailed nurse appears from nowhere, running on her squeaky rubber soles.

'Christ, fuck, it's leaping out!'

The doctor hesitates and steps forward. The nurse picks up my wrist and takes my pulse. Burns stares into my face, so that I can smell his breath and see the dark hairs in his nose. He checks my ECG and assures me it's stable.

'Just a few wee palpitations,' the Scottish bastard says, taking a step back. 'Perfectly normal.'

'But in my throat! It was beating in my throat, it was trying to fucking escape!'

'Well, you've had a sternotomy, haven't you? We sawed open the bone of your chest and wired it back together. You've got the wires to prove it. Your heart's no longer fixed into place – that's the space around it that we told you about – so it will quite literally move around now, and you'll be able to hear it beating in different places.'

'Oh my God,' Helen says. 'Patrick.' She sinks down on the chair beside my bed. 'They sawed you open. With a saw,' she says.

My other hand is still at my throat, clutching. Beneath it, the damned heart is really thumping; beating there right at the site of my Adam's apple, pushing, forcing. Helen pours me some water from a jug on top of my cabinet, and hands over the plastic cup. Her eyes, searching mine, seem to be swimming in tears. I drink the water with my hand at my throat, unable to hear what she's saying, or understand. Only when I've forced a few hard swallows do I feel reassured – I've pushed it down, I've shoved it back down my throat like a big pill that won't be easily swallowed. I rub my hand over my throat and the beating quietens.

Helen breathes out loudly, forgetting herself and reaching for my hand. I haven't held Helen's hand in a long, long time. It's soft, and strangely young, and my fingertips feel cool against its warmth. She no longer wears her wedding ring. That's fine, that's as it should be, of course, of course.

'How come you're not at work?' I suddenly think to ask.

'It's Saturday.'

Ah. From somewhere in the back of my brain I hear the *Grandstand* theme tune on the telly, see myself running downstairs in my stockinged feet to watch it with my dad: Saturday. *Grandstand*, banana sandwiches and a lemonade shandy. And from long ago, after Mam had gone, I feel the power of his attempt to use this like balm, this routine: TV and food, the radiators on, the smell of beer and male feet in socks. Comforting.

'Alice said . . . she told me about *your* work,' Helen says.

'Ah.'

'It was bound to happen one day, wasn't it?'

'Thanks a bunch. Your belief in me is touching.' I don't know why, but I'm grinning.

'Well, modern girls. They don't just shut up and put up, you know.' She bats at me with her hand, striking my arm lightly, and adds: 'And you're still managing to look pleased with yourself. You look like that photo of you at the top of your slide in your back garden when you were a baby. Two years old, waving your willy around. Look at me, look what I can do!'

This makes me laugh, Helen remembering that photo.

'OK, OK. But Daisy was hardly a girl, Helen. She was a grown woman, a mature student of thirty-four. And *harassment*. I ask you. Where do they get this from? It was a relationship. I ended it. Possibly a mistake.'

'I believe you—'

'You do?'

'Yes. That all sounds plausible. That she was being vindictive, I mean. It doesn't change my view. Your behaviour. Someone finally making an official complaint to the university about you was an accident waiting to happen.'

I close my eyes. Helen's remark strikes me as true; no need to defend myself against that. I might have done once; in fact, I would have protested with all my might.

'So. How has it been left?' Helen asks.

'Well, I was ill, wasn't I? I couldn't attend the hearing. I was off for several weeks and then left in a hurry, as you know. And now. Now. The fight's gone out of me. There are rather a lot of emails and correspondence about it all and I – I don't care to open them.'

Helen considers this and then, after a pause, asks: 'That was horrid, just now. You must feel very – it's frightening, isn't it? Do you feel really strange, knowing someone else's essential body part is inside you?'

'Can't bring yourself to say the word *heart*, eh?'

She smiles. 'Well, do you feel strange?'

'No. Apart from panic attacks that something might go wrong – I feel fine. It's just a pump, you know. A helpful contractile organ, keeping me alive.'

'You don't look fine.'

'Jeez, that's what Alice said! I've just had major transplant surgery! Go easy on an old fella, can't you? Have you got a cigarette on you?'

'I thought you'd given up. I certainly have. Back in 1996. I think that's the last thing you should be doing now, don't you!'

'Yes, yes, of course. As always you're completely right. And I doubt you have smuggled in any whisky for me either or nymphets from the Royal Courts – if indeed there are any working there these days?'

She smiles again, but the frown is still there. 'Alice said you were talking about – that you said you might pack it in. What will you do, rattling around that bachelor pad all day, drink yourself to death?'

'I could work on my book. My book about the Boy General: Custer.'

'Blimey. You're still working on that? But you could apply somewhere else, you know, once this has all died down. You can probably leave with some kind of pay-off, emeritus, that kind of thing. Would Cambridge have you, do you think?'

'Actually, I'm . . . I've been having a rethink. I – feel I might do a course, retrain in some way.'

This remark is more surprising to me than Helen can know. Retrain? In what?

'Wow, really, Patrick? That's a bit – radical. Mid-life crisis.'

This mild mockery and dismissiveness is irksome. I close my eyes again and lean my head back against the pillow.

'Well,' Helen says. 'I really thought you would be there foaming at the mouth and railing against the young woman who'd ruined your glorious academic career.'

'I know. It's as much a surprise to me, Helen.'

I can't help smiling at her. She really is looking good. She always was a beauty of course. Fine bone structure, long legs.

'God, I'm hungry,' I say.

'There's a menu here somewhere. Shall I stay while you order up lunch?'

She seems to be wondering whether she's overstepping the mark. Is this a bit maternal, perhaps? She fiddles with her necklace; a little silver locket that she'd always worn and . . .

well, perhaps I even bought it for her long ago. Though I can't now remember.

'Yes,' I say, picking up the laminated list. 'Chicken and broccoli,' I say. 'And juice in the absence of a decent whisky.'

'You hate broccoli!'

'Well, I fancy some now. And lemon meringue pie for afters. Marvellous.'

'Probably a good sign that you're getting your appetite back,' Helen says, returning to her sensible self. 'You need to exercise. Walk around the ward. Dr Burns says you have to make it beat faster. Have you seen that exercise bike thing that you can use in bed? And they're saying two weeks. Two weeks, tops, because they need the bed.'

'Two weeks? Where will I go?'

'The flat. I told you. The hospital flat right next to Papworth.'

'Bugger that! Once out of here, I want to be *out* of here.'

'You know, if you keep swearing and shouting, that scary Burns will come back on the ward and tell you off and this time I might not be around to protect you.'

She's standing now, fishing for her keys in her bag. She slides her arms into a thick chocolate-brown jacket with furry lining that looks expensive and new. She suddenly seems like someone I don't know and might even fancy if I saw her for the first time (if I didn't automatically screen out women her age) – an attractive divorcee in skinny jeans with a nice backside, with lovely dark eyes, shaking her shiny red hair. She's ready to leave. To detain her I say:

'I found out something. You know you asked me? From Maureen. My donor was a boy. A boy of sixteen. Motorbike accident near Littleport. I even know his name: Andrew Beamish.'

Helen looks startled. She sits back down.

'Well . . .' she begins, then can't seem to think of anything else to say. 'A boy.'

'I know. It was – I don't know why. The same age as Ben. I wasn't supposed to know – the donor family is promised anonymity but there was some kind of cock-up. Maureen says I should write to the family. Thank them or something. Apparently that's what people do.'

'Will you?'

'What do you think? Not really my style, is it.'

'I guess not.'

I sink back against the pillows. I *have* wanted to contact the family, and I have thought about them. In fact I keep thinking about them; about him. Actually, my curiosity is intense, but it seems transgressive somehow. I should just accept this astonishing *gift* – Maureen's word – and be done with it.

'Are you in a hurry?' I ask.

'Honestly, Patrick. Five more minutes, then.' The furry-lined jacket comes off again.

Helen. She never was able to say no to me.

Part Two

Name is Willie Beamiss. Both my parents was illiterate, but full of wise sayings. I was eldest of six. We all of us got some schooling on a Sunday from the the Methodists in Prickwillow, the Ranters who like to sermonise in a field or empty barn and fill the air with their ravings. Learned enough to read my Bible and *Robinson Crusoe* and *The Compleat Angler* by Izaak Walton, bought from Mr Burrows in Ely, and long a favourite. In my blunt view that last book is all a boy needs.

Circumcised on the kitchen table. Never much happening on that table – just a barley loaf or a dish of potatoes. Snip went the scissors and the foreskin thrown to the dog, who snapped it up. Mother always had scissors at hand; a snip for the animals one minute, and next for us. Always sewing and pinning something, making a dress for Jenny or a bonnet for Annie, she was.

Shared a cottage with Ma, Pa and five sisters and a privy with several other families. Always been in farming, farm labouring, threshing, picking, whatever and whenever. All the fields was forked by hand and that was a job for me and my friends when any other chores was done; the dykes was newly made back then. Was never idle: there was plenty to do to keep cart upon wheels, as the saying goes.

Kept always a pencil in my pocket, bought from a Cheapjack in a caravan outside Ely Cathedral; and was always drawing or writing or stealing into the garden to clap something down on paper in private, using every morsel of brown paper

Mother had her tea and sugar wrapped in from the shop. Had a trade too, for the winter season when work was slack: Father had been apprenticed to a shoemaker. The Beamiss family was skilled shoemakers. That became my sometime trade too, by the time I turned twelve and schooldays over. Our table always had some Knotty sum on it, in Pounds, Shillings and Pence, written by me, as the quickest brains in the family.

The reading of books, my mother said, would fit me for 'nothing but the Poorhouse' – she saw how it gave me an itching after everything: a Beamiss trait if ever there was one, she said. It was my fate to be born at the end of the century and the French Revolution was still Pa's favourite topic by the time I was out of my crib and walking. All have liberty to think as they please, but me, I confess, I was quite in the suds about Politics. Pa loved rebelliousness and his ballads. Over a horn of ale in the Globe, with a stamping of his feet and a cheer at every line, he'd sing:

> *The law locks up the man or woman*
> *Who steals the goose from off the common*
> *But leaves the greater villain loose*
> *Who steals the common from the goose.*

Countrymen is no rebels, they love the seasons and the land and fear the new, but Pa was the exception; he had a talent for whipping up others, and when labour is back-breaking and stomachs growl empty you can rile the sleepiest and loyalest of farm labourers to sedition.

In the Globe all talk was of the Enclosures that was robbing us of the little plots of land we worked, instead parcelling it up for the Farmer Martins of this world. Then was rumours of a drill-plough that would do the work of twenty men and horses, or, worse, new wind-pumps that would drain the meres and rivers in double time and rob us of the fish or eels that might sometimes turn our potatoes-and-bread supper into a banquet.

I let such talk wash all about me. I had a little tame sparrow, Dickie, that I'd trained to sit on my hand and take crumbs from me. I would sit myself under Pa's table while he drank and spieled and watch Dickie's patterning pecks, thinking of how it was like the beat of its tiny heart, and fall into raptures. I heard the talk in the pipe-smoked air above my head; heard the praising of the Great Fen that some fellows went in for, heard how it had become, according to Farmer Martin, instead of a waste and howling wilderness, a garden of the Lord, but I remembered, as if I seen it with my own eyes, Pa's own dear memories of the place, just how he told it.

Those black ugly flats, the black-gold of Farmer Martin's soil, Pa said, had less than twenty years earlier been silvery, pale-green reeds, vast miles around a broad lagoon that stretched from Ely to Peterborough. Men – only a small number, the Fens was never what you would call *populated* – lived in houses wattled with reeds and looking just like the nests a bird might make: dotted around on platforms upon piles above the water. Or else where the lake ran shallow they walked with great long poles and called themselves Slodgers. The door of each home had a ladder and at the ladder was a boat. There was no proper roads to speak of, only skating in winter, or rowing.

In those days before the wind-pumps drained the land the sedge-bird sang, and high overhead was hawk, buzzard and kite. (To a Fenman like Pa such birds could only ever mean food, or quarry.) Pa would lie on his punt boat on the mere, invisible due to the flatness and white paint of the boat. Then – a puff of smoke and the blast of his stanchion-gun; and overhead rushed and whirled the skein of terrified wildfowl, screaming, piping, clacking, croaking, filling the air with the hoarse rattle of their wings. Above all sounded the wild whistle of the curlew, and the trumpet note of the wild swan.

Knew and loved *all* my birds from an early age. Knew their names, their calls, their habits. The jay's warning chatter, the clap of a woodpigeon wing at dusk, the *boom* of the bittern, like the sound a boy makes blowing over the mouth of a glass bottle. From a young age I had me a leaning towards tiny things: the cracking of the corn stubs in the sun, the bounce of a grasshopper. Best of all I liked to walk by myself in the marshy Fen, watching the heron that hunched like an old fisherman at the water all day, trying to learn his lesson of patience.

When he wasn't agitating about the draining itself, Pa used to rile himself something terrible about the *Commissioners* who profited from it. And as a boy hiding under the table, with the warm belly of the little tame sparrow resting in my palm, I soon learned to quake when the *Those Bloody Bugger Commissioners* was mentioned, as then the thump of Pa's fist would land on the wood above my head. Every man who owned a few score acres in the Fens became a Commissioner and could squeeze rates out of other men for the draining of the land. So those like Pa who opposed the draining in the first place now had the further insult of having to find the penny to pay for it.

I fell in love with Susie Spencer when sixteen years old and she a girl of one year younger. I was in love at first sight. She had a witching smile and perfect lingering form, shining black curls and hazel eyes. I saw her outside Ely Cathedral on the same day I bought the pencils from the caravan stationed outside it: the day of St Etheldreda's Fair. The local girls was all flocking around, giggling and chittering, hoping to bid for a comb or a ribbon or a package of orange flower pekoe tea all done up in silver paper, and my schoolmate Tom (we called him Tom Foolery though that was never his name) says to me: 'Ain't she just a stunner?' and nudged me in the ribs. We knew who she was: Susie Spencer, the daughter of a small-time farmer. That is to say her father owned a few acres of land in Prickwillow and employed labourers to work them.

Prickwillow Farmhouse had once been no more than a reed-walled cottage that showed above the water for a few weeks in July and then again when rainy season ceased. Grandfather Spencer had been a canny old devil not afraid to use his fowling piece on any who opposed him and he had claimed some dubious rights to this place of willows and osier beds. Once the land was drained the wily old grandfather borrowed some money and made a cross on a piece of paper and made sure his son once of age became one of the cursed Commissioners – it being in the family interests to keep the land dry and the house sitting atop it like an ark. There, then, you have it. Even though I knew more of my ABC than Susie, she was a cut above the Beamiss family. And now began some of the happiest and some of the *unhappiest* days of my life.

Susie Spencer was trying to look like she was too much a lady to be interested in what the Cheapjack had for sale at the same time as cocking one ear in case a good price came up. Tom got it into his head to try his luck with the Cheapjack's daughter – another stunner in his view, with green eyes and chestnut hair and a manner both tart and queenly. He yelled at the gypsy girl, what price a kiss? The crowd roared. 'I don't sell,' says she, smartly, and Susie and her friends look scandalised and turned their heads and began to walk away from us. Tom had jumped up onto the platform of the caravan and was saying if she wouldn't sell he'd *steal* a kiss instead and there was an uproar from the crowd – temptation was something

Tom rarely resisted. The girl's father appeared from inside some curtains at the back of the rows of goods and started bellowing, while the girl, as unmoved as it's possible to be, picked up a flail and threatened Tom with it.

Had half an eye on him but the main pull was from the back of Susie Spencer's curly head, her slender waist, as she slipped her arm inside her friend's and walked out in the direction of the Market Place, where a line of bullocks and horses – the real business of the Fair – was being driven towards Stuntney. I walked just behind them both at a distance.

Something in the way that Susie Spencer held her head, something in her walk, told me she'd begun to notice me following. Soon enough she turned, and said with great impudence: 'Is there something I can do for you, Willie Beamiss?' because of course in a place like ours we was all known to each other. Her stout little friend – a good head and shoulders shorter than Susie – started to titter and make some bad jests towards me and the pair of them put their heads together and tried to run away from me.

I had to cook up something quick and my brains did not let me down.

'I'm drawing you both, to sell at the Fair. Wait!' and I pulled a pencil from my pocket along with a scrap of paper, and bending one knee to rest the paper on, I sketched a quick likeness. It wasn't the best drawing I ever did but Providence played fair with me and it was good enough to draw cries of 'Oh see, Susie, he's really caught you – a look of you,' and that's how I got to talking to them, and they allowed me to walk alongside them, down the hill, following the bullocks.

By the time we'd reached the Stuntney road I knew at least that the girl I favoured (who put me in mind of a willow, because she was long and tall and rare in these parts; a girl with long limbs, uncommonly tall) could be made to smile with a cartoon or a witty remark. I knew that she was frank and not coquettish like her friend and I knew too that she thought me and Tom 'Fen louts' since she said as much, though she was not afraid to talk to us directly and made the strange comment that why did folk in those poor huts in Littleport live six to a room like sheep in a barn? Which allowed me to know that she herself would expect more.

Tom told me later that he knew a bad house where the Cheapjack girl had taken him, after she had put down the flail, and for a few coppers we could find it again. But Pa had warned me against such places, and such diseases, and anyway, something new had happened to me and couldn't be undone. Now that is the trouble with us Beamisses and it's the family trait that's most likely passed down and the one I should confess. Fixed, when we set our hearts on something. Constancy is our middle name. Fierce stubbornness, some might call it, and it takes a different shape in each of us: with Pa it was politics. With me it was love.

I worried that I'd wait a long while before clapping eyes on Susie Spencer again, but hadn't reckoned on the Peace signing with France in the summer of 1814. Of course we didn't know then that the banishing of Bonaparte to the island of Elba was not to be the end of it; we only thought of the coming party thrown on the Nut Holt at Ely, of our plum puddings and beef, our donkey races and promised ale. All at the expense of the Bishop of Ely – a Peace party thrown for three thousand of 'the poor inhabitants of that city'. Us. The doors of the Red Lion Inn was about to be thrown open and the streets filled with rockets, mines and other fireworks.

Woke to the ringing of bells in Ely Cathedral, walked the few miles along the drove from Littleport to Ely with Tom, sharing a pipe, filling it with grass from the roadside. The grass burned black in an instant and satisfied no one; we looked for poppies but it was too late in the summer for them. All we'd had for breakfast was the boiled, peppered water coloured with soot that our mothers called tea but Tom said the Bishop of Ely had promised an ounce of tobacco for every honest citizen. I said I'd believe that when I'd smoked it. Our stomachs rumbled and we discussed when last we'd had beef. Tom thought it was last May, on his birthday.

Then Tom sang for a while – he had only two notes, like a cuckoo – the most insulting and vulgar tunes he could dream up. We started a fancy in which we had beef every day and pheasants and duck for supper, and our mouths began to water, and our stomachs popple like a pan of water on a stove, though we had full six hours to go before the lunch. We watched a heron stand guard at the river and wished ourselves half as talented at spearing a fish. Tom threw stones but could not distract the bird.

I spied Susie at the moment the procession began, when twelve men carried a stage decorated with laurels and roses and began solemnly to parade, carrying Susie Spencer, atop the platform, all dressed up with a crown of fruit on her head and a wheatsheaf in her hand and a stone lion at her feet, and followed by a band playing 'Rule, Britannia'. The dress clung to her witching form. I felt my face turn red as flame. There was nowhere to hide.

Her dress was flimsy, made of some kind of pale cloth, and Susie sat straight as a pound of candles, then waving, then laughing, then shouting to the crowd. After I'd done with blushing I fell to laughing as I didn't know what else to do. Tom dug me in the ribs and tried every kind of coarse word on me, to see the blood rise in my face again. (Tom's jokes was like a pack of cards: always the same but told in a different turn.) He said it was his 'favourite spectacle' to see me redden – better than all the fireworks and flags of the day itself. Tom said, with a sideways glance at me, that on the other hand she was indeed a fine-looking lass and he wished he could reach and knock that crown of fruit off Susie Spencer's dark head and have a nibble.

'I'll knock *your* head to the ground!' I shouted, and Tom and me locked arms around each other's heads and scuffled, though only in fun, and the singing parade trooped passed us. Pa was with the crowd, full of strong ale and merriment. Susie was carried off, high above us. Nothing could have better expressed how out of reach she was to me. And yet I followed, dodging after her, elbowing others in the crowd, shouting, leaping and ducking when my view of her fruit-crowned curls was threatened. The smell of tobacco smoke was the only thing powerful enough to distract me from pursuit of her. We filled the clay pipe and someone at another stall offered Tom and me a tot of Tant Brown's ale. The tables – set out along the Market Square – groaned with food but you had to fight to get it.

'What sort of a lass sets herself up as Britannia?' Tom mocked, his mouth now full of hot mutton. He was being Tom; that is to say, provoking. The only answer could be 'a popinjay', or 'one above her station', so I said nothing, filling my own mouth with the plum pudding that Henry Rickwood's wife handed me. Struck me that Tom was teasing me for cocksuredness in picking a beauty like Susie Spencer, because surely she hadn't set herself up as Britannia, but been *chosen*. Tom contented himself with plainer girls, or ones who charged a half-shilling and was within his reach. Was a rare novelty to feel myself envied by Tom. So I swaggered across the Market Square back towards the cathedral, trailing behind the band members in their poke bonnets who was banging their drums and singing 'Rule, Britannia', hoping to get another glimpse.

Seemed her stint of duty was soon finished because suddenly she was shoving her way towards me in the Market Square through the crowd, still in her flimsy dress but with a blue cloak tossed over it. She waved and grabbed my arm and – here I confess, I looked behind me, as if to see some other lucky chap the object of her attention.

'Quick – there's donkey racing starting down Fore Hill,' and as if she was but a school-friend or perhaps a sister, she took my hand. Little could she have guessed the chill that ran from her touch, and struck directly at my heart. I felt it hit like a bell.

Such foolishness . . . Why choose one lass over another? Until that moment I'd not fancied myself a romantic at all, but only a Beamiss with brains and more book learning than was common in Littleport, a stubborn streak, a love for birds and a resolute temper. Wasn't prone to self-reflection but the matter of the suddenness and the stuck-fastedness of the choosing of a love-object: that interested me wonderfully.

Was more than beauty, though, that drew me. Something in the way she tore at things, so heartily, pleased me too. All was impulse, loudness and vitality with her. When the donkeys lined up and was ready to race Susie shrieked with laughter. She ventured a bet at once, tossing her hair around her shoulders and shrieking again more loudly still, when I admitted I had not the shilling she needed. Kept seeing her as she'd first appeared as Britannia – held aloft above the crowd, queenly and magnificent, but giggling wildly behind her hands and then foolishly waving, and accepting all laurels and praise without a simper, more of a slapping of her thigh. To any question she had an impertinent answer – to my timid 'What would your father say if he saw us?' she laughed and pushed me in the shoulder and told me, 'Bear up! Be more gallant!'

Amused myself then, imagining what sport Tom would make of me weighing her so thoughtfully. His view (to know it I need not trouble myself to ask him) would be that it was an animal feeling, nothing more than what the bull feels for the cow, that was drawing me to Susie Spencer. Pa no doubt would say the same. Had Pa ever felt this way for my stout, grey-haired mother, nowadays crooked from pricking willows and half blind from her sewing? What did people marry or couple for in the Fens? To bring children into the world and to be companions to one another in old age. That much I could fancy. But to feel anything more – to feel warm affection like this, or this heated, gathering feeling, this wildness that swept over me whenever I looked now at Susie and her lively, hazel eyes or heard that lusty, ridiculous laugh – did everyone feel this?

Susie held my hand throughout the races. More clutched it than held it, truth be told, and I began to wonder if she knew she did, or was it to her some warm object to be squeezed in excitement whenever her chosen donkey came close to winning?

When the poor beast straggled in and was declared the winner she leaped on her wooden bench and jumped up and down on it, utterly heedless of the people to the left and the right of her, and the ways that her dress became transparent, allowing me full appreciation of her lovely jiggling form beneath. She swept my hand right up to her mouth to kiss it.

Then the crowd bellowed and more fireworks was fired and the scent of smoke and gunpowder filled our nostrils and it seemed as if the whole of Ely celebrated with me. She never left my side the rest of the evening. She flung herself into dancing all the reels and country dances with me, screeching anew at my poor technique, she shared a pot of ale with me, she showed no shame when her friends spied us together, nor when Tom came threatening more mischief. The miraculous

51

thought began to shape: that luck had just dealt me the best hand. Susie Spencer was as smitten with me as I with her.

And there was more. Later that night I learned that Tom's swaggering knowledge of the fair sex was more limited than we knew, because he'd always assured me that they none of them had interest in letting you get your tarse out, except to laugh at it. His assurances – that only if you showed them a coin would a lass even pretend an interest (an interest she didn't truly feel) and that 'Farmer Spencer's daughter', Susie, would be 'tight as a drum' to unpick – proved untrue.

We lay ourselves under the stars near the area we called the island of Babylon, as the evening celebrations rolled on. We could hear the voices from another party in a boatwright's shop, and the clacking of the geese, and felt the slide of their droppings everywhere underfoot as we picked our way down to the black river. The lanterns along the bank was full bright, glazing the water with fire, and we thought we'd be lucky to find a darkness to hide us, so we climbed into a boat, untied it, and pushed it out with only the softest of splashes to betray us.

And there on the cold wooden base, with the fireworks and the fires of Ely blazing against the cathedral, a glorious sight, more lovely than ever I saw, Susie Spencer showed me what true joy there is, in the warm flesh under her skirts and the sweet pleasure when she gathered me in her arms and kissed my ears and my throat heartily and made us ply one another fiercely with all our might and main, all the time with my mouth hot on hers and my hands on the firm flesh of her buttocks, acting for all the world as if we was both desperate, but she wouldn't let my tarse find its home; she would hold it and prevent it as it knocked to gain entry, she whispered that this would be painful for her and could wait for another day and she showed me that even her touch, her hand, would make my pizzle leap and play, and we went on like this, and she took my fingers and guided them to a wet dark place, until we was both gathered up in an approaching sweetness and then just as suddenly, shockingly, was spent; and then she called me her darling, and whispered that never had another made her blood rise like that and that if I would only be hers I would be surprised.

'You will collect frequently, Willie Beamiss,' she said, 'you will rise up.'

What a girl was Susie Spencer! A girl like no other. I knew I was in love now for ever, for how could another ever win my heart with an explosive start like that? And if Tom was to be believed about a feminine nature and aversion to passionate feelings, Susie Spencer's talent for joy was a rare gift indeed.

Didn't have to wait too long before coupling with Susie again. Later that summer when Pa's rheumatics was playing up it fell to me to make enough to buy bread for the family so was working hard in the fields, loading hay, forked and spread on the field onto a cart and in between times beating the flies from the horse's arse with a flail. Sweat poured down my back and my hands steamed raw and red from the hauling; Tom was at a short distance from me, doing his own pitchforking, and further still, at tidy distances the length of the field, could be seen the dotted figures of a dozen boys of my childhood. Rowed up, we called this. The Fens is divided with ditches to mark them, not hedges, and when we needed to relieve ourselves we strode over to these, mindful that if we was caught luxuriating in this necessity by the farmer we would have our wages docked. I often found myself ruminating on what used to be beneath the fen. I knew the banks of some dykes at fen borders was made by the Romans and the legions of that army passed by my fancy on many an occasion.

The task was to make a big heap of hay on each cart and,

after a time, despite the tiredness, and the aching in your back, there was satisfaction in seeing the mound of hay grow and smelling everywhere the heat of it and feeling the buzz of flies in your ears and the hay-dust clogging your nostrils; if we had not been so empty in our bellies and so longing for our docky we might have been charmed by the sun and sweat into some kind of delirium. I looked up, in this exalted state: there she was, dazzling her way towards me. Seems her father had sent her on some errand.

Naturally my face flamed redder than a setting sun and Tom was not slow in noticing it. I was clownish and shy and could do nothing to hide it. Susie gave some message to the oldest member of our crew – man named Cornwall – and seeing her point with one slender outstretched arm towards her father's barns at Prickwillow a hot liquid seemed to flow suddenly through my veins – as if the memory of her flesh under my hands was the most fiery of liquors still firing up my blood. Picked up my fork and threw myself into the work so that I could look down at the ground and not meet a soul's eyes. Tom stared queerly at me but quit his beefing and chiding me, and Susie turned on her heel, picking her way through the hay still lying over the ground in a way that reminded me at once of her dainty way of picking through the goose-shit that night.

Her father's barns at Prickwillow was away over the other side of the fen. There was a row of black wind-pumps on the horizon. Once she'd put some distance between us, I looked left and right about me, and then followed her. It wouldn't do for the others to see how keen I was; nor her father either. I reached the rickyard at Prickwillow and gasped aloud at the stacks of wheat – two, each forty paces long, with a lane between them. Suddenly, from behind one, there appears Susie.

Her face is flushed. She has a guilty look and I feel my tarse harden at once, thinking on its own, obeying some law of nature I've no control over. When she comes close and kisses me and looks about her, she laughs at this (putting her hand in my britches, boldly fetching it, like it was some muscled eel) but then she pushes at it, calling it naughty.

'There's no time for that, Willie Beamiss. I told you you'd rise up – but not like that!'

And there's something she says she wants to show me. 'Look to the house. That sign means a curtain is drawn; Father takes a nap at this time of day after rising at crack of dawn. Here would be the perfect time to bring your friend – the saucy one – and look, did you ever see such ricks as these? There are rats and mice in here, feasting, while your families starve! You could come with a horse and I would distract Father—'

I sweep her up in my arms then, kiss her all over her neck and face, and then I put my hand over her mouth. I'm almost crying, so great is my joy at discovering that Susie Spencer would risk all, for me, like this.

'I'd hang for it,' I tell her. 'We all would. Don't you think the fancy tempts us? Look at the young stock – the bullocks and heifers. They have more meat on them than we do!'

I spin around in the rickyard, fearful of her father's return, or overhearing us, out here in the sun like this, pressing her against me, kissing her feverishly. Daring my mouth further and further down her neck, pulling at her dress to kiss at the brown freckled skin of her breasts.

She ruffles a hand in my hair, tries to lift my head from my intense task, saying: 'There's turf. Look at that. Father has piles of turf too, there for the digging, some ten – fifteen – twenty feet of it. That could warm your cottage. I've seen how you live – your ma is like a sow with the pigs all pulling her to pieces – you could dig it out and take that turf to market and sell it for sixty pounds an acre.'

In between kisses I say: 'But what will it help anyone, any of them, Ma, me, you, if I'm thrown onto the Hulk and sent to Botany Bay?'

Susie's eyes fill with tears. She takes me by the hand to a spot behind the hayrick and begins pulling at her stockings, ruffling up her skirt.

'Come, be quick. I'll let you.' She lies back on the straw-specked ground, and licks her fingers and, to my astonishment, begins rubbing at herself under her skirts, saying, 'This will hurry things along. You're a good man, Willie Beamiss. An honest man – who would have thought it? I think I love you. Ten minutes. Can you manage it in ten?'

Needless to report, I managed it in five. I exploded in her like a dam bursting. She laughed at me and told me she would teach me ways to make it last longer but I was proud of my work as a lover, I thought I couldn't be bettered. Time was short. I was back in the fen with the others before our docky break was over, with only the smell of me and the stain on my britches to hint at what had happened.

Susie asked me to meet her at one of the wind-pumps, she told me which one, she pointed it out, the black-winged mill, the one slightly larger than the rest – Black Wings, she called it, and said she'd be there any night or morning – she'd sleep there most nights under pretence of taking care of the pump, she often did this for her father and there was a wooden cot there for the purpose. I could come to her late at night and leave early morning before the rest was up, if I could arrange it.

'There's not a man alive could stop me,' I said.

So that was where we met and conducted our loving, and that was where I discovered the wonders of the body of Susie

Spencer and the thousand different ways she could please me, and I her. I soon learned to smell that sedge that grew around the mill and stiffen automatically in my britches, before I'd even reached her, the way a dog begins slavering as soon as you put the meat in the bowl. The rush of wind in the sails, the creak of the wheel turning, the grinding of the cogs, the paddle hitting the wooden box that covered it and the splash of water as it was scooped up, and thrown from the dyke to the lode; the moaning and sighing of Susie Spencer. Those became the sounds and flavours of my days, and the happiest ones I'd known. I might be starved and skinny but I had a great youth and vitality where Susie was concerned. I never tired of her. If she suggested horseback mode or facing away from me or putting her mouth around me or me climbing on her back and crawling around on all fours, bucking and behaving like animals, or any new approach, I was always willing, if surprised. I never knew a girl could have such an interest; such a craving after life and variety as my Susie had.

One day the inevitable happened and her father appeared among the line of black painted wind-pumps on the horizon just as the sun was flushing the Fens pink. The dog with him was barking, we knew he would run to our platform high inside the framework of the mill and give us away. We lay barely breathing, and then Susie said the oddest thing.

'Pa would turn a blind eye, you know. He's not the bad sort. That's why I tried to show you the wheat. Pa's not like Farmer Martin or the landowners. The Bishop of Ely, or Reverend Vachell. This is just a small tenant farm – he works hard too, nobody granted it to him.'

This was news to me. A farmer was a farmer, someone who had land when we didn't, someone far above us. I hadn't truly thought about the shades and degrees of farmering until then. It was an important lesson. Have told you it was Pa who was the seditious one. I was only ever a reluctant, one might say, accidental rebel. At heart I was tender; that was the character and nature of me, and too late by then to change it.

Days did not pass with my benefit in mind, however, and my entering the lists of Cupid made no difference to the way my life in the Fens continued. No. Not long after the Peace celebrations Old Boney was up to his tricks again and we was back at war with France, as some of us readily predicted. And more soldiers and seamen was needed; this would bring us better fortunes than farm labouring, Tom was told in the Globe. Also how the French had reached Northampton, but even he was not fool enough to believe that.

'If we wait until eighteen years of age they can force us to go for nothing,' Tom whispered to me from over his pot of ale and we agreed that the better choice now would be to be taken as Volunteers for the bounty of two guineas. Tom and me had reached our seventeenth birthdays at around the same month. We convinced ourselves we could pass for eighteen.

So we set off for Peterborough and our mothers acted as though we was leaving for Botany Bay. Pa was still mouthing his rebellion, and he had an injured foot too, unhealed after a skating accident that winter past, so he stayed at the cottage in Littleport. Pa was angry with our decision. Sat up from his cot where he was coughing and resting his raised foot on a plank. Shouted that Boney was nothing to us and only a fool would fight for a country where wheat was stacked sky high in the Farmer's barns and feasted on by mice, but never sold at a fair price to the poor buggers whose hands was raw and backs bent double and foots broke from its harvesting. (We did not dare point out that his injury could not be blamed on the Farmer but on his own high jinks on the ice when he was pulling Jenny, the youngest, on her sledge, never heeding her screams to slow down.)

Tom and me got out of there fast and shut the door heavily behind us. We got as far as the fields at Oundle. Was a multitude of lawless fellows there: a great stink of male flesh – all of it unwashed and sweating in the summer sun and farting to make a stench like the great bad-egg smell that comes off the rotted reeds in water. Over a thousand of them. The Captain was trying to sort us into some sort of companies. Me being short, my only chance could be the 'Bum Tools', though Tom might be lucky and be classed a 'Light Bob'. Both of us dreaded ending up in the Awkward Squad, which stamped you with the distinction of uselessness for the rest of your soldiering life. But we was found out.

On our stepping forward, the louse-looking Corporal barked, 'Names! Date of birth!' and Tom always had a voice as high as a girl's when he was nervous, and piped up, 'Where's my two guineas?' The Corporal screwed up his face and screamed at us. Air puffed out of him for some full two minutes. The main theme was who was in charge and that we was not old enough to have balls that was dropped and other familiar insults about us being web-footed (on account of living not long ago in houses on water) and about our opium-addled mothers and our Fen hovels.

So that was a long walk wasted. Facing the return one, we decided to spend our last few pennies on a boat-ride down the river for some of it and Tom was silent and in a black temper and it was the first time I ever saw him take fright. Evening, and a flock of geese flew over us honking like hounds in chase, and the mist was drawing in over the river, and Tom said he was sure it was Black Shuck hounding us towards the Pearly Gates. When I called him a fool (enjoying the tables turned) he screamed that he'd seen a 'will-o'-the-wisp' on the water in front of us and cried for his mother.

59

On my hearing this, hairs started to tickle on the back of my neck. The boatman was rowing, chewing on a pipe, at the other end of the boat from where we two huddled. Somewhere out on the water was a sudden light, flickering wildly, and a crackling sound like pea straw burning. Maybe they was lanterns held by someone on the bank. The mist wrapped everything so it was hard to tell. It looked to be hovering over the water, not the land. Kept my eyes on the pallid light for a while – was Tom right, was it the ghostly villain we called 'Jack with the Lantern'? Always was a disbeliever in ghosts but when you find yourself lonely and rejected by the army and no hope of bettering your impoverishment, and your belly empty, your mind will clutch at fancies.

Pa had told me will-o'-the-wisps was a natural phenomenon and I forced myself to repeat this to Tom now. 'It's something to do with the gases from the stagnant water,' I said. Then a scream ripped through the air. The boatman dropped his pipe in the water and cursed.

'Damned badgers,' said he.

Tom did not stop his shaking. I could not easily make him out but had the feeling that his red hair stood up like the head of a brush. His ready handful of jokes and ditties was for once lost to him. The hairs on my own neck did not lie down either, nor my heart quieten its drumbeat. Badgers screaming when you are deep in a Fen mist sound exactly like a woman being strangled or horribly mangled. And fear – the fear of being further from home than we had ever ventured, being in fact over the other side of a horizon that we knew as flat, flat – meant we had surely dropped over the edge of the world, into a next life?

So, as we huddled and the boatman set his teeth against his lack of a pipe, I stared at the pale, guttering light – like a flame caught in a bladder, whisking along – and watched it closely, hoping by my boldness to extinguish it. Yet as I stared, something more horrible still occurred. The light reshaped itself into the figure of a man. Though what kind of man I could not tell. Tall and dark and atop some kind of terrifying horse, the like of which I'd never seen. Behind him the light fanned out and turned red, the way a drop of blood will colour water. Closed my eyes for an instant to shake the terrible vision of the spectre flying fast towards me and I swear there was a strange roaring sound too, like a thousand lions, and when I reopened my eyes, he was vanished. Put my hand to my heart, to check whether it had stopped in fright. But no, all was still there. I was alive and on a boat on a misty river, I was Willie Beamiss, a Fen lout in love with Susie Spencer, travelling home.

Tom and me did not speak of the will-o'-the-wisp and I never troubled to ask him if he saw the terrible man.

By the following year when the crops was bad and we had finally squashed Old Boney for good, most of the soldiers returning now all ravaged and one-legged from Waterloo, Tom and me not having signed up to the Awkward Squad turned out to be important. If you was a soldier you was barred from receiving the poor relief when you was desperate poor. A time which came much sooner and sharper than anyone predicted.

That night began much like another. Tom and me went to the Globe tavern on the high street for ale. We'd saved and scrimped but barely had our eightpence entrance fee for the meeting since the main business of the night was to decide who needed assistance that year. Beneficiaries out of work or incapacitated receive seven shillings a week.

Pa was there too, and taking a leading part in the meeting. His foot had healed but the time he'd been laid up had increased his vexation, and politicising. While he'd been resting the foot he practised some of his old trade, shoemaking, hogging the candlelight to sew the leather. 'Wherever the spirit of reform is stirring you find a cobbler,' he was fond of saying. Time when your hands was occupied but your brain idle meant that you got in the habit for thinking. Pa's spirit was strongly knitted with independence and if truth be told it was a lifetime of hard labour had crippled him by forty-five, but he refused to see it because he was stubborn as you know already and he still had little mouths to feed. After making shoes at night he would put stones in the ruts in the road in the morning for five shillings a week, alongside all the hairy-bearded, returned-home seamen, and that only worsened his rheumatics further. There was just too many men swarming everywhere, grubbing after the same mean work.

Tom was in a huddle with a friend of his, Aaron Layton, a twenty-year-old bricklayer covered in pockmarks, and no favourite of mine. That night the Globe was full and the door to the street was wedged open with bodies. As fifty men jostled for space none could sit down. Mud from labourers' boots coated the floor and the stink of sweat mixed with the smell of ale, pipe smoke and snuff. The May day still hung warm and bats flitted above us in the thatch of the inn, like they was suddenly diving down to eavesdrop.

All talk was of events at Hilgay and Southery where there had been rucks aplenty in recent months. Barns burned down, a riot in Brandon. Give us bread or blood this day! 'The Norfolk Banditti', Aaron called them. He was a strangely powerful figure in his fustian jacket and fancy blue stockings. Seemed like I was the only one in the inn to stifle a laugh at the labouring men of Norfolk being given such a grand title.

'Bring us another pot,' Tom shouted, spellbound.

This Aaron was a mystery to me. He was an ugly bugger with his freckled and pock-pecked face and he had work too, unlike the rest of us, being a skilled brickie, so why was he full of sedition? He liked a ruck, was all. Robert Johnson, the landlord of the Globe, thumped two pints down on the counter top and told us to shut up, and pay up, or he'd pour ours over the cat's head. He was growing weary of our shouting about the price of bread. We could never afford it and yet everywhere we looked there was wheat piled high in farmers' barns, that was the complaint, over and over, though we tried it in different tunes.

Some talk and laughter fell upon a fellow's slapping the *Cambridge Gazette* on the wooden table and pointing out that if we was accused of 'liberally partaking at the shrine of Bacchus' (the very words the newspaper had used to damn meetings such as ours, although ignorant that this particular one was taking place), what about this fool parish clerk who had fallen over in the middle of a service? Someone repeated the true tale of Anne Green – sentenced to one year's imprisonment for breaking off the limb of a walnut tree and trying to carry off some branches bearing nuts – and we damned the mad clergymen who sat on the benches and passed down such laws to us.

'Damn all the parsons to hell – what have they ever done for the poor!' shouted Aaron. Then we damned the clergy with all our might, and farmers and millers too. 'Whether enclosures or old Bonaparte – not a thing remains in common hands!'

I found myself fearful of Susie's father being blamed – he was small beer, a tenant farmer, as Susie had explained to me. I was sure I was not the only one in the Fens who had not until then been mindful of the differences. Hadn't seen Susie in a while, yet when we did meet up things between us was sweet as ever. It was Farmer *Martin* who had much of the land for miles around sewn up. Where it wasn't him it was the Commissioners, and, if not them, the clergymen who owned the rest of the land and controlled the charities that was set up to help us.

'I remember when wheat was only fifty-two shillings – only earlier this year!' Aaron said. Wheat was now over a hundred shillings a quarter.

'Henry Martin just laid off three more, including our Jack . . .'

'Shirt on his back costs him more than three men's wages!' This was Pa.

'Aye, but what's to gain by—' This was me.

Tom burst in, his red hair all abristling with excitement, the way a dog gets when a bitch is in heat: 'Over in Denver they've had a ruck . . . said they'd join us, show us how it's done—'

'Damn your eyes, no Denver men here – let's have a fray ourselves!' Aaron thumped his tankard down on the counter top and pushed his way out onto the street.

Someone – perhaps pock-pecked Aaron – had a seed-drill spout that he was holding over our heads and trying to use as a horn. No one heard him above the racket but I saw his cheeks puff in vain. He shouted once – 'Bread or blood!' – disappeared again and the jostling grew, with each man voicing some new grievance, and the sound of pots of ale smashing down onto wooden tables, and that deep sound of rabble that gives a mob its name.

Men streamed out onto Crown Street. I thought for a second that I saw Susie in the crowd of fifty men with her vivid head bobbing above the rest the way a poppy stands out in a field of corn, but then I wasn't sure. There were two girls, one dark, one fair, but it was a glimpse only: was one of them Susie? Aaron and Tom was blustering and yelling and everyone's blood was up. Each was possessed by their own devils, bellowing into each other's faces, not listening but spitting out their complaints. Violence scented the air. An ale-house brawl, a boxing match, a cockfight – the smell, the first glint, when men knew a ruck was on its way – I followed it, two steps behind.

We poured down Crown Street, and now Aaron was blowing a lighterman's horn, and the sound blew out over our heads, calling the whole of Littleport to join us. Looking about me, I saw others was carrying weapons: pitchforks, cleavers, clubs. Tom had a long pole with a piece of cotton print attached – a flag of sorts – and he waved it drunkenly. Searched the faces for Pa, but could not then see him. Searched for something to arm myself and spied a piece of broken beam propped up against Mingey's shop. As I went to grab it there was the sound of glass shattering and at first, startled, I thought it was me who'd caused it. Glanced behind me and saw that a rock had been thrown by one of the youngest with us, a small fellow and a real hothead: John Badger. A cheer followed it. No light shone in Mingey's shop. If anyone was home there was no sign. The clamour in the street grew: looking around I now saw more had joined us, perhaps fifty more men, with lamps lit, and held high.

Perhaps some people rushed into Mingey's shop at this moment. I did not. Others had quickly moved on, further down the street, and, as a tide, I surged with them. I remember Tom beside me, and the moment I first saw him with a butcher's cleaver in his hand. It was dark by then, around ten o'clock; he had dropped the flag on a pole. The silver blade glinted in firelight from a lamp held in his other hand; he must have snatched it from Mingey's shop.

Already the picture blurs. So many times I was asked to tell it. Where next? Mr Clarke's shop. What did you do there? Nothing, sir. Did you throw his wares onto the street? (I remember the drawers. The small wooden drawers with their hand-smoothed knobs – so familiar to all of us who had used his shop every day as children – and every one of them opened and dashed to the floor like a gaping mouth with its teeth pulled; and sawdust and blood, and the contents: nails and string and every kind of nut and bolt, the contents of every drawer spilled.) Then smashing the windows of Josiah Dewey, surging in through the broken-down door of his home, Aaron demanding a pound. *Not me, sir.*

Once the breath from Aaron's lungs filled the horn, was already too late. The notes rang out. The long, loud, thrilling joy of it. The lighterman's horn. The same one that called to us as boys to tell us that pleasure parties was going to Downham Market Fair and we should run along the river chasing the boats and waving. We always obeyed it unthinkingly: like whistling for a dog. Our ears pricked, our hearts drummed, our boyish selves leaped into our limbs. Before too long the hundred or so of us numbered two hundred, and the touchpaper for the night's bad deeds was lit.

What next? The Reverend Vachell reading us the Riot Act. His tiny eyes, squinty with sleep, his well-padded body and the hatred he produced in us, how the sight of him in his nightgown outdoors on that May night, well fed; cowardly behind the figure of his wife – did nothing to quell our anger but flamed it to boiling point. What did he know of our privations? Did *he* have six children at home with nothing to put in their bowls but water and potatoes? Damn old bugger did nothing to help the folk of Littleport. This was Pa. Pa now at the head of the crowd, inciting.

Didn't see Reverend Vachell scurry back to his house, like a dog with its tail tucked, but not long after, we followed him there. The vicarage door had already been smashed by the time I arrived. Tom said that the damned Reverend Vachell had brandished a gun and run out the back, but I never saw that myself. Now men swarmed in the dining room, knocking over candles and the smell of wax and seared wood was in the air.

Found myself with others in the storeroom where the stocks could not fail to amaze us: and seeing so much, seeing it all there, the boxes, the food, the silver, the beer, well, my eyes was bedazzled and my heart ready to burst with outrage and yes, I picked them up, I picked up the four silver gravy spoons and I remember looking at them and feeling their weight in my hands and in the light from the candles marvelling at their beauty and all slowed down while I thought about this, how lovely things lived with unlovely people, and just as I'm about to take them, to pack them into my waistcoat, there above the crowd I spy the fair slip of a girl I thought I saw with my Susie, it's the Carter girl, a servant of the Waddelows, and she's calling to me, saying, 'Beamiss! Give them to me!' – Vachell has sent her to carry back his goods.

'He's sent a girl! What a man! The Reverend! He sends you, does he?' I shouted.

Tom was beside me. Tom heard it. He heard what I said but he didn't see Elizabeth Carter mouth her reply. Was full aware of that cleaver Tom held, the frenzied chopping, the smashing he had achieved with it. The sound of wood creaking and breaking; of table-legs snapping, all around me like a crackling fire. And the blood pumping, pumping hard throughout our bodies so that we beat as one.

Elizabeth Carter begged me. She took fright at the mayhem in the room and she mouthed something in all exaggeration. Something hard to read across the heads of others, but something like: 'Mistress *Susie* says . . .'

I held the spoons out to her. The court record shows it. Elizabeth Carter, the servant girl, under cross-examination, told it so in court. *Beamiss held the spoons out to her to carry home. The moment she asked Beamiss for the spoons, he endeavoured to give them to her; she verily believed he meant to give them to her, but he could not reach her.*

Those spoons. Four silver spoons. My life hanging in the balance, all of me a-dangle in that kitchen, and the four silver spoons, glinting. But it wasn't the servant girl Elizabeth Carter I saw there. It was the dark, lovely, glowing face of my Susie. Susie who could do nothing quietly, nothing stealthily. A girl all riotous herself and hot as blood: it was her lovely figure that was trying to hide behind Elizabeth – the mob would molest her, her being a Spencer, a Farmer, the enemy – and her dark head that bobbed and ducked and sent its message to me. A look that flew through the room like an arrow, and saved me.

Witness on the night of 22 May 1816 through the window did spy Beamiss with several spoons in his hand. There were other persons in the room. About ten minutes after, saw him in the garden with the spoons in his hand. While he was coming in the house, there was an alarm of horse-soldiers coming. Saw Beamiss with Thomas South in the garden, the one they call Tom Foolery though that is not his Christened name. Some conversation took place between them. Spoons afterwards found in the thatch of a house of the mother of one of the rioters.

And throughout all I heard the chop of Tom's cleaver, like a madman's.

How did the spoons come to be there?

I cannot tell you.

Cannot or will not?

I cannot properly recollect it.

But you were there, and you held the spoons in your hand, you cannot deny that.

Yes, I was there, sir, but beyond that, my mind is bare.

At what point did your father, Mr William Beamiss the elder, join you?

I cannot recall, sir.

Was he with you at the point when you broke into the house of the Reverend Vachell? Or perhaps at the moment when the riotous mob smashed their way into Mr Dewey's house?

I—

You cannot recall. So you all say. And the main charge, that you and your father later held up a chaise with farmer Henry Tansley of Littleport, Ely, in it and put him in bodily fear – what recall you of that?

Witnesses called as to the character of the prisoner. They all stated they had known me from a child, and that I had always been peaceable, honest, and industrious, that I was by trade a shoemaker. One of those same witnesses, James Loddington of Littleport, mentioned that he had asked me, the prisoner Beamiss, to keep the mob out of his house, as he had a child dying. The mob went to his house, but Loddington told how Beamiss the younger said: 'Go back, you shan't go in there,' and they obeyed.

So you had influence over the mob?

I'm just a boy, sir.

You had enough influence to prevent them from going in a house where a child was dying?

I cannot recall—

So you say. Witnesses claim you were a good man but if you had some influence we can assume you could have stopped them. And if that had been the case, neither you, nor your father, would be in this courtroom today.

That was how it went.

The learned judge did not think it necessary to repeat what had already been said about my good character. The prisoner, he said, acknowledged that he went in the house but did not take the spoons. A witness agrees. He later, with his father – who others named as the 'cashier' in the operation – opened the door of a chaise with passengers in it but did not take any money from those inside. Henry Tansley spoke up, saying in his measly little voice that Beamiss the elder was the cashier for the mob. That, Henry Tansley squeaked, Henry Tansley was certain of. The jury immediately returned a verdict of guilty.

I was the only prisoner who answered the questions put to me in court. Terror silenced the rest. Mr Hart spoke for one or two of us. The rest had no defence. We all knew what dangled in front of us. We had been brought in, our legs in chains. We saw the monstrous Ely Cathedral rise up above us and can you imagine, in a place as empty and featureless as ours, how fearsome that building was to us, how much power and majesty it commanded? I used to think of it as a great whale rising above a white foamy sea and me on a tiny wooden boat in its wake . . .

The occasion called for Special Assizes – we did not know what that term meant – and for the trial to be rushed through and judges brought from London and elsewhere in view of the great significance of the trial. We, placed standing on the grass, had to watch the Bishop of Ely make his slow and certain way to the Cathedral, with his sword of state carried by his butler in front of him. All pomp and ceremony was laid on, to make the point to us. 'Tell it out among the people that the Lord is King,' sang the choir. We remained outside with our gaolers and guards, but we heard every word of the sermon that Henry Bate Dudley made: 'The Law is not made for the righteous man, but for the lawless and disobedient.'

Then we was ushered to the town hall with another speech, this time by Judge Abbott, telling all of how it was of the highest import not just for the peace of our Isle of Ely but of the whole nation that an awful lesson might here be taught. You can imagine the black dread struck in our hearts at that; and then the trial began.

Their questions come in the cold light and our night had been all bloody and inky-dark heat. And their intention: to set an example. To crush 'those very daring acts of outrage' – to show that none of us who rioted would be spared. To show it had nothing to do with poverty or need and to point out that the inhabitants of Ely is more 'rude and uncivilised' than anywhere else. The conduct of the rioters was not due to poverty, or bad crops, the courts was told, because all the prisoners was robust men receiving great wages, too frequently wasted in drunkenness.

They read out a letter in court that was meant to shame us. It was an ignorant letter full of curses so foul it would make your mother faint, they said. Listening to it, 'You do as you like, you rob the poor of their common right, you plough the grass up that God sent to grow, that a poor man may not feed a cow or pig . . . we intend to have things as we like and we will fight you for it,' revealed to me that it was rage and impulse that fuelled us, yes, but older grievances too, going back to an earlier time. I thought of Pa and his strong feelings and politicking and whether it was possible that, despite the difference in our natures, he had sometimes succeeded in passing them to me. Where do *Feelings* live? Inside us, surely, in our hearts. Where do they end, where do they stop? Pa's feelings sometimes made such a vivid spark in my nature that I believe I shall not forget it in my grave.

The trials lasted a week. Taken in chains afterwards to Ely Gaol and was barely enough room to stand up. Face to face, like animals taken to market. I breathed in George Crow's breath and heard him mutter, why am I standing in these shoes, when Aaron the pock-pecked bastard escaped to London, when Henry blasted Benson escaped with a misdemeanour?

I said to Pa, damn the eyes of the bugger who spoke so freely in court against him, Henry Tansley, but Pa was quiet and shook his head. I said, a bare year ago, didn't you share a pint of ale with him, at the Peace celebrations, didn't you sew shoes for his daughter? But again Pa's eyes only filled with tears, and he said nothing. Was he not our own neighbour, had I not gone to school with that same daughter, hadn't Pa once helped him drag his horse from a ditch, I whispered, still hoping to raise Pa's ire, his lively seditious spirit . . . This, I thought, would surely rouse Pa to fury, but again it was met with only tears.

I hung my head in weary pain, trying not to weep myself. Could not recognise this quiet Pa, this Pa who was beat, and that was most frightening of all. My neck was sore, my stomach growled with hunger, but Pa's strange spirits was the thing that pained me most.

And then two mornings later, and a message came to the Bishop's Gaol in the form of one of Judge Bate's junior men. We was all assembled in the Felons' Hall and was screamed at by the gaoler for silence.

Tom shuffled to his feet, dragging Isaac Harley, bolted at the shins, with him. A tiny breath of fresh air and a smell of spring blossom came in as the young messenger and a small troop of military men with guns entered the prison, then was quickly snuffed as the door locked shut behind them. We was told a message was delivered and would now be read to us.

We shuffled and clanked into some kind of silence. The stink of straw soaked in sweat and the stench from the privy in the yard choked the room. George Crow had an iron spike around his neck, on account of the trouble he'd caused last night, and was rubbing at his throat and staring at his hand, which came away spotted with blood. The rest of us lay slumped, defeated, on the straw mattresses, or struggled to our feet. The gaoler watched us warily, sucking on a clay pipe. Extra men had been brought in from Ely for the task of watching us 'dangerous felons' and they stood either side of the gaoler, their hands nervously stroking the smooth wooden truncheons at their sides.

The youth was trembling and took fright of us. The old gaoler put aside his pipe and grunted, 'Read the notice then!' and silence fell. We held our breath. A mouse could be heard scratching in the straw.

I had manoeuvred myself next to Pa. His bad foot had swollen within his constrained irons and the skin was shiny and almost blue. I stared at this. I tried to listen, but the names read out seemed unearthly and wavered on the youth's voice, like a bird cry, not like human speech. I only heard Tom's soft crying, and looked up and saw his red head dropping forward, and remembered the day we had climbed the tallest tree on the banks of the River Ouse to peep inside the buzzard's nest, and Tom had let go his grip and fallen from it, dropping like a stone into the water, and how I had jumped down and run alongside the river, crying out: Tom! Tom! until his head broke the surface again. Being Tom – Tom Foolery – he resurfaced with a madman's laugh like the honk of a goose.

I kept my mind on that; closing my eyes. As I did so it was Susie's face that filled my mind. Her little pointy chin. Her vivid hazel-coloured eyes. Her liveliness, how all around her was always glittering, bright. Was this true, or a fancy, my own thoughts colouring her so?

Nineteen of us was reprieved. I heard the words at last: they drove into my thoughts, like a stake. Pa they deemed too seditious, being in possession of some intelligence that should have made him know better. Tom too violent with cleaver and his feverish chopping. John Dennis they said was a leader, and without need and therefore greedy. The deeds of George and Isaac unforgivable. But seven was to be transported. Twelve was to stay in Ely Gaol for at least one year. I was one of those.

Pa and Tom, Isaac Harley, John Dennis and George Crow was to be hanged.

They came for Pa, Tom and the others in the morning. Light scoured our eyes early, streaming in through the one square window, falling to the floor in stripes. A cuckoo piped its bum notes, the most detested bird, singing for all the world as if there was joy in the air. Staggered to my feet, tried to speak. Pa hugged me and nodded and touched my cheek, and he looked soft, soft, his face melting in front of me like the softest of clouds, as if he was already fading.

'I can see you now in your little pink frock, sealskin cap . . .' Pa muttered, in his embrace a madness that seemed to grip him, that made him want to babble sweet nothings in my ear as if I was but two years old. The gaol chaplain stepped between us and we was rudely parted.

The same armed men from yesterday gripped at Pa's shoulder. He showed no resistance. We felons could hear the crowds that waited outside the gaolhouse, hear the clop of the horses ready to carry the condemned away to the swampy grounds at Parnell Pits. We knew without seeing it of the waiting cart, draped in its black crêpe. Even in gaol news had reached us, how troubling they found it to purchase horses, so strongly did locals feel about it. There was barely a man in the area Pa didn't know. Men he grew up with, drank 'good Ely ale' alongside, played cards with, sewed shoes for. Boys he had swum with in the River Ouse; skated beside under Sandhill bridge, when the river iced over.

Tom wept openly and noisily. Gave me a last beseeching look, wild with fear, and all jokes wrenched from him. Why Pa? I could only think. Tom – it was clear to all that Tom would one day come to the bad, but Pa? In the courtroom it was said that his position in life should have restrained him. The fact of his job as a shoemaker. His age. In the end, they wanted to make an example of him.

'Bear up, Willie!' Pa shouted, one last flare of his old spirit as he was bundled from the gaol.

We could hear the horses' impatience, hear them snorting and stomping. Pa's words rattled around the empty walls.

The iron doors clanged behind them. I only wanted to die myself.

I fell then into some kind of faint, a dreaming state, where I lay on straw in a corner of the gaol and felt myself neither living or dead. Wondered if I was a horse: was that why I could smell straw in my nostrils? Was I already in heaven, or had I fallen into a dark deep well? Once again the will-o'-the-wisp came to me, this time skating across the gaolhouse floor as if on ice, and on its face the most terrible expression and it seated astride a creature nothing like a horse . . .

I do not know how many hours or days I lay in this place, willing myself to die too. The pain in my heart was so great I believed it would surely complete the task and break in two.

One night I dreamed a most fearful dream: of the noose hanging and Father's head, looming at me, expanded as big as a bladder. I began shaking and weeping in my sleep. But the strangest thing: Pa spoke to me, and it was just as if he was beside me. Bear up, he said again. Your death is yours alone, it belongs to you, it is contained in the first seed of you; none can take it from you, not even your killer.

I thought this a nonsense remark and wanted to strike him. Where am I? I asked him, in the dream. You're just a twinkle in my eye; you're a star, you don't yet exist, Pa said. I tried to will myself awake, to continue this conversation with him, so comforting was it. Where am I before I'm born, then, and after my death? Pa smiled, and told me not to fear. I was where he was now: in dreams, in the memories of my children. Pull your children in sledges over the frozen lake, never stop them from squealing from joy.

I woke with my ear pressed to the floor, feeling the cold brick seep through, and I felt as if I'd been straining to hear more, to catch Pa's voice. I covered my head with my shirt and jacket for warmth, and tried not to listen to the gossip of the other prisoners, but could not prevent myself from hearing as how Tom South was the most vexed and agitated; how Pa's last words was to forgive Henry Tansley who spoke wrong in court against him. That struck me. That shocked me and infuriated me at first.

And I heard too how the women of Littleport was allowed – no, *invited* – to come and weep over the bodies of their menfolk as they lay in the house next to the prison, awaiting burial. I closed my eyes against the picture this drew for me of the five men in the cart with the black cloth draped over it, white caps on their heads, slumped there like shot birds. And thoughts of my own dear mother. Her bonnet and her calf-leather slippers, sewn for her by Pa.

They had had to build a gallows new and fast, to make their point, I knew that much. Parnell Pits – a swampy place, old Fen, quag, they call it, foul-smelling water; a place to avoid since all Fenmen knew it gave you the ague: Marsh fever. There was a crowd, the others whispered. Women carrying babies, mothers iced over with shock. A few infantrymen to keep the crowd in order.

I close my eyes and ears but still I'm there with Pa, with Tom, in my mind. I see it clear: the morning sun making finger shadows across the marshy spot; we've all seen that round here. How the reeds look, spiked with the blood red of the summer's last poppies. Their silky paper petals drooping their sorry heads. A woodpigeon tooting fit to burst. I know Henry Tansley would be there. John Griffin, our gaoler, praying. *May their awful Fate be a warning to others.*

A hush. A crow rummaging in its feathers, searching for something lost. Nettles and the sharp juice of grass and that stink of bad Fen water. My breath held at the hour they did it – the exact hour – five men are paraded on the wooden platform, hands tied, white caps covering heads. The dark seeds of their eyes.

Pa would be bold, I know that. Stare out at the Fen country-side he loves. Hear the geese honking overhead – there's always geese honking overhead; hear the bittern booming. He would be dreaming of lying low on his stomach in the boat on the river with a punt gun.

Perhaps he thinks of me, of his son Willie back in Ely Gaol, or of his daughters, or his wife, or the future. Of a first grand-child he's never going to see. Or the far future – of a long line of Beamisses. He had modest aims, I think, did Pa. He wanted a fair wage and a fair price for flour. He didn't plan on being supernatural.

Those fragile poppy heads – a sudden breeze lifting them from their stalks and scattering red petals and seeds and black hanging figures everywhere. William, Isaac Harley, John Dennis, Thomas South the younger, George Crow, taking their leap into the dark. A stain upon the Fens.

They whispered that Pa cried out as the drop fell, 'I forgive Mr Tansley that he swore falsely against me.' Finally I knew it was just Pa being Pa, a man hotly rash but full of forgiveness. Fair, and straight: a good man.

'Might as well be hanged as starved,' muttered Richard Rutter, from his bed of straw in the gaol.

'His heart continued alive for a full four hours, expanding and contracting after the body was cut down,' whispered little John Badger.

'Its powers was visible past one o'clock.'

'Preserved his rebellion until the last gasp.'

Did not need to know of who they spoke. Who had the Fen Tiger's heart that could continue to pump like the wind-pump with its steady inexorable task when all life from the body was gone? I knew anyway, knew without asking. William Beamiss the elder. Dear Pa. Now launched into all eternity.

Thought then that my life would fade to nothing and that be the end of me. Gaol rations, sickness, the ague; longed for one of them to carry me off. But one day, an icy day, when frost coated the cobwebs in the gaol and lit the trees outside the window as if with heavenly light, a new prisoner was brought in. A thirteen-year-old boy, one week for trespass on the Spencer farm in Prickwillow. And with him, something queer. A note. Blue paper. Folded small and thick and hidden in the boy's breeches. He hands it to me with a sullen, dull-eyed face.

Dearest Willie,

I do not know if you can read this. I have risked all to send it and bribed the boy you see before you. I endeavour too to send money each week to your mother and sisters. Little Jenny has been very sick but she is recovering.

Willie Beamiss. Dearest one – know that I am waiting
for you. I am yours. If you will have me. I would run away
with you, whatever you ask of me I will do. Know that
my middle name is Constance and that my heart is
constant too.
    Your
        Susie Spencer

(Mother, being superstitious, had taught me that book learning was the blackest of Witchcraft, and now I rejoiced once again that Pa had always been such a ticklish devil, full of disobedience, and had allowed me, as I have said, to learn my letters.)

Susie Spencer reached into that darkness like the white finger of a winter tree-branch and saved me once again. And so I endured that unspeakable year and when the gaol door opened, Susie was good as her word, and had learned the date, and stood outside waiting for me. We defied her father, who cut off all funds and never spoke to her again.

My Susie was bold and fierce and original. We was married the day I quit Ely Gaol, 7 July 1817.

Part Three

'Before you know it, you'll be swinging your legs over the side of the bed and getting ready for your first walk outside the hospital.'

'Jeez, you think so?'

It's Maureen again, the knitter. She's nodding towards the physical therapist, a stocky local girl who has left me in a state of near collapse after asking me – no, seriously, wanting me – to *cough*, and cough hard, meanwhile holding a pillow over the incision in my chest to 'splint it and muffle the pain'. Muffle the pain! Muffle the bloody pain. Hold the wretched thing, more like, lest it pop out and do a triumphant dance over the entire ward.

Anyhow the malicious fascist has gone now, leaving me with Maureen the minuscule knitter and her murmurings about happy futures and, what do you know, her plans for Christmas. Christmas! We're still in November surely, or have I been here longer than I think? A hilarious piece in *Transplant News* (so bored now that I've resorted to flicking through it) tells me that 'patients may resume sexual activity after their transplant. In the first few weeks after surgery, however, they might find that pain along the incision will limit activity to a certain extent. During the first eight weeks after surgery, any activity or position that causes pain or pulling across your chest, such as bearing weight on your arms, must be avoided.' This helpful instruction conjured up such a powerful image of Daisy sympathetically lowering herself onto me, carefully bearing the load of her own featherweight form on those slender freckled arms, I wonder if I didn't groan out loud. Certainly the departing physical therapist – a pasty Fatso as they invariably are – threw a startled glance over her shoulder at me.

Daisy. I have not been thinking about Daisy. Daisy is over. She was over months ago – months before she submitted the offending letter, that vicious trick that she'd kept up her sleeve, the lurid emails she'd carefully saved, with me twittering on about her tiny waist and huge breasts and other deeply embarrassing things, not to mention the poetry – those tossers on the Complaints Board would have had a field day, laughing at how I'd tried to pass off quotes from Keats's letters to Fanny Brawne as lines of my own.

The day I finished things with Daisy, she burst into my office, where I had another student, a very promising young American post-grad called Elizabeth, sitting with me.

The door opened with no warning. Daisy's hair was filled with static, rising from her head like a shock of feathers.

'You wanker! You're dumping me – by *text*?'

'Elizabeth, that will have to be all for today, thanks, yes—'

Elizabeth scuttled to gather up her papers. We'd been making great progress but this wasn't the time to mourn that. She dropped her bag, offering me a glimpse of a girlish bra as she leaned forward to pick it up. She was practically running. But I thought I saw a smile, too. Perhaps we could resume our discussion later. On the other hand her smile might mean that the girl couldn't wait to tell her post-grad group.

'Daisy, I only said—'

'You said you needed to talk to me. I'm not an idiot. I know what you're going to say.'

'Well, do *you* feel things are going well between us? Is this your idea of how you'd like things to be?'

'You created this, you bastard! You make me angry, you mess me around the whole time, I never know where I am with you.'

And then she was crying, and I admit it, some little part of me withdrew. It was the tears. I hate tears. Tears make you the villain and the unfeeling one, regardless of what you feel, simply because you can't produce them yourself. And whatever they say, I know women use them to get their own way: Alice learned that trick by the time she was two years old. If some boy was misbehaving in the park and she said he'd pushed her and Helen didn't go and tell him off right away – bursting into tears would do the trick every time.

I offered Daisy a tissue. I made sure the door was closed properly. I put my arms around her and stroked her long, baby-soft, hair, trying to smooth it down so that she looked less like an angry cockerel. I noticed for the first time that she was wearing thigh-high boots, (which seemed to me a little over the top for a young academic).

'This is exactly what I mean,' I murmured. 'It's all – a bit much for me. Not sure, you know, I'm not sure the poor old ticker can actually stand all the drama—'

And then right on cue, the old ticker started to do something shocking. The pains, the breathing difficulties, the dizziness, the worsening of my condition: I'd been ignoring it all for weeks. Suddenly I could feel an invisible waistcoat, *inside* my skin, and it was tightening and tightening, cutting off my air supply. I crumpled to my chair.

Daisy was still talking. It was that word 'drama' that so offended her. I was accusing her of being a *drama queen*, she said, of over-reacting, or worse – making it all up. She seemed to take the strange noises I was making as my only defence and eventually she stormed out. I sat there, trying to breathe.

I undid my trousers. I reached for the telephone, wondering, like a child, if this was the right moment to call for an ambulance. I considered checking that Daisy had closed the door properly behind her – the indignity of being seen like this – but in the end the pain in my chest, the tightening brace inside my shirt, was too gripping. Sweat made my palms slippery on the phone. I gave up and instead found myself kneeling at my desk drawer, throwing out pens, clawing at the packet of heart pills.

When I could breathe again I was able to think calmly about Daisy. I resolved to find a tasteful way to end things cleanly and completely between us that would make it possible to sit in department meetings with her without embarrassment. What I didn't reckon on was that she would get there first.

Now I disguise my erection under the sheets with *Transplant News* and manfully try to steer myself away from vivid, pointless thoughts of Daisy.

'I wonder if there has been anything more in the local paper?' I watch Maureen's face for signs that she's hiding information from me. More details about the donor? An obituary perhaps?

'The *Cambridge Evening News* is still on about the fires. Sabotage, they're saying now, but they can't find out anything more about a perpetrator. No leads. They're giving up on that.'

From the cabinet beside my bed, I pick up the paper she left me, the one where I had a starring role, and read the headlines – the front-page article – for the first time. 'Arsonists are suspected of setting fire to more than thirty thousand bales of straw in a blaze in Cambridgeshire. A further fifty thousand tonnes is now understood to have caught fire in a field near Ely, said Cambridgeshire Fire Service. The fire service commander co-ordinating the operation said he believed the fires were "suspicious".'

'How strange I didn't take this in. I think Helen mentioned it too. I guess I thought I was the only thing happening in the news that day.'

'Yes, and in fact you were only a small item and photograph on page five.' She smiles. 'One of the nurses says you look like George Clooney.'

She blushes faintly then. Looks horrified at her own loquaciousness.

'But I look better now, I hope? That was a very bad photo,' I say.

She laughs: a snort, a loud laugh, unabashed, like the laughter of a twelve-year-old boy. She had been hesitant, as if unsure I wanted her to stay, but now, encouraged, she takes off her coat and sits down in the visitor's chair.

'I imagine you've looked him up,' she says, nodding towards my laptop.

'I couldn't find anything. There are Andrew Beamishes on Facebook but none recently deceased from Littleport. There's stuff about Littleport Historical Society. Did you know it means smiling with optimism? The name Beamish, right? I've been thinking . . . what you said. Writing to my donor's family. Here, I've given it a go. Perhaps you could pass it along to – well, his family, his parents, I don't know, whoever you think would like to hear from me.'

Maureen beams at me. 'That's very kind. I'm impressed. It's – well, in my experience people usually don't hear back from the donor family, but it's a great comfort to them to hear from you and to know that you – the recipient – are grateful.'

The moment she says this, I regret what I wrote in the letter. Selfish. That's what Helen would say. It's always about you, isn't it, Patrick, that's the difference between men and women (her complaints never just addressed to me, but in my unasked-for capacity as representative of the male sex), men being so hopeless at thinking about anyone else's feelings except their own.

'Well, maybe I need to give it a little more thought,' I say.

Maureen is staring at me, without picking up her knitting, and her hand goes back in her bag for the envelope I just gave her. She turns it over. 'Where did you get this?' she asks.

'What, the envelope? Alice bought me it. My daughter.'

'You see, you've sealed it. And I need to be sure you haven't included any personal details. You know, the town you live in, your name, that kind of thing. And no religious sentiments! The donor might be Muslim for all you know.'

'Are there a lot of Muslims in the rural Fens?'

'Or even the name of the hospital. You shouldn't put that.'

'Jeez. So much secrecy! If I don't have any identifying information how the hell are you going to send it to the right donor family?'

'The proper procedure – as I'm sure I explained to you – is to put it in an unsealed envelope. I'll bring you another one if you like. Then you put your name, date of operation and hospital on an accompanying piece of paper.'

She's ripping open the envelope as she speaks, and I have a childish fear of her opening it and reading it in front of me. I snatch back the envelope: 'OK, I can do that. Give it here. I can do all of that.'

She looks startled. To hide her confusion she begins rummaging – red gloves, flower-patterned glasses case, crimson-suede diary: garish teenage choices, all – placing them on the grey coverlet on the bed. She finds what she's looking for, a folded page, printed from the internet.

'Here. I meant to give you this. You know, a sample letter to help you know what to say. It's from this website for transplant patients. I'll just pop this here and . . . well, there.'

I stare at the sheet she gives me, a poor-quality print-out.

Dear Donor Family, 'Thank you.' These two words seem so inadequate for the gift of life you have given to me.

Oh Lord. I get the idea.

You have given me this astonishing gift of a second chance and many tomorrows. Endless possibilities. I will be able to see the faces of those I love, hear the birdsong. I will be able to hug and be hugged.

Many tomorrows! To hug and be hugged!

I promise you that I will do my utmost to honour this truly wondrous gift. I will try to do all I can to make our world a better place.

Really? Is that what's expected of me now?

Do let me assure you that not one day, not one hour, not one minute will go by without me remembering and wondering about my donor.

Well, that bit's true enough, but somehow not in the way that's meant here.

Please know that if there is anything at all I could do to make your suffering less, I would, and you only have to ask. Thank you from the bottom of my heart, the recipient.

Good God. 'Thank you from the bottom of my heart.' Are these people strangers to irony? *Whose* heart?

To Maureen I muster: 'OK, I get the idea. I'll give it another go.'

'Next time I visit we'll go to your flat. That'll be nice, won't it?'

The flat. I've been here a while now and they need the bed back. I'm doing 'beautifully' according to Dr Burns, but I need constant daily monitoring; hence the plan to move me to the flat on the hospital grounds, used for this purpose.

There's something about Maureen, and I can't fathom what it is. Is it her desire to help me all the time, or something else? She's sort of eccentric, I suppose. (Not a quality I usually admire in a woman.) Today she is wearing this long fringed skirt in a deep-red colour, beads, a black silky blouse with some kind of flowers embroidered on it – all she needs is a guitar and a wig and she'd be Joni Mitchell. Her strange job; her role as go-between. Presumably in her role as transplant co-ordinator she even sat with the family, held their hands at the point they made the decision, switched off the machines, whatever it is they do. How can she stand it? She must be made of different stuff than other people. Than me, perhaps.

'How do you know for absolute certain if a brain-dead person is really dead?' I ask her.

'Sorry?'

'Radio 4. This woman has written a book about, you know, the ethical questions around organ transplants. That's one of the issues.'

'I think that . . .'

She picks up her long beads, fiddles with them, drops them again. I can see she's worried about upsetting me, but I'm fine, I'm perfectly calm.

'Every test is done,' she says. 'I can assure you – apparently more tests are done on donors than – you know, non-donors – before pronouncing them – dead. There's no way . . . Mistakes can't be made—'

She gestures, a shake of the hand, as if to brush away any possibility of doubt.

'Actually,' I tell her, 'I was thinking about my mother. She died in a car accident – oh no, don't worry, it was years ago. I mean, I was a kid. About eleven. I just mean Dad agreed to switch off the life-support when we were told that. And now, just now, I thought, What does it mean? At what point do we really know?'

'Well, I'm not a doctor, of course; you could ask Dr Burns. Brainstem dead. It doesn't sound very nice, does it, but I think it means, you know, all activity in the brain has ceased for ever. Legally, that person is dead.'

'*Legally.*'

'Yes.'

So that I could *legally* take the donor's heart and make it mine. I'm not a thief after all, then. No stealing involved. It's all legal. We're not in some primitive era where we cut open the chests of our enemies and eat their hearts in order to steal their courage, their vitality. It's interesting now to see Maureen a little . . . what? Flustered? Less professional, somehow. Her hair this morning, now I'm lying here and considering her more closely, must be newly washed, or perhaps it's a bit damp outside. In any case her hair is slightly less Jack Russell in texture – short and harsh – and instead she looks . . . ruffled. Her hair is tufty and girlish. Like I say: it's a strange job.

'Funny how it's always the end of brain activity now that signifies the end of life. In the past it was the heart, surely?'

'Yes,' she answers, with the same worried expression. Then: 'It's perfectly normal, I think, to worry about the family—'

'I wasn't. Like I say, I was just thinking. About Cushie. My mother. And how, in the old days it was the heart that was considered, you know, the centre of things, where the self was located. Aristotle wasn't very impressed with the cold wet matter of the brain. These days neuroscience is king, isn't it? That's where people think emotions are located. Cranio-centrism over cardio-centrism. The brain has won over the heart, you could say.'

91

She looks uncertain then, as if I'm involving her in some sort of tutorial or oral exam that she's about to fail.

'Sorry. Going off on one rather, aren't I? Used to drive Alice – my daughter – insane. Why can't you just *talk* to me, she'd say. I'm not one of your students.'

'Well. I'm sure she's very grateful now. I wish my dad had ever – you know. I can't imagine it! Taken me seriously. Talked to me like an adult.'

'Really? Try telling that to Alice. I've been thinking a lot since I've been here. It occurs to me that I deserved a mug. *World's Worst Father.* You know. For Father's Day?'

'I'm tiring you,' Maureen says.

I stop rubbing at my eyes. 'No, no, I'm fine, really.'

Stay. Damn fool. What's wrong with me?

Maureen runs a hand over her hair, patting it down a little and tucking her beads down her blouse, where they rattle away between her breasts like a happy snake while she puts on her raincoat.

'I'll bring the keys to the flat tomorrow,' she says, forcing a smile.

'Well . . .'

(And here it comes, the professionalism again, I see it re-form, somehow: *it's been a very trying experience for you.* Or: *the post-operative period is full of ups and downs.*) But instead she says nothing, buttons her coat, and nods to me as she leaves.

The lamp is dark beside my bed and I close my eyes.

The place behind my lids is black but dotted with lights. Chester-le-Street, County Durham. The night of Cushie's funeral. (Mam. As a little boy, I called her *Mam,* but the Geordie word later carried a sizzle of – what? shame? – and was replaced.) Four days after they switched off the life-support machine, I heard her singing in my bedroom. I'm upstairs, hiding, the room is full of shadows: Airfix planes dangling, wobbling. The family, the visitors, the sandwiches and sherry I'm supposed to pass around are all downstairs. The body was in the coffin, my mother wore a yellow dress, the coffin passed through the curtains in the church, I saw it myself. And yet here, I can hear her singing, her beautiful Dusty Springfield voice, her favourite song: *yesterday when I was young, the taste of life was sweet as rain upon my tongue* . . . I hear it so clearly I put my head out from under the pillow, I stop crying, to listen. A model plane flutters as if someone just walked past it. The sweetness of her voice, the Geordie lilt in every note. And then I don't hear it. And I know that she's gone.

Dear Donor Family . . .

Fuck. I bet it's a mother reading this.

I do hope this correspondence is not unwelcome. I am Professor Patrick Robson (his parents will know my name, they must have read the newspaper reports), *the recipient of your son's heart.*

Scratch that. *Your son's organ.* No, sounds somehow sexual. And sends my thoughts in unsavoury directions. A young lad's dick? A shot of Viagra? I can imagine Helen admonishing me. For God's sake, Patrick! *Your son's heart* will have to do.

Jeez, I can't get any further than that. I've got a splitting headache. The memory of Helen saying (more than once), 'You think with your dick, Patrick, you always have, that's your trouble.' That consciousness might be located there of all places never struck me as insane or insulting, the way Helen intended.

Last night I had the weirdest dream. My heart was talking to me. And, after all, the heart does indeed look – if we're talking about the skin of it, the surface texture – like the dark purple head of a giant skinned cock – you know, taut and looming – and it was *talking* to me. And then, other things in the dream. My heart was on the screen – the monitor – and it was yelling, and it looked really weird, like a little screaming monkey. And then it was jumping out and running all around the hospital. In another dream there were all these birds around and there was a barn owl – an absolute beauty with a heart-shaped face and it was called Ted Hughes. I don't know how I knew this but you do, don't you, in dreams. It was flying alongside my car, peering inside. Next I'm at Westminster Abbey and someone is telling me Hughes is dead.

So, despite the unlikely nature of Maureen's forecast for me ('Before you know it, you'll be swinging your legs over the side of the bed and getting ready for your first walk'), that day is here, and I've walked round the wards and even through the door to the outside world and yes, my legs do function and the bugger inside me hasn't stuttered to a halt, and – surprising how strange I feel about this – I'm not in prison. No one has rushed to stop me. I pause just at the door, finding myself in Papworth Hospital car park. Outside is exactly as Helen reported – all unseasonably fair, stunningly bright, the sun making lattice patterns on the vivid green grass, a yellow ambulance, bright as a child's toy, a few scattered leaves on the ground glowing in cornflake colours, and on the horizon – the edge of the known world – aspen trees waving their wispy branches, as if to say: Come over here, see if your doctors aren't wrong with their dire prophecies of infection and rejection.

That ridiculous thought seems par for the course these days. I'm thinking in ways that are unfamiliar to me. Pathetic fallacy is not a concept I've ever embraced, and once again the horrible idea occurs that my IQ, or rather my general ability as an intelligent, educated person without clichéd or religious or other superstitious beliefs, has forsaken me. As I stand there, shuffling to a stop in my trainers, putting one hand out on the acid-green-painted door to Reception, surveying the pristine golf-course world outside of the hospital, a quiet little voice trickles through to me. *Yep. I'm still here.*

Two steps forward and my feet find a concrete path. I have an urge to reach that unreal grass, to take a closer look. A few steps more and I'm there. Crouching down isn't easy, but I'm intrigued. My foot has nudged something in the grass.

'Hi, Patrick – out and about, are we!'

Fuck. It's Maureen. And as I look closer I see that it was a circle of toadstools, honey-coloured, fine wobbly heads on fragile stalks, like something from one of Alice's childhood books. A fairy ring. I straighten up. I'm aware of a strange sense of wanting to look at it again; to bend down, to pick one, and see if under the cap is the fine crumbling flesh I imagine, a stalk trailing threads from the earth that sprinkle spots of soil, but stronger than this desire is the one to appear, well, normal.

'Were you on your way to see me?' I ask Maureen, straightening up. And then: 'I like your hat!'

She looks embarrassed, unsure if I'm teasing her.

'No, actually, I'm on my way to a . . . to meet . . .'

She seems reluctant to tell me. She nods instead towards a small hill on the hospital grounds, topped with a grand cream-coloured building flanked by pillars. My eyes are drawn to a sign next to it: *'Stop! Check your pockets for patient data.'* Maureen readjusts her heavy duffle bag, hoisting it with a strange jutting hip gesture, and acknowledges the sign.

'They don't like us to go home with your files in our bags!'

'My file? Do you have my file?'

'Well, as it happens . . . I just meant . . .'

'What month is it? The weather's all wrong, though, isn't it, too sunny for . . . November, is it? I should go back in.'

She nods; she seems relieved I've let the question drop. She's wearing a red woolly hat with a bobble and her cheeks are pink, healthy, her eyes glittering. She's an odd mismatch of fabrics, shapes and colours, a garden gnome: yellow, scarlet, brown. She's knitted herself up, I think: a little doll. Even her bag is knitted: dark green and orange squares. The colours of the heaps of leaves I used to pile up in the back garden as a boy, my job to rake them and help Dad to burn them. She's already marching up the hill towards the building – *Corporate Affairs and Chairman's Office*. I follow her, clutching the letter in my pocket.

In the end I kept it simple.

Dear Donor Family,

My name is Patrick Robson. I am the recipient of your son's heart. I don't know if you would welcome a letter from me but have been advised that it might comfort you to hear from me. I will keep this brief. I am fifty, a retired academic, father of two grown-up children. In the months preceding the operation I had the most appalling health problems, was constantly exhausted and in pain and had numerous tests and endless inconvenient hospital visits that had a detrimental affect on my working life. The diagnosis was cardiomyopathy and in a meeting with my cardiologist earlier this year I was given only a few months to live. Your son's decision to carry a donor card and your agreement to this has changed that prognosis. I am profoundly grateful to you.

Yours sincerely,

Patrick Robson.

Under a hundred and fifty words and harder than any abstract I ever had to write. It took me five attempts. I changed 'I am very grateful' to 'profoundly grateful' but that's the only concession I've made to mimicking the fulsome tone of Maureen's sample letter. I was determined not to ask Helen or Alice for help either but then could hear Alice's criticisms in my head anyway: 'Dad, don't put Professor – that sounds so pompous and cold!' In an earlier draft I'd also mentioned that I had a son the same age and thought better of that, too. Surely that would be rubbing this family's nose in it – *I still have a son, yours died.*

Strange not knowing who I'm writing to. I realise – pen in hand, third attempt, staring glassily down the ward – that I have been picturing, while writing, a father and mother reading it. Also, perhaps a sister. About the same age as Alice. I realise I'm even picturing them in this Cambridgeshire village, Littleport, whatever the hell that's like: some sort of generic countryside, a thatched cottage no doubt with rag rugs and gun dogs and muddied wellies in the hall, a Barbour hanging on the coat peg and a Range Rover outside. Admittedly this doesn't fit with the one detail I have – that it was a motorcycle accident.

I catch Maureen up. I'm now waving the letter and she's walking at quite a lick: she has a brisk trot, and a funny gait, she almost hops. She's wearing impractical shoes, that's what it is, and is having to pick her way among the muddy leaves. Red shoes with a high heel. They keep sinking into the ground and she's in danger of losing one.

'I have this for you!'

My voice is feeble and I feel ridiculous – she's not looking back at me and I'm going to have to break into a trot to catch up and give it to her. The weakness of my body, the pains in my chest from breathing hard, the woolliness in my head . . .

'Maureen!' It's the first time I've uttered her name. She looks surprised that I even know it, stands still and smiles.

Wipes at the muddy heel of her shoe with a tissue. She's very nimble. She stands on one leg, bending the other, like a stork. She waits for me to catch up.

'I wrote it. The donor family. I haven't sealed it this time,' I tell her. I think my forehead must be sweating. Up close to Maureen I smell something nostalgic, a smell from childhood. Sweets? Pear drops, is it?

'Great, thank you. I'll make sure she gets it.'

She. *She*, Maureen said, not *they*.

Maureen accepts the letter without a glance; she seems preoccupied, flustered; the momentousness of my accomplishment lost on her. I stand panting with cartoon-like noisiness and leaning against the building as she goes inside, putting the letter in her pocket along with the muddy tissue, and the huge doors bang shut behind her. An after-image of Maureen's pixie figure remains in my gaze, after she's disappeared. *Come back early or never come.*

I am expecting somehow Maureen's concern – how quickly I've become dependent on it – anticipating that she will pop back out to enquire after me. The heavy wooden doors to the building are firmly shut. They are quite hideous. The handles are two enormous carved green hands, made from copper. Giant's hands with the fingers flopping downwards: what a God-awful joke. Standing where I am, my skin all at once provoked into fierce goose pimples, I have the horrible impression that someone is trapped behind that door. Some monstrous creature with unnaturally large hands is dangling horribly, cut off for ever, stuck between one world and the next. And, worse, I have the dread certainty that the figure is me.

The little flat that Maureen takes me to is curiously thrilling. The village is called Papworth Everard or something equally bizarre and inexplicable, and the feeling of Toy Town or that film Helen mentioned, *The Truman Show*, continues. We're standing at the door with Maureen showing me the key and saying, 'Well, it's handy that it's walking distance from the hospital but you know it's going to be very – spartan.' And then the door bursts open over its corn-coloured carpet and we step over the shiny new threshold.

The smell of new paint, nylon carpet and pine-fresh chemical cleaners greets us but has no impact on my cheery mood. This is the best I've felt since the operation. I put a hand out to the wall and touch the ice-cream-coloured surface; I have a strong desire to lick it.

Doors open stiffly, jerking over freshly laid carpets – all in the same nylon sweetcorn-colour – and Maureen bounces from room to room, saying, 'Dishwasher there, obviously, there's your fridge-freezer and there's a Hoover kept in here but a cleaner comes once a week, your shower's pretty basic,' and opening and closing squeaky cupboard doors. She keeps checking my face as if she expects a sarcastic remark or a complaint – 'It's very small, of course; it's only temporary until you go back home when you won't have to be monitored all the time,' she says, staring at me and standing still, awaiting my response.

But in the end my excitement seems to infect her and she laughs as I whirl about, saying: 'Wow! All so new and on such a mini scale – I feel like a Lilliputian!'

'It's only a single bed, I'm afraid.'

We're standing in the doorway of the bedroom, surveying the plain cotton bedspread, with its stewed green colour, its dimpled pattern. I can see she doesn't want to linger here, doesn't like the way I'm testing the bounce of the bed and laughing. Next to the bed is a wardrobe, with one door partially open. I spring from the bed – Maureen takes one step back – and I put out my hand to press the wardrobe door closed, and instead it resists, opens still further, slowly, as if someone is pushing it from the inside. I try to close it again and it pops open again; on closer inspection there is no catch at all. I start to giggle; Maureen watches, and then coughs, goes back into the kitchen.

She puts down her paperwork on the kitchen table and then goes outside. For a strange moment I think she is leaving and wonder at her brusqueness, the lack of a goodbye, or anything much at all, and am puzzled to find myself stung, but then I realise she is going out to her car, parked outside the flat, to fetch a box of things. She struggles in with it, pushing the door open with her knee, heaving it to the table. Tea bags, bread, toilet paper, apples, coffee, milk, a bottle of something. She stands behind it, a little embarrassed.

'Just to get you started. You can do your own shopping once your wife drops your car off . . . or, there's a shop in the village. For the exercise.'

We both stare distractedly at the box. An advent calendar. A Cadbury's advent calendar.

'Ex-wife.'

'Huh?'

'Helen. Bringing the car up. You said *wife*.'

'Oh. Yes. Sorry.'

'Are you married, Maureen?'

'Yeah, I'm divorced as well. About three years ago.'

'Kids?'

'Two girls: Cassie and Chloe. Year Seven and Year Eight.'

I nod, as if I know what Year Seven and Year Eight means. She seems reluctant to leave. The kitchen door is open and I see her look towards the window, the kitchen tap. After a hesitation she picks up the kettle in there and starts filling it. A splutter before the first stream of browny water runs clean.

100

'Shall I make us a cup of tea? I need you to sign the lease and I think I've got . . . now, where did I put it?'

I feel like a student. The day I arrived at university it was Dad who took me to the college, delivered me to Corpus Christi, dropped my things off with the porter; shook my hand in the courtyard, clapped an arm around my back and then buggered off immediately. I knew Cushie would have done things differently. I was eighteen – not much older than this boy, this youth, this Drew Beamish. I considered myself no longer a boy, of course, but I remember sitting down heavily on that tiny student bed, feeling the mattress give entirely, the weight of so many previous hopeful youthful occupants having knocked all the stuffing out of it. Cushie would have said something like: 'Ee, well, there won't be much hanky-panky going on in that little bed – no bigger than a postage stamp!' She would have pinched my cheek, smiled, tried to chivvy hope rather than dread in my youthful breast. She would have done that womanly thing of leaving me with gifts. Home-made raspberry jam. A clean pressed tea-towel printed with Durham Cathedral. My own small kettle. New razors or underpants. A packet of Jaffa Cakes, stuff like that. I would have pretended not to like being babied.

Yet this time, for no reason I can fathom, the little room, the sense of a squeaky new life unfolding in front of me, excites me. Feelings I don't remember having back then, when it was – relevant. When I was a youth going up to Oxford, for God's sake, not a middle-aged man, moving into a utilitarian hospital flat in Papworth Everard. This thought makes me grin harder. I sit myself down, pulling out one of the flimsy chairs for Maureen. The chair squeals on the rubber floor-tiles. I urge myself to thank her as she pushes the mug of tea at me – not just for the tea but other, unknowable things – but she speaks first: 'This came, here—' Handing me a letter. 'You don't have to open it now. Maybe when I'm not here?'

When I say nothing, just stare at the letter in my hand, then place it carefully on the table and stare at it a little more, she looks around the kitchen for a change of topic. Her eyes light on the advent calendar.

'It was on special offer. I know it's silly, sorry. I thought you might not know that it's the first of December tomorrow. Time stands still a bit when you're in hospital, doesn't it? And there's a CD player. Over there. I don't know if you listen to music but I could lend you some CDs if you like?'

Blimey. There's a thought. Eva Cassidy? Joni Mitchell?

'Um. Thank you. I think Helen said she would bring me some stuff from my flat . . . my iPod perhaps.'

The handwriting on the envelope is neat, and unmistakably female. Rounded letters. Regularly spaced. *Patrick Robson. Papworth Hospital.* Clearly hasn't been posted, but hand delivered. Once again, a surge of irritation about the secrecy; the feeling that Maureen holds all the knowledge. All the cards.

I reach out to the letter. Pick it up. Turn it over in my lap. 'I'd quite like to visit this place. Littleport. See – you know. See what it's like.'

Maureen looks startled. 'Really? Littleport. God, there's not much to see. It's a typical Fen place. Bit bleak actually.'

'Are you from there?'

'I live in Ely. Ely's pretty. A cathedral and a river.'

She sips at her tea, bringing the mug up to her lips and looking at me with big eyes over the top of it. Her eyes are brown, a hazel brown with stubby, short lashes. She has a frank, exceptionally unguarded gaze, and clear skin with an outdoor quality to it: fresh like the freckled skin of a brown egg. Many times I have the impression that she's about to say something, and thinks better of it. I have wondered if this is something to do with her training, with the thought that she shouldn't overstep the mark. Now she gets up to fetch sugar, offers it to me. I shake my head, so she spoons a dash into her own tea and begins stirring. When she puts the cup down I notice a lipstick curve on it, a pink arc just at the rim of the mug. I find myself smiling again.

'You have to take things slowly,' she says. 'With the donor family, I mean. If you go to Littleport – you wouldn't . . . Don't look his house up, will you? That would be – I don't think that would be welcome.'

'God, no. No, of course not. I'm just curious, that's all. I'd never heard of the place before last month. I'm just curious. And I've got stuff to do! I decided this morning. I'm going to put my flat in Highgate on the market.'

Another startled look. 'Oh. You're moving?'

'I thought I'd . . . consider my options. Grown-up kids. Job . . . Um, well I also, I made another snap decision. Early retirement. New start, you know.'

'Wow! Did you plan that before – was that what you—'

'No. But just yesterday I woke up and thought, it feels – right.'

'Wow. Big changes. I suppose, that's what happens. Major surgery. Makes you reassess things?'

'No, no, I don't think that's anything to do with it. Just feels right, that's all. I find I've no desire to go back to London. I rather like it here.'

She looks surprised. 'You haven't actually seen any of it, have you?'

'Well I know that, but, I plan to.'

'You won't be able to drive, either, for a while, you remember that, don't you? A couple more weeks, possibly more, Dr Burns said. I can help you with shopping but, you know, walking will be good for you, too.'

'Yes, yes.'

I wonder how old Maureen is. She seems younger today. She's wearing an old-fashioned yellow dress. It looks like the kind of dress Alice would get from Oxfam and wear with her big boots and a leather jacket but on Maureen it's . . . worn without irony. It all adds up: pink lipstick, brown freckled skin, cute haircut. I don't want to open this letter in front of her but we both know it's burning a hole in my lap here. She glances at it, at me; stands up.

'Now, various nurses will call in for the first day or two but after that you can pop over to the hospital for your obs. Observations. Get your dressings changed and talk to the cardiologist. See how your – chest – is healing. Well. I'll leave you to it.'

She picks up her bag from the back of the chair. Puts the key down on the table on top of the lease.

'Well, I'll see myself out. Give me a shout if there's anything you need. The physio should be in later today. Cleaner comes Tuesdays.'

The front door makes a squeaky new click behind her. I have the letter opened before it closes.

Dear Mr Robson,

Thank you for your letter. Maureen gave it to me. Drew was a lovely boy and we all loved him very much. I don't know what more to say right now. I am in shock. I never wanted Drew to carry a card. I still don't know what I think about that – but it was his own decision so when it came to it I thought I'd better carry out his wishes. Though we didn't give any other organs. But they did ask us. Eyes. Cornea. I said no. My husband died only a little while before so I'm on my own now. Well, I'll say cheerio now and thank you for getting in touch. I hope you

continue to make a good recovery. Perhaps that can be a
small comfort to me. It's too soon to say.
  Yours sincerely,
  Ruth Beamish

Ruth Beamish.

Cornea. Eyes. She didn't want him to carry the card. It is a
sad letter. Pathetic. Cheap paper, old-fashioned writing, blue
ink, probably a fountain pen. I read it several times. I turn it
over. There is an address – Black Drove, Littleport. Nothing
more. The picture I had, of the cosy father-mother, Barbour-
coats and Range Rovers, melts away. There's only a second-
hand motorbike, and a boy and a long, lonely road: this new
word, a Fen word. A drove.

Just after midnight I return to the box Maureen left when I
feel sleepy but scratchy too and discover with a leap of gratitude the screw-top bottle of red that she brought me. I pour
myself a mugful – can't find the glasses right now – and lie
stiffly on my back on the outside covers of the student-sized
bed.

As I close my eyes a young man is staring at me. I open
them again; the skin on my face prickles icily as if someone
just touched it. My heart thumps.

It's a long time since I've been afraid of my dreams, afraid
to close my eyes. I fight the drowsiness but the moment I go
under he's there again, the same man, the same fierce stare,
and other things. A barn owl, wings outstretched, flying into
my face. A lake with a light leaping on it – some kind of glowing insect that turns into Jiminy Cricket from the Pinocchio
movie. A man astride a strange roaring horse, or is it a motor
bike? Nooses in a theatre. A bale of straw on fire. Graduation
Day again at UCL, or is it King's College, Cambridge? Anyway,
this time Daisy is on the platform, hair fanned behind her in

an Indian headdress, wearing a short yellow dress and a sash with LITTLEPORT written on it like a beauty queen. She's weeping and weeping, she can't stand up and accept the rolled-up qualification being held out to her. Her name is called and the mortarboard won't stick on top of her headdress, she's furious with it, weeps afresh. She sinks to the stage and disappears through a little trapdoor, right at my feet.

I open my eyes, switch on the lamp beside the bed and reach for my mobile. At the other end a mechanical tone rings and rings, somewhere far away. I'm about to abandon the call when a voice picks up.

'Hello?'

'Daisy?'

'God. Hello. Patrick.'

'Sorry. Did I wake you?'

'What time is it?'

'I don't know. Sorry. It might be late. I'm really sorry to call so late, if it is, I just—'

'What the fuck do *you* want?' Her voice sounds clotted with sleep. Intimate. And young. Wary, rather than furious.

'I just – wondered – wanted to say. How are you?'

'How am I? At this hour? Fuck!'

'It's just that . . . well. I was thinking that—'

'If you're calling to ask me to drop the harassment case, forget it. I already have. Don't you read your emails?'

'Oh! No, that wasn't why I was calling, but, well, thank you.'

'I didn't do it for you, right? I did it because. For me. Because I need to move on and being angry with you, hating you, thinking about you, is not helping me. OK? So fuck off and go back to where you came from, I never want to—'

And then she is crying, and her snuffling and gasping breaths fill the line. The phone is warm against my ear. I listen for a while helplessly. I'm ready to click the off button. I'm *so ready* to click the off button. I force myself to stay connected. I listen for as long as I can stand, and then I interject.

'Actually Daisy, I – you remember, I'm not in London? I had an operation. I'm still here in Cambridge. I'm not really in touch with the department, I haven't been keeping up . . . but thank you. Actually I rang to say something else.'

Her sobs continue but she struggles to get a hold of herself. Then a soft, breathy silence and I realise that it would be cruel to prevaricate. That her held breath might denote . . . hope. (I never crush a relationship dead, I once boasted. Meaning: I always leave something in case I want to pick it up later.)

'I just wanted to say sorry. If I – I mean, I think I *did* behave badly. You are young, and . . . well. That's it. I really am sorry.'

A crackling pause. Her shock is palpable. Then: 'Why the fuck? At this bloody hour! The sound of your voice. I suppose you're on some medication that makes you nicer, or something!'

'Daisy. You're a lovely young woman with so much going for you—'

Click. A cut-off sob as Daisy puts the phone down on me.

I lie on my back on the bed and stare at the white ceiling of my anodyne flat, leaving the phone on the pillow beside me. Not even a spider for company. You asked for that, I tell myself. But still. There *is* some satisfaction.

Once, as a boy of seven or eight, the teacher had made the entire class miss playtime because no one would own up to writing a rude word on the blackboard. And I told my mother at home that weekend in outrage, railing about the missed playtime, the making us *all* suffer, I think I was actually pacing round the kitchen, balling my hands into fists, while she was prinking the edges of a pie with a fork. I stared at the tied bow on the apron at her waist. Her back was still to me as she said in a measured, floury voice: 'Well, that child should probably listen to his heart. We all make mistakes, do bad things from time to time. That boy – whoever he is – will feel better if he just owns up and says sorry.'

Did she know it was me – that *I* wrote the bad word? I was glad she was preoccupied with making a leaf-shape in the pastry and couldn't see my face. How clever she was! I was more outraged at the injustice of it than if I'd been innocent.

'Sorry's just a word. It won't change a thing,' I said, sniffily. 'It's done. We still missed playtime!'

'It's just the right thing to do,' my mother persisted.

I never saw the sense of Cushie's advice until now.

'So, you're in grand fettle! How are you feeling, in yourself?' Dr Burns asks, two weeks later, after the battery of tests are completed. We're in his consulting room and he seems unhurried. Like he might genuinely want to know. I hesitate. That phrase: *in yourself*.

'I imagine you're a wee bit curious about your donor,' he continues. 'That's natural. It's your transplant co-ordinator's job, mind, to protect the family.'

Has he been talking to Maureen? That meeting she was rushing to, the day I met her in the hospital grounds and she mentioned not taking my file home with her. Was that about me? I suppose I'm quite the phenomenon around here – only the third time a transplant has been performed this way.

Dr Burns is watching my face. 'Notice any changes? Feel . . . you know, any personality changes, food preferences, that kind of thing?'

'No, nothing at all,' I say.

'No – strange cravings, or new tastes or behaviours?' Burns asks.

108

'No, not at all. Should I have?'

'Some transplant patients mention these things, that's all. Vivid dreams – new dreams they haven't had before.'

'Well, dreams,' I concede, self-consciously. 'Yes. I have had some funny dreams. The medication, no doubt.'

Burns pounces. He seems thrilled, leans forward, stops staring at the screen in front of him.

'What do you dream of?'

'Oh, I don't know. Barn owls. Flying. Littleport. Nooses seem to feature a lot.'

'Wait on this. There's a whole theory. That patients having heart surgery *change*, take on the personality of their donor in some way, and maybe their dreams, their memories too. There's quite a well-known study and a book by this woman who started craving chicken nuggets and green peppers and what do you know – turns out her heart donor was a young lad who loved those foods.'

I'm not sure how to reply. Is he expecting me to take this seriously?

'Do liver transplants report the same kinds of changes? Or is it just those who've received a donor's *heart*?' I ask.

'Well, yes. Quite. Only in China, apparently, where the liver has some of the same cultural significance that the heart has for us! *Ha*.'

I have the strange sense that he's disappointed. That – rationalist though he may be – he almost wanted me to disprove his scepticism.

'Maureen Gotobed has some funny ideas,' he says, as if I should know that it was Maureen who mooted this. 'She's not a doctor of course, and this – cellular memory, the concept that the heart carries memories, has a wee "brain" as it were – a good many folk seem to go for it. And it's strange for her, knowing both the family and *you*, I suppose.'

Gotobed? Maureen's called Gotobed. What a name! My back aches. The skin on my chest, at my wound, itches. I have a scraping feeling in my throat and aching shoulders and, well, I'm tired of hospitals. Of medication and the smell of hospitals and death. Of strange theories and general strangeness. I don't want to come here any more.

My little flat and my advent calendar – yesterday I opened the second window and ate a Dairy Milk chocolate: that's where I want to be. I woke in my skinny bed and felt eighteen again: a student. The chemical smell of the cotton sheets, the plainness of the slatted window-blind and the clean new day in front of me. Lonely, at first. Profoundly lonely. Alone. With nothing to do, nothing to attend, no one to meet. *Like a leaf on a river, floating towards its end*. And then something I never felt back then – excited. Not a leaf at all, but maybe the river itself. Why so linear, such a linear image? It's not all progression, progression, forward, forward. I know that.

Burns is watching me closely, while pretending he isn't. He's around the same age as me, I realise now. His ugly great conk, his beer gut notwithstanding. Might be younger, even. Funny how when someone has power over you, you think of them as older, like a parent. But, see, I'm right, doesn't time sometimes reshape itself, move in other directions? And, boy, did that man – who lifted my heart from my chest in his gloved hands – have power over me.

'Cellular memory is one theory. Much more likely, though, is that very occasionally,' Burns is saying, and he's animated, it's as if he's been wanting to get this out in the open, 'and I'm categorically not saying this was the case for you, mind, very occasionally, in major surgery there is a wee moment where lack of oxygen to the brain might cause . . . might bring about what we might call the most minuscule, *infinitesimal* amount of brain damage – I'm talking a split second, mind, but these neurological shifts could account for *personality* changes.'

He seems to be waiting for me to reply.

'So you haven't noticed any *personality* changes? Unfamiliar *feelings?*' he asks.

I watch his hand hover over his keyboard, as if he longs to type something, to record 'Patient's Response'.

'No. Sorry. I've always been a rationalist,' I answer.

He sits back in his chair and spins it around a little.

'Ah.'

'I do understand the – mystique around this particular organ. The special status,' I offer.

'When I was a student, no, a junior doctor. When you see your first heart, beating there. It's a grand thing, and pretty! Vivid, you know. Like something you might see in a coral reef.'

I struggle to imagine this.

'And you think of the past, of how crude operations must have been – or of battlefields, that's what I thought: you know, spears and swords and, aye, face-to-face combat – people would have seen chests ripped open, and – you know, they might have seen the heart still beating inside a body, so of course it being the only thing *moving*, the only wee thing that seemed to be *alive*, so that might explain it, as you say, the special status. Things like the idea that if you ate an enemy's heart you gained his strength . . . if you know what I'm saying.'

'Yes.' I do.

A pause while we both think of this, picture someone eating a heart. 'Are you signing me off? Will I need to come back?'

'Not entirely, no. You will have to – it will be many a long day – you'll have a lifetime of monitoring, mind. But it has all gone remarkably well. And that means, you'll be pleased to know, you'll be seeing a lot less of me!'

'I've put my flat in London on the market. An agent is showing people round for me today. I might stay in the area. The Fens, I mean. London doesn't seem so appealing suddenly.'

Burns looks surprised, but he takes my lead; there's no need to talk about it. 'And what will you do, these daft days?' he says and, when I don't understand, adds: 'Christmas? Go on the bash, now you can?'

He grins. His pale blue eyes seem watery, and tired, suddenly, and I wonder – it's the first time I've given Dr Burns' private life consideration – if he's been up all night. Perhaps on another six-hour, life-saving operation.

'I haven't given it any thought,' I say. Then awkwardly add: 'I don't think I've said thank you, yet, have I, doctor? Not very good at that sort of thing. I'm sorry if I was – I'm sure I've been – a difficult patient. But I am. I would like to. I *am* grateful.'

Burns' ginger eyebrows shoot up again and disappear into his hairline. A tap on his door rescues us both: a nurse to tell him Dr Bryan is here to see him.

We shake hands as I leave and I notice how cold his hand is, despite his overheated office. *Cold hands, warm heart.* Impossible to stop these phrases from forming in my mind; ones I never knew I knew present themselves hourly. Just left-over metaphors from the Galenic model when hot-bloodedness or cold-heartedness was thought to be literally true. The four humours. Which type would Burns be? Phlegmatic, no doubt. And Maureen, maybe the same. Or choleric perhaps. (All that yellow.) And me? Melancholic, I might have said, once. But now – ah, that's the rub. Now, I'm not so sure. Sanguine maybe. Pleasure-seeking. I was always that.

Arch rationalist I may be, as Helen says, but what Dr Burns alluded to, this idea of cellular memory, this account by a transplant recipient of changing, taking on the qualities of her donor, it did rattle me for a second or two. Or perhaps it was the thought of Maureen holding this belief, considering this valid. Maureen Gotobed – quite a sexy name, now I've got over the strangeness of it, all ruffled and newly knitted and colourful – talking about me to Dr Burns, the realisation that my behaviour, my reactions, every aspect of my recovery and my response to the operation has of course been discussed between them. Of course, of course. I'm a phenomenon. And they have the advantage in that they know the other side of the story, the donor's side, the bit I don't, and long to discover. They know the story of my heart.

Daisy believed there was no such thing as falling in love. A construct, entirely. Daisy of the baby-fine blonde hair so full of static – hair that provoked a boyish desire to rub a balloon against her head and watch it stand up. The language of love: all a load of bollocks, according to Daisy. The concept of *falling*, of giving up will – a human construction to support the basic desires of lust and gene advancement.

Did I agree with her? Lying on that faux-leather couch in my office in UCL with a chair shoved against the door and my pants and trousers thrown over a chair, the blind down against daytime sun and the phone off the hook and my foolish sperm making their ridiculous journey to oblivion aided by that last, convulsively powerful thrust; yes, all Daisy said seemed true. Genes want to advance themselves and people want to fuck. Sex is a problem to be solved. People also want to dress this up in nicer language. Women in particular (if you ask me) perhaps need the romantic gestures and terminology so they feel themselves to be less like little hamsters on heat raising up their arses for you on the rare monthly occasions when they let you near them.

But love – falling in love. I know about that. I knew for instance that I wasn't in love with Daisy. That my affection for her was ordinary; more like fondness. I knew it by a process of elimination. That it was nothing like my feeling for . . . for Helen, as an example. Throw your fond in a pond, Daisy once said. Lines from some God-awful poem. What I actually thought was this: Daisy doesn't believe in love because she's never yet experienced it, and so to her it is unimaginable and therefore can't exist.

But then, how to explain Daisy's behaviour afterwards? Was it that I'd taken her at her word and assumed that she would prefer our break-up to be in rational language – not dressed up in the rhetoric of love or regret? (My brief foray into romantic language in my emails to her, the ones she showed to the Board – was that my mistake? But at some level I'd thought that Daisy, given all she said, Daisy, an educated, cynical young historian, would take them in the right spirit, would see the *irony*.) What had motivated her complaint to the university about me if it was all so . . . rational? A four-month affair. Plain vindictiveness? A desire to punish me?

An accident waiting to happen, Helen said. Meaning, I suppose, that I had broken a heart once too often. Or that I should have kept my affairs out of the workplace. Grudgingly, I know that she has a point.

Helen and I met at Oxford. She switched to Law in the final year. I clocked her in that first year; several of my friends fancied her. I was learning, at eighteen, something peculiar and I swear it was an unasked-for gift. Girls seemed to fall for me. I never had to try, I never really understood it, but just enjoyed how it was all – strangely easy. Helen had her own theory, of course. She swore I knew damn well what I was doing and that even if I'd been as thick as shit (which, she conceded, I clearly wasn't) I'd have had an easy time of it with my brown eyes and naughtiness and how I could make her laugh. Plus 'all those masculine straight lines'. She would look at me sometimes, and come out with comments that let me know she was musing on this: 'I wonder if it's just that you're so cocky, so certain, like sort of solid and hard, maybe that's what women like?' Or other times: 'It's your teasing. Maybe women like to be teased.'

In darker days she'd say; 'God's gift. That's what you think you are.'

Those comments came later. In the Lucy years. In the beginning Helen was much sweeter. Skinnier too. She used to wear this elongated striped scarf, *Doctor Who* style; wrapping it around her so I thought of her like a barber's pole or stick of rock – red and black, long and slim and endlessly shifting, never still. She was studious even then, harder-working than me and resentful that she had to be, that things didn't come so easily for her. I'd had every chance in life, she said, expensive education, well-off family. Her other favourite phrase for me was 'You don't know you're born.'

I suddenly long for photographs. I don't seem to have any. Nothing to match the strapping, brisk Helen I know now and the girl I seduced that first night, as I crept into the sleeping bag I'd rakishly offered her on the floor of my Corpus Christi room. I remember smiling into her face, white as moonlight; the ripping noise of that zip as I unpeeled her for the first time. Her eyes were alarmingly young without her black make-up.

She was shivering. She had a real fit of the shakes, as I tried to slot my naked self into her, and I had to pause for a bit and defrost her with slugs of brandy. I regretted immediately my clumsiness, my attack on her, the unruly shapes of my desires. I tried to go more slowly, to be more precise. I kissed her breasts and her white neck. She closed her eyes. But in the end

I'd drunk too much for restraint. I felt huge and swollen, made what felt like a feverish, unadulterated assault on her. She didn't protest. In my eighteen-year-old way it seemed to me that she liked it.

I remember that it was a new LP we listened to: *Boys Don't Cry* by The Cure. And afterwards I made us a snack of tea and raw mushrooms on crackers because that's the only thing I could find in the fridge. Mushrooms: white dense flesh, the butter cold and salty. Water biscuits splintering on your tongue. Glowing Helen, sleeping beside me in a damp patch of student semen; the delicate taste of mushrooms.

To my surprise Helen told me shyly the next morning that she sang in a band, would I like to come and see her sing next week in town. I expected something smoky and obscure, all fierce guitars and shouty: Siouxsie and the Banshees, The Slits. I felt the dread that she might be no good, wondered how easy I'd find it to continue shagging her if she was talentless.

It was a pub in Oxford. I waited for her to come on stage, glad she couldn't see me – standing at the back, pretending to eat a packet of crisps.

She stood in a strange pool of light in heels, elongated; looking like somebody else. Her auburn hair was piled up. She wore a bottle-green dress – straight up and down. A slender, glass bottle. Or a fragile red tulip atop a stalk.

I couldn't have been more wrong about the kind of music her band played. Not The Doors or punk or any of that druggy stuff. No. She sang my mother's favourite Dusty Springfield number in a voice that rolled through me like blood. Dark, coarse, a voice cracking slightly in the range just above middle C, a crack she exploited – it seemed to me rather deliberately, rather pointedly – for all its power and poignancy.

Helen gave up singing in the band not long afterwards. She was beginning to think about switching to Law, beginning her transformation from smoky siren to the fixed form she eventually took. I had asked her to marry me and we'd both stopped smoking the roll-ups, progressed to Benson and Hedges. She asked me to promise not to unpeel other young women from their sleeping bags.

All of this brought on by the simple email from Helen this morning.

I'm bringing your BMW up. I'll leave it by the flat and push the keys through the letterbox, then I have booked a cab back to the station so that I can be back in court by 9 a.m. So I won't be able to pop in and say hi. You probably won't be up.

I remember that student room again, the smell of hyacinths floating up from the courtyard at Corpus Christi, blue and dizzying the next morning, and moments after coming Helen sitting up and letting the sheets fall off. She started rolling a cigarette.

'How sad,' she said, 'that we'll only have this moment once.'

I felt the blood drain out of my face. My limbs turned icy.

'Hey, honey, we can do that again, any time. Give me ten minutes – I'll be right with you.'

'Never exactly the same,' she said. 'Nothing is, is it? No two moments. *Exactly* the same.'

Helen – so clever, so infuriating, so unlike anyone else. How could I have known that then, at eighteen? It needs time, perspective, to show you that someone might be original. And yet what do you want to do when you start out? Make a comprehensive study. *Compare.* Never pick the first restaurant on arrival in a new city. Wander round a bit – do your research. Make sure there's not something better round the corner.

Hard to know if that's self-justification or the reasoned perspective of age. All I know is that it's a long time since I remembered that student bedroom. The hot squeak of the bed. I mean really, of course, since I thought of Helen with affection; with indulgence. Remembered my own part in things. I wanted always to enter Helen like a dream, like stepping through a boundary. I loved that she could do that to me. That's what I wanted: what she could do to me. And then it stopped.

So, when Dr Burns mentioned the daft days or whatever he called it, it got me thinking. Christmas. Christmas in this tiny flat, on my own, with only my new ticker for company, and no doubt a few ghosts. I email Helen. Her reply comes back pleasingly fast.

Sorry, Christmas Day itself is out – but Boxing Day would be fine. Alice says that's great. Can she bring her boyfriend (his name is Jake)? I'll bring the rest of the turkey and we can make a risotto. Perhaps you could get the rice and something to drink? The right kind – arborio rice.

PS. Why don't you invite Ben and Lucy?

Ben and Lucy. Jesus. Has she gone mad? We'll already be pushing it to squeeze four of us around this card table, which might well collapse if we actually put plates on it. It chafes me, this PS of Helen's. I find myself furious, somehow, all thoughts of a moment ago melting. Why does she always have the moral high ground, what is it about women, always behaving so well and thinking of things we should have thought of first and shaming us?

In the end I text Lucy on my BlackBerry. Her reply, too, comes quickly.

Sorry. In India 4 xmas with Ashok. Ben on his own. Says he'll come. Send him directions.

She's leaving our seventeen-year-old son on his own over Christmas, while she swans off to India with her new bloke? And if I hadn't texted (admittedly, only at Helen's prompting) I would never have known. I fling the BlackBerry on the sofa and myself down after it. Once again all my failings as a father – as a person – are writ large. *What she could do to me.* Helen. Reflecting me at twice my natural size. Yes, that's all very well. But when the mirror breaks . . .

It bothers me that Helen is suddenly willing to see Lucy, too. Ben I can understand, but Helen was never subtle in what she said about Lucy over the years, the years when we tried to stay together and limped towards our divorce. There could be no doubt what she thought of her. Especially the fact that I ended up paying, sending money every month, and yet Lucy was still living in that Housing Association place and still coming up with wacky ideas of starting a stall at Greenwich market or becoming a lesbian or whatever.

'Flaky', 'neurotic', 'the world's worst mother', 'that dreadful woman', 'hopeless', 'a nightmare': just some of the things Helen said about Lucy, long after our divorce, long after she had any reason, in my view, to continue to hate Lucy, since there were so many other women Helen could more justifiably have hated (students mostly, sometimes wives of colleagues). Helen, a pull-herself-up-by-her-bootstraps kind of person who despises weakness, especially her own. That incident. On the roof garden of the old flat.

Theatrics, I remember saying, later. Bloody emotional blackmail. She wouldn't get me that way. I was in love again by then; my heart beating to a different drum as the cliché goes. The drum – well, the arse, to be strictly accurate – of *Lucy.*

Remembering that incident now makes me close my eyes as if I had just glanced into a livid wound – something red and shocking. I haven't thought of it in years. We've never mentioned it. Both women quickly had children, small children. I stayed married to one and kept shagging the other. It's all a blur of mess, mess. Helen – and Lucy – shouldn't have put up with me, given me that glimpse of power. I was just . . . I was . . . Where was I in all of this?

Maureen turns up and suggests we go 'out and about' for a 'change of scene'. She must know Helen has dropped the car off; it's there outside the flat. She's looking rather cheerful – this time she's wearing a bright yellow woolly hat (no doubt also knitted by her own fair hand) and a fluffy scarf in the same Easter-chick colour. I find myself wondering about her ridiculous surname and how soon I can get a reference to it into the conversation. Also: if she has so much time for knitting, she can't be going out much? Must still be single? (Unless she knits during dating or sex, as Helen, with her superior logic, would no doubt suggest is at least a possibility I ought to consider. Why do you always assume everything is the way you want it to be, Patrick?)

Maureen's brought me something. She hands it over rather sheepishly as she gets into the passenger side of the car. 'Dr Burns mentioned that he'd told you about this, so I thought you might like to borrow it.'

A book. A hardback, looks like a library copy, lurid green cover. *Claire Sylvia – A Change of Heart: The Extraordinary Story of a Man's Heart in a Woman's Body*. I turn it over, suppress a groan as I stare at the back, read aloud from the puff by Bernie Siegel MD:

'While I can't necessarily explain the amazing things that have happened to Claire, I have no trouble believing them.

That's why I enjoy speaking with astronomers and quantum physicists, who are continually dealing with mysterious and unexplained events . . .'

I throw it onto the back seat of the car. Maureen closes the car door on her side and says nothing. To cover any dismissiveness in this action I quickly add: 'Thanks! Looks great. I'll read it later.'

Maureen is putting her seatbelt on and chatting; she doesn't seem offended. (She's difficult to offend, I've noticed, despite my best efforts). 'This woman, Claire Sylvia. After her transplant she has all these strange dreams. She dreams of a boy called Tim and she's convinced that's the name of her donor, though, like you, no one told her anything about him. And in time, she gets to meet the family and discovers – yes, that is the donor's name.'

I take a deep breath, soaking up all that is familiar and beloved about my car: the dangling piece of Chinese jade – gift from Alice; the specks of crisps on the dashboard; the familiar grey leather of the seats, the pleasant heaviness of the key in my hand, the pulse of that engine revving up beneath me.

Maureen is still talking. It's like the floodgates have opened or something, me giving her permission to tell me about it.

'She mentions that, after the operation, she reported peculiar changes like cravings for beer and chicken nuggets, neither of which she had a taste for prior to the transplant. She later discovered that these were favourites of her donor. She even learned that her donor had chicken nuggets in his jacket pocket when he died in a motorcycle accident.'

'Are most donors young men who die in motorcycle accidents?'

'That's just a coincidence.'

'St Ives, is it?' I ask, going through four gear changes as fast as I can, just for the pleasure. I'll have to take it easy, this first drive. That's why Maureen's coming too, she says. In case I pass out in the car park, or something. Of course that's just an excuse. Her excuses to see me are cute. I like that she has pride and doesn't come right out with it.

'And after this book was published, there were more studies done. One by this Dr Pearsall who was a transplant recipient himself and so more open to listening to the ideas his patients expressed. He says in one a forty-seven-year-old man received a heart from a fourteen-year-old girl gymnast who had problems with eating disorders. After the transplant, the recipient and his family said this man had a tendency to be nauseated after eating, a childlike exuberance and a little girl's giggle.'

'But it's just – anecdotal, yes? No offence, Maureen, but it wouldn't exactly hold up in a peer-reviewed, scientific journal, now would it? Has this theory been advanced in *The Lancet*?'

'One thing I've noticed about you, if you don't mind me saying,' she begins, and I see out of the corner of my eye that I've finally succeeded; she's bristling. 'You don't find it easy to value the opinions of women, do you? I mean, it's all about the opinions of your colleagues, esteemed peers . . . by which you mean: other men.'

'Jeez! Where did gender come into it suddenly? I don't think I said anything about women or men, did I?'

'Anyway, what about this example? A baby boy was transplanted with the heart of a dead baby who had had cerebral palsy. And the baby developed some shaking on the left-hand side, the same side as the donor baby had. How can that be anecdotal? The baby's not old enough to be cooking up the evidence, is it?'

'No, but it was the parents presumably who noted these changes? And the parents would have known or been told about the donor baby and so – they imagined they saw shaking in their own child. Or even maybe this doctor asked them questions in a leading way: did you notice anything in your baby after receiving a heart from the donor baby with the cerebral palsy who shook on the left-hand side of his body?'

I can't see her face but it strikes me she's crestfallen, so I change tone: 'On the plus side, there is a lovely fluffy angel protecting me. I definitely think so.'

'You're cynical, aren't you?'

'It has been noted before. Should I take this left?'

The route I'm driving is a dizzying assortment of mini-roundabouts. I keep hoping for a glimpse of the countryside, and wanting to interrupt Maureen's discourse on transplant recipients and their changed personalities with facetious remarks and whoops of joy: 'So this then is the beloved Fens of which you speak?' But it's a short journey. We arrive soon enough at this market town of St Ives. I remember Helen mentioning it now, on her first visit to Papworth. I follow signs to the Cattle Market car park, trying to think of ways to get this conversation with Maureen back on track; on friend-lier, neutral territory.

'My ex-wife did once accuse me of treating my own needs as if they were instructions and everyone else's needs as impediments. She says this is the fundamental difference between men and women – men don't acknowledge their feel-ings as much but they act on them without compunction.'

That should mollify her. Always worth a good quote, Helen, since at the very least her arguments are coherent. (Unlike Lucy, who would just yell a bit and then pop like a balloon and dissolve into tears.) We're out of the car now, and I'm surprised to discover I have a giddy, thrilled sensation – like bunking off school – mixed up with a nauseous one, as if there's something wrong with my stomach. Maybe the drive, the unaccustomed exhilaration. Obviously I'm a bit delicate. Maybe even ropy. I'm still on medication and am likely to be for the rest of my life. One theory (mine) is that the drugs themselves might have a psychotropic effect. Be affecting my consciousness and my moods. I mean: giddiness. Excitement. Joy. Not characteristics I'm especially known for.

So, our purpose in this odd little town is to buy plates and cutlery so that I can serve a Boxing Day dinner to five people. (I don't know if this is within a transplant co-ordinator's remit or if this is on Maureen's own time. I've figured out by now that her job is part-time and she's employed by the Hospital Trust but pretty much freelance. She's some sort of counsellor the rest of the time. And I know this is vain of me, but she fancies doing a bit of overtime, in my honest opinion.)

'Don't you have that sort of stuff in your flat in London? Couldn't someone bring it for you?' Maureen asks; perhaps glad to change the subject. I explain that the flat has already sold. Cash buyer came along immediately. The stuff is going into storage. All arranged via phone and email and being packed up by a removal firm as we speak. Like Helen and Alice, Maureen seems to want to make this into something momentous. She actually stops walking and says: 'Your entire flat? You didn't want to wait and do it yourself?'

'I'm not sentimental. Helen got the best stuff when we divorced anyway. I'll get it out of storage when I find somewhere permanent. Or longer term at least.'

Maureen seems curiously concerned by this.

'It's radical, though, isn't it? Leaving everything behind like that?'

'Maybe. But it makes sense – ah, here we are. This is the High Street, is it? Look at that. *Cadge:* Gentleman's Attire. In my day cadge meant scrounge, you know, cadge a lift. Weird name, for a clothing shop.'

It doesn't looking promising. A bookmaker's, a pound store. East Anglia's biggest bridal wear shop. The usual war memorial dedicated to the Brave Men of St Ives. A green statue of Oliver Cromwell on a raised plinth, pointing at someone. (I follow the line of the statue's outstretched finger to a bloke sitting on a bench eating a sandwich.) A bistro aptly called Nuts. Unlit Christmas lights already festoon the street-lamp beside it. There's a busker in the doorway. He's singing *Wild World*. Wild indeed. His version is the tamest I've ever heard.

I stop, hand on the door, and find myself smiling while I rummage in my back pocket for a quid. How soft this man's voice is. Although now I look at him, he's more of a boy than a man, despite the fifties effort with his clothes: the denim jacket, part-quiff and the roll-up parked above his ear.

I stand and listen: it's so quiet. Not just his voice: I've never heard quiet like this in a town before. I am sure I can hear a bird twittering. I definitely hear a plane rolling over and the tick of a bike as somebody wheels it past; the swish of a push-chair being pushed. Soft ticking. The sound of watch enveloped in cotton. This busker is singing really, really softly – it's exquisite. He's giving it his all; he's really – what's the phrase? I lean against the doorway to listen. And as I look up from the strum of his guitar, glancing at the stetson on the floor at his feet, hearing my pound coin make a tiny – a jingly, tinny *splash* – I feel something shift.

I see Maureen looking at me. I'm standing half in, half out of this café and she's waiting for me to join her inside. She's taken off her hat and is ruffling her hand through her tufty haircut, her cheeks glowing; she's fresh and luminous and brilliantly coloured: just the same way Helen looked when I first saw her in the hospital. My actions feel strange to me, a dim memory of how as a little boy I sometimes asked myself: am I really doing this because I thought of it – lifting my hand, tapping my fingers – or is someone else, something else, directing me? (That was back in my religious phase, again, no doubt.) My ears are cocked, the blood is pulsing in my veins, the strange little town of St Ives is presenting itself to me; music trickling under my skin. The busker is so young that he is reddening, it's clear that singing in public is embarrassing to him, that he only half believes he can do it. But his voice is good: he hits all the notes.

I realise I'm blocking the doorway; a woman with a push-chair is trying to get out. I hold the door for her, mumbling apologies. And then I reach for my wallet and find all the money I have – forty, sixty, eighty quid, four twenties, and bend down to put it in the stetson. The boy stops mid-strum, reaches down and pockets it instantly. His mouth is open.

'I love that song! Cat Stevens,' I say. We grin foolishly at one another.

Maureen has found us a table. She makes no comment as I drag out a chair and sit opposite her, though her eyes are wide. She hands me the laminated menu. I put my hand to my chest and take one or two deep breaths, putting the wallet back in my pocket.

'Well, I guess I'd better buy the coffees,' she says, 'since you've gone and given all your money away. Or have you got another stash in there?'

I try to figure out the tone of her voice – is she mocking me, admonishing me? My heart is racing slightly.

'Thanks. I – I like that song. I *really* love it. I – well—' I murmur, turning my attention to the menu, trying to get back to some sort of ordinary feeling.

Maureen stares at me for a moment too long. Then, 'We're obviously celebrating,' she says, sitting back with a big smile. I'm grateful to her. This habit women have – a role Helen often claimed not to want – of telling me what I'm feeling. Tremendously helpful. Like having an interpreter at hand to translate you to yourself.

I glance shyly at her. I notice that smell of sweets again. Pear drops, sweets that smell like nail-varnish remover to me. Where has that smell come from? Has she been eating them? I wonder if I should tell her that her cardigan is done up all wrong, there at the centre where the buttons are pulling rather tight? I don't want her to think I'm staring at her breasts.

'You just know the coffee here's going to be terrible,' I whisper instead.

She follows my eyes in any case, looks down at her chest, laughs; unbuttons and rebuttons the cardigan (she's wearing something underneath though. Some sort of camisole). 'Got dressed in a hurry,' she says. An image then of Maureen at home, perhaps the shadow of some dark male figure lying in her bed, buttoning up her clothes.

The busker is singing again. A jazz number. 'Out of the tree of life, I just picked me a plum.'

'He sure did!' I say, nodding towards the stetson where I laid the notes. I'm euphoric somehow. So happy to be somewhere new. Driving again, doing ordinary things. Maureen laughs.

I find myself smiling widely. The boy sings in the same mild way, with the same absence of flourish, but in its place he offers plainness, precision. Yes, I love his singing. It's joyous. I'm tapping my fingers on the table. Fantastic. *Out of the tree of life, I just picked me a plum.* Isn't that a Frank Sinatra number? Tum tum ta-dum ta-dum ta-dum ti-ta-ta-duum. Maureen gives me another funny look, and then returns my smile. That was a bit *random*, as Alice would say. Yes, but, poppet, at the danger of sounding corny, you must admit: I do have so much to celebrate.

After the café, I go to a cash machine, and Maureen waits while I get more money out. The sale of a two-bedroomed flat in Highgate makes a balance in there of a ridiculous sum. You could buy a six-bedroom house in St Ives for less, I notice, after staring in a few estate agents' windows.

We buy the forks, knives, plates from a small department store. Maureen makes small talk about her girls, her plans for Christmas (I notice that no man is included in these, no boyfriend or partner or ex-husband) and while she chats we wander down towards a river, pass a Methodist chapel in a disgusting, shit-coloured stone. Opposite is a low stone building. It's some kind of local museum and Maureen suggests we go inside. It's free, she says.

We enter via a little courtyard garden, the wintry trees decorated with children's drawings of snowmen and Santa Claus.

The usual flickering yellow light; glass boxes full of bones; damp smell; lumpen plastic shark hanging from the ceiling. Fading leaflets, closed blinds and no visitors. History. About as dusty and foreign as it's possible to make it. Maureen points out a framed newspaper piece about John Bellingham, pinned to a wall in a windowless ante-room with other newspapers and a few dark oil paintings. It looks as unappealing as any museum display could ever hope to be.

'Assassinated the prime minister? I never knew we had a British prime minister who got assassinated!' Maureen says, diligently reading the notes.

'Yes. Spencer Perceval, wasn't it? In 1812. Bellingham was a nutcase. He meant to shoot someone else, I think, some ambassador he had a beef with because he said he had been unjustly imprisoned and they owed him. I didn't know he was from round here.'

Bellingham was from St Neots, the newspaper report says. I read the display. He was hanged.

'There was a buzz at the time by some of the crowd to cheer him but it was a far greater number who called: *Silence*.' And some Frenchman in another document suggests: 'Farewell, Bellingham, you have taught ministers that they should do justice, and grant audience when it is asked of them.'

'They're a rebellious lot round here, aren't they?' I say. Maureen agrees with me. It's a noted Fen trait.

'Depressing, isn't it,' Maureen says, back in the car, 'how they suck all the life out of history? No wonder kids hate it.'

I mumble something in defence of history. In defence of teachers.

'Yeah, but good teachers are like hen's teeth,' Maureen says. 'Each school gets only one, if they're lucky. I don't know who it might be at Cassie's school.'

'Was she – is your daughter at this same school as the – as this boy Drew?'

Maureen gives me that look again. The one that says I've transgressed. But after a pause she says:

'No, Drew went to the other local school. But he was expelled. I probably shouldn't tell you this. But there was – a lot of gossip about it. He ended up at the Pupil Referral Unit in Littleport – that's what happens when kids are excluded. Something happened. Littleport's a small place. At his funeral—'

'You went to his funeral?'

'Of course. In my role as support to the donor family—'

'Oh.'

'I'm getting tired of keeping secrets.'

'Quite.'

'You did ask . . .'

'Yes. I did indeed.'

And unbidden, it all comes to me now: a funeral. A modest turnout, a modern church, small, one of those buildings lacking in sacredness; that feels like a village hall, that doubles up for jumble sales and tombolas. More than the usual amount of young people: girls and boys, friends of his, kids just a bit younger than Alice and Ben. Girls from this Pupil Referral Unit place who look and speak like the physiotherapist at the hospital, girls I've learned to think of as 'Fen girls' or local, with names like Cassie and Chloe – the names, I dimly realise, of Maureen's daughters. Plump girls in tracksuits who never wear coats, even in the coldest weather.

This is how it happens. One thing leads to another. One image, one name, one phrase, tumbles another along, like beads on a necklace. You are not sure if you are dredging them up, or making them: it feels like the same thing, and you know that whatever these details are, they're it, how it's done, they're the story, the truth.

Now I can smell the place, too. Lilies, of course, waxy and haunting, a jasmine smell. The smell of coffee too – for later – and chemicals used to clean the carpet. The feel of narrow benches under the buttocks. Running your hand underneath and feeling the scratches under your fingers, someone else's graffiti. And the sounds. Coughing and shuffling, the odd stifled burp. Papers rustling as the hymns are announced. What would he have, on the order of service, a boy like Drew? 'The Lord's My Shepherd', perhaps? No. Some verses. A prayer. *To give and not to count the cost.* That's what he did, didn't he? And at that line, murmured softly by the elderly vicar, the family vicar, the same one who did her husband's funeral, and her son's christening, this Ruth

Beamish, dark, vivid, heaves into view and turns her long sharp gaze on me: *you*, she says. That's all. She looks at me. She has dark eyes and she looks a little like my own mother, she's a woman of uncommon beauty, she throws her gaze the way a fisherman throws his hook. I'm sorry, I say. Or: What can I do?

'*A new heart also will I give you, and a new spirit will I put within you; and I will take away the stony heart out of your flesh . . .*'

Ezekiel. Chapter thirty-six. 'And I will give you a heart of flesh.' Funny how I remember that, but I just do.

I raise the blind to a misty morning and know that today is the day I'm going to re-read the letter from Ruth Beamish. I tell myself I'm not interested but I've nothing else to do and, apart from a solicitor's letter to deal with, nothing to occupy me. After all, I'm just checking the address: Black Drove, Littleport. It's too soon to see if I can visit this woman, satisfy my curiosity a little more – Maureen's right, that would be insensitive – but no harm just in *looking at where it is,* now, is there? I get the map from the back of the car, venturing out in the cold in my pyjama bottoms and socks. I'll have to change them, they're so wet. Returning to my bedroom I pull on pants, T-shirt, jeans – I pull the belt tight, I've lost weight – but in fact before I know it I'm outside, locking up the flat, punching a postcode into the satnav and starting up the car.

On the back seat I notice the book that Maureen gave me and I decide to take it out, and leave it in the flat. Then I start up the car again.

But I'm soon frustrated. The day is so foggy it's treacherous and there's nothing of the landscape to see. Pointing the nose of the car down the long empty roads is like staring into a deep well with white smoke billowing up towards you and trying to see the bottom. And then the sudden rearing of two yellow headlights like the glinting eyes of an animal. I give up, drive back. My first drive on my own since the op. Probably better if I come back from it in one piece.

And then a funny thought forms: better for *whom*?

The answer comes back: this Beamish woman. Better for her, perhaps. That I treat her son's gift with respect. *Perhaps that can be a small comfort to me. It's too soon to say.* Her first Christmas without her son. I can't think about that. I can't imagine that.

My first Christmas without Cushie. I got drunk. Eleven years old and home from school for the holidays and I found my Dad's whisky bottle in a cupboard and since it tasted disgusting and Dad had forgotten about all essentials like tangerines in red string and a Christmas tree with an angel on top and ginger wine and a brandy-soaked cake and cards strung up on little pegs, I poured the whisky into a mug with lime cordial and that seemed to do the trick, I could slug it down in one. And then – this bit I had to be told about, later – I apparently went into a bakery in Chester-le-Street to buy a Christmas cake and said to the woman who wrapped it up for me: Will *you* be my mam? I was brought back home in a police car and was sick on the front steps, while every Christmas-lit window in the neighbourhood twitched its net curtains as one.

'This isn't the flipping exchange department in Marks and Spencer,' the woman had said.

Dad promised the policeman he'd 'give the lad a good talking-to; or, better still, a jolly good hiding'. He never did. I'd been a weekly boarder; he said I could change to day boarding. He made that concession. The *Grandstand*-theme-tuned Saturdays continued: frankfurter sausages out of a can. Him on the sofa, me on Cushie's armchair, the smell of unwashed socks and cigarettes. Later we progressed to watching the snooker: the soft clack of the ball against the cue, those long silences when someone walked around the table, looked at it from another angle, walked around it again, stuck their bum in the air. We both preferred the safety play of the clipped Steve Davis to the brilliant mayhem of a player like Alex 'Hurricane' Higgins. 'He'll press the self-destruct button one day, you'll see,' Dad liked to say. We disapproved of Higgins. The passion, the risk-taking. The naked desire. Nothing held back at all.

He was right about Higgins, though it took a while. He died last year of throat cancer, I think. Same disease that took Dad, though Dad went sooner in the end, for all his *conserving*. Fifty years old, the same age as I am now.

Somewhere on a slip of paper I have Maureen's mobile number. She gave me it when we arranged our trip to St Ives, in case she was late, she said, or got delayed. I dial it now and she picks up almost immediately. I ask her if she would like to come to dinner sometime, try out the new cutlery. Maybe in the New Year, when this malarkey with my family is over. It will have to be something simple, I say, like pasta: I've got limited pans and kitchen stuff. I hope you like pasta, I say.

'I can bring a colander,' Maureen replies.

Part Four

Nobody ever called me Andrew. I was Drew Beamish, the first Drew in a long line of Williams, like our ancestors, or Billys, like my dad, and somewhere along the line our family name Beamiss got an 'h' where that last 's' should be. Yes, I knew about the rioters, I loved hearing about Willie Beamiss. We learned it all in Reception, along with Cromwell and Hereward. I was in Hereward, that was our team. Mum was the busy type. Hyper, you know: in and out like a dog at a fair. But I had a strong personality, too, as *Beamish* as the days when the Soham mere was forming, she said. The first words I spoke made Mum laugh: I would point my finger at whatever caught my eye and shout: *mine!*

I was born at the Hinchingbrooke, Huntingdon. Mum told me it was an easy labour: she bloody nearly popped me in the car. The old boy – my dad – would have been driving: one hand on Mum's arm, trying to keep her calm, and her squirming and clawing and squealing at the window like a cat trying to escape its basket. He should have been at work, a busy time a late harvest. October 24th 1995. They didn't get paternity leave, farm labourers, so it was a stolen day, and would have to be made up later. I was their first baby. They'd been married a bare two months.

Mum had already been on the whist drive with Dad before they married, as the old boys say round here. Dad was thin as a yard of pump water in photographs from those days. I never remember him like that. Solid, he was, by the time I remember him. Secure. Safe. Drove a tractor and moved hay bales around. Every day of his working life; he loved it. If Mum ever started up with: 'The way they treat you,' he would just laugh and ruffle her hair and call her his little firebrand. Was he a lily-liver then, my dad, too easygoing for his own good? No, he was on a slow fuse, that's all. He was fair. He thought the best of people. Soft-hearted, you might say. Kind. That's not a crime, is it? Mum was the clever one – top of her class, she told me. Mum liked taking tests, I knew that much; always trying to prove something, she was.

I think boys aren't meant to know if their mum is, you know, nice looking and that, but I did, somehow. Or maybe they can know but they're meant to hate it. I saw the way men looked at her. It didn't make me feel sick, or hate her. It was just the way it was. She was a person, I knew that, she wasn't just mine. I don't really get why boys find it so hard to think this way about their mums. She was a good mum, she made a great shepherd's pie, she took too much interest in your home-work, she had some funny sayings ('Half the lies you hear aren't true'), she wasn't too strict, she was a good laugh. And she was still young, and nice looking with these very dark eyes, and I think she was probably a real looker at the point Dad met her and she didn't change much over the years, not that you'd notice, anyway.

I once brought a mate home, Jezzer it was, and it was school holidays, summer, and Mum was sunbathing in the garden in her bikini. Jez was the year above me in school and straight as a pound of candles; Mum wandered in from the garden to the kitchen to offer him a glass of Ribena with her freckled bare skin like *really close* and he sort of stopped in his tracks and blushed and Mum was just smiling and pouring water into the glass and the drink was pink and then deep-red coloured as she stirred it, just like Jez's face. Really made me want to laugh, but I didn't, because I could see that would make matters worse and that scalding kind of blushing's a bit – well, it makes you feel sorry for someone, doesn't it?

Mum, Ruth Beamish, was descended from a Fen line too – her grandmother was one of the Ice Maidens, a champion Fen skater – that's probably why she had such good balance. We used to walk to this barn in Farmer Martin's field to try and spot the barn owl that lived there and there was a skinny plank sticking out over the ditch and she would always challenge me to walk it and she would do it, no trouble, but I'd get spooked by the owl, it would appear suddenly out of one black hole of a window like a ghost and sweep out over our heads, the exact same colour as a loaf of bread, making me wobble and hurry to the other side of the plank, looking like an idiot. That's maybe her contribution, Mum's bit of the DNA, good looks and good balance, but she could be snarky sometimes; liked her own company. Loving, yes.

It started in Year Nine. Jo was a new teacher and I noticed her on the day of that first assembly, I noticed that she was bursting the seams of her pink fluffy jumper. Small with this head of blonde curls, like one of those cherubs in St George's Church – and big grey eyes behind these sort of owl glasses – how could any boy not notice her? I didn't know how old she was and I didn't care; she just made me feel long-legged and hot whenever I walked past her, adjusting my tie or rolling up my shirtsleeves, swaggering, Beamish-style, you know.

I towered over her already. That was a great feeling. At fourteen I'd shot up – five foot ten and counting, my feet way bigger than Mum's dainty ones, I already took the same shoe size as my dad, and being able to look down on a teacher's head, on a blonde, cute teacher's head – seeing the little pink tips of her glasses frame through her hair, and how the ends curled, sort of *tenderly* around her ears – a new feeling, totally new, it made me stop in the corridor and want to think about it, what the—?

I remember heat flooding me and a tightness in my chest and then whoosh – as if something was . . . I don't know, swooping. When I came across Jo – when I saw the back of her dandelion head from across the playground, or her arriving in that funny yellow car of hers and climbing out, books, folders, flattened hard against her chest; when I looked up in class because I heard her snap open her glasses case and knew she was trying to disguise the way she was staring at me – it happened again. Like something had swooshed down and gathered me up, like when you see a marsh harrier swoop down on a mouse over the fen; nick it, lift it away. I almost wanted to look up, it was so totally weird. Was something falling on me? I couldn't tell if it came from inside me, if *I* was making this feeling myself, or if it was – well, I know this sounds funny – if it was landing on me from somewhere, like a brick. I wanted to tell someone, talk to someone, ask Dad maybe. Well, I did and I didn't. Dad might laugh. And . . . it was mine, this weird feeling, I didn't want it spoiled.

I thought maybe I could tell Jo. I somehow thought: Well, this is stupid, yeah, but not *totally*. I thought that she should be the one I should tell. So one day I saw these little earrings in Peacocks in Ely. Cheap. Cute. Little gold-coloured birds. Not real gold, of course, but sweet. I thought about her ears and the feelings washed around me again and I paid ten quid and they wrapped the blue cardboard box in yellow tissue paper.

And she goes at once, pushing the box back at me, 'Drew, I can't take these.'

And I'm a bit sad but I try not to show it, and just say, 'Why not, Miss?'

140

Funny to call her Miss. Doesn't sound right. I'm almost sick with nervousness. Inside I'm shaking and spluttering but on the outside I'm all . . . I'm . . . I put my hand up to my chin, brush it against the little soft hairs while I wait for her to say something.

'It would be—' she goes and I know before she says it, I hear it – that fucking awful word: 'inappropriate'. So I snatch the bird earrings. I shove the box in the back pocket of my school trousers and act like I don't give a shit.

But as I'm going out the door I say to her: 'Thought your ears looked a bit bare, Miss, that's all,' and at that word 'bare' she blushes, and I stand there for like two seconds, looking at her. She's biting her lip. She's widening her eyes and making a funny little gesture, sort of lifting her shoulders up towards her ears like she's trying to, I don't know, disappear inside her own body or something. Whatever. She can't hide that pink flush. So I grin to myself, turn my back. I'm safe. The swooping, the lifting, the feeling like I'm being carried off. I'm not on my own. It's not as if Miss Lavender feels *nothing*.

So then the next day, I try again. I leave the earrings in their yellow tissue and the little eggshell-blue cardboard box on her desk. Now she'll have to go out of her way to give them back to me, look for me, after class. Single me out from the others and how will she manage that without it being . . . inappropriate? I spend all day thinking of her, imagining her bothered about it. And four o'clock, coming back to collect my tie from the classroom where I left it dusting the floor behind my chair, she says – as if casual, as if she hasn't waited for this opportunity all day – 'Oh! Drew, a word, please.'

I come to her desk. I stand there. I'm so tall these days, like honestly from one day to the next I don't know what size I'm going to be – a bit like my voice, will it come out high and squeaky or gravelly, low – so I just actually feel like I'm growing, stretching like a shock of wheat as I stand there. She looks at the door, which is closed. She does the hunching-shoulder thing again, like she's trying to duck away from me, duck out of it. Then she lifts her chin and puts her hand on the box of earrings. She picks it up and pops the lid open and the gold birds sit there on their blue cardboard, beaks trained on us.

'It's very sweet of you. I'm – touched, to be honest. I don't know if you knew – if you'd been told? I've just lost my mother – cancer – I've been feeling wobbly.'

This I didn't know, and didn't expect. And there's more –

'And, well, I don't know – I probably shouldn't tell you this, but my divorce came through last week too. I'm actually – I'm really, you know, "*Miss*" Lavender again, though I know you all call me that in school anyway. I never took – his – Bob's name.'

She smiles. Small teeth. A real smile, very quick, though, and then back to seriousness. Squeezing at the place where her glasses usually sit on her nose with her fingers. Tired, she looks.

'Anyway. So. I'll keep the earrings, as long as that's the end of it. No more presents, Drew, you know? It will get me into trouble. It will give people – the wrong idea.'

The blue box is flipped closed; the birds in their dark nest.

'Yes, Miss.'

Innocence. All innocence. I just stare at her like I've no thought about what this 'wrong idea' could be. But I stare at her all over, if you know what I mean. Up, down and all around. I stare long enough to see if I can make her blush again. I stand there long enough to smell the perfume she wears, which is very faint but sort of silky and – feathery. I don't know how else to describe it. It's pale. It tickles my nose.

'Oh and Drew, Mr Roe said you didn't hand your History homework in this week and you got detention? I – well – if the detention is Tuesday, I wanted to warn you, I'm supervising. I mean – just so you know.'

Just so I know. Fuck me. What on earth is that about? To *warn* me? Sounds more like – somehow, *preparing* me for the fact that we're going to be on our own in a small sweaty room together. Me, her and those hefty tits of hers. I mean, right away I picture them. The fluffy pink sweater, some kind of wool, I think Mum calls it *angora*, that sweater lifting over her head. A pink bra, the kind with little wires underneath that sort of force them up, in your face, really hard. A bra made of lace so you can see the dark nipples nosing through. Oh God. That's the sort of bra she'd wear, I'm sure of it. She might as well be naked now – I've got a hard-on so fucking enormous it's practically tapping on the desk.

'OK, Miss. See you Tuesday.'

I stumble out the door somehow. I have the weirdest impression that she's smiling about something; she could even be laughing. She's so quiet, Miss Lavender, such a soft voice and a secretive way about her, it's hard to know. In any case, I'm concentrating on swaggering out without bumping into any chairs. And thinking that I'd better try and get some fags before Tuesday so I can bribe Stokey – the other one with a History detention – not to turn up.

The detention day, the longed-for day, comes at last, like a birthday. The days leading to that Tuesday I spend so long in the shower before school that Mum is banging on the door, shouting: 'God's sake, Drew, what you doing in there?' Listening to the Plain White T's on my iPod . . . *Oh, what you do to me, it's what you do to me* . . . and picturing Miss

Lavender, her little mouth with its small tongue, her perfect heart-shaped face, that tickling scent of her, the way it settles on me like something just breathing on my face, just as I fall to sleep. I love her! I whisper to myself. It isn't a shock to me. I grew up under this and around it – I don't know if my mates feel like this – for me it's always filled every crack in our poky old house: the way Dad looks at Mum, the way she touches him – so here it comes: my turn, and though it's powerful it doesn't surprise me, it's just my due.

Why her, though? Why not Poppy Martin or some other girl in Year Nine? What is it about Miss Lavender and the grey ring-binder files she carries pressed against her chest, like someone's out to prise them off her; or her little wrist with that slim gold watch that seems to swim around it, way too solid, too big for her; or that little yellow car of hers sliding between the school gates, nosing into its regular parking spot, and making me think about a tongue slipping inside a mouth?

I don't say anything to my mates. I don't tell Stokey, though he must wonder why I want him to miss detention and no doubt earn himself a second one as a result. I don't tell Ricky either, though he'd probably just make some disgusting joke about someone's mum. Mature pussy's the best, he'd say, trying to sound as dirty as possible and like he knows anything at all. The Mum thing is gross – especially when I think back to that day when Jez was in our garden and suddenly got all embarrassed about Mum in her bikini – but Miss Lavender's younger than that! And she's not even married and she's nobody's mother and – well, that's just crap and no one really believes in it, do they – our English teacher, I remember him saying, and he was stuttering, you know, and blushing – his advice for finding 'Freudian imagery' in any text was: 'If it's longer than it's round it's a phallus and if it's rounder than it's long it's a womb' – A phallus? Like any of us knew that word!

144

We just laughed. Threw paper aeroplanes at him. Says it all, though. If you fancy a girl in Year Seven you're a paedo and if you fancy an older one you want to shag your own mum. Fuck off.

I know mothers who are old boilers, dried old. I know boys who could never in their wildest dreams imagine their mother doing it – too disgusting to go there. But I'm not like that. I've seen her underwear, hanging on the line, she never bothered to hide it. Purple. Lace. I'm not saying I think about it, but you can't avoid it either. Music. Underwear. Beer and smoking on the back step when he came in from the farm, him with his shirt off, her rubbing sun lotion on his shining brown back that looked like wood, like an oiled wooden tree – and her taking the cigarette out and resting it next to her beer, and saying, now, Billy, don't do it tomorrow, don't work all day without a shirt, what about skin cancer? Her hands all over his skin, after – what, twenty years together. I'm not stupid, that's all I'm saying. I've got eyes in my head.

So, Jo's in the History classroom with the history books piled beside her on the desk and wearing her glasses firmly pushed up her nose, and there's a smell in the room like Christmas. Satsumas. These neat little cups of peel beside her, one inside the other; and she's popping the last segment into her mouth as I step in.

'All right, Miss.'

'Drew. You know what you have to do. Do you have the letter from your parents?'

I hand over the letter that states that my parents know I've been given a detention and give their permission for me to stay after school. *Mrs Ruth Beamish*. Mum signed it. Best handwriting.

'Don't suppose they were very pleased, were they now?' she says, in her teacherly way.

I shrug. 'Dunno, Miss. They know I'm OK. They don't worry 'bout me.'

'OK, well, sit down.' She's sort of flapping one hand in front of her the way you shoo the coopy hens, as if to say, go then, go away from my desk. It pleases me just to stand there. To put my hands on the desk and stand over her, looking down at her and forcing her to look up at me. And then I see it. See them.

'You liked the earrings then, Miss.'

Her hand flies up to her ear, as if she wants to cover it. She's all panicky. She's frowning and her big eyes, the pupils inside them darken, sort of filling up the grey colour with a deep dark black.

'Look—' She glances towards the door of the classroom like she'd like to escape. The door is firmly shut. The backside of a poster blocks the glass. We're safe in here. No one can see us. Oh, that's if you don't count the window to the school field, which is behind me.

A beat starts up, a drum-tap, fingers tapping on a table while I wait for her to right herself again.

'Yes. Thank you. I do actually – I really like them.'

A smile. A rare smile and I notice she has this tiny thread of satsuma resting on her blouse. Resting there just above – just in that awesome place where I really shouldn't be staring. Her T-shirt is black, so it's hard not to notice. I could pick it off and see if she slaps my hand away? This would be my most daring act so far, a make-or-break gesture, should I risk it?

'Go and sit at the desk, Drew. Don't hover round me.' She glances down at herself, her eyes following mine. Picks off the thread of white. Grins. 'Shoo! Sit down! Get on with – whatever it is you're supposed to be doing.'

'It's about John Bellingham, Miss. I need some help.'

'Well. Bellingham? Is that what you were working on? You know that – that really is my topic. I actually work in a museum over at St Ives on a Saturday – I'm in the local history society. Don't get me started, Drew, I'm afraid I'm rather obsessed.'

And that's how it goes and that's how it begins. She slaps me down if I act out of order. But she's friendly and smiley and the feeling I have around her is just of that, of friendship and easiness and like there isn't the usual screen there, the teacher–pupil screen that makes you feel there isn't a person behind it that they really want you to know. OK, I have a massive crush on her and she knows it. But we sort of agree to ignore it. It's impossible not to know that she likes me right back. She can't help herself.

One time she says, 'You're a very unusual boy,' and I grin and grin, and later, another time, she says, out of the blue as if thinking it through to herself, 'You're a very popular boy, Drew, you're lucky. I felt very lonely when I was in school.' Another day she laughs, really laughs at a joke and covers her mouth with her hand and says that she hasn't laughed like that in years and it's weird watching her, I mean she doubles up, she really laughs, her eyes are watering. I can't even remember what I said, I'm embarrassed by then at the sight of her, at the – lack of control – it's just odd. And she pushes her hair away from her eyes and her hair is all messy and she suddenly sobers up and says: 'God, I think I'm cracking up.'

One time she says: 'You're so clever, Drew. You should think about A levels. University.'

'University. Is there one in Ely?'

She laughs at this. 'No, you'd have to go further afield. There's Anglia Ruskin in Cambridge. That's where I went.'

'Cambridge? I can't imagine it, Miss. I just sort of picture myself on a tractor like my dad.'

She comes close to me then and takes her glasses off to clean them. She picks up a bit of her T-shirt to do this. Does she do this deliberately? My eyes go straight to the little place above her waist where I can see flesh, pink flesh.

'That's the hardest part, Drew. The imagining part. Picturing it. My mum was a hairdresser. I do know exactly what you mean. I'm just saying that you're clearly very bright. Your life could in fact be quite different.'

I picture Dad then, while I'm staring at that patch on her tummy, while she's speaking. I once stood in a field with him, after he'd let me sit up front in the tractor while he ploughed it, and he jumped out and picked up a clod of earth and put it under my nose and said: Smell that, Drew. Rich as chocolate, it is. Doesn't it make you want to lick it? Do you know only five per cent of the land in this country is classed as first-class agricultural land – but all of ours is!

Ours, he said. He thought it was his because he loved it. Bread basket of Europe, the Fens, Dad would say. Black gold.

So, that's how I get into History. Jo teaches it and she tells me I'm clever and good at it and I start to like it, simple as that.

One day she organises a trip for us to Ely Gaol. Ely Museum as it is now. We're all arsing about. Stokey digs me in the ribs and says *mature pussy* in this stupid voice whenever she's in view but I'm actually paying attention, I'm reading the little notices about the exhibits. The Bishop's Gaol. The Felons' Night Cell. And then I see this thing, this amazing eerie thing, and that's it – that's how I get it. A piece of wood. I read the notice:

'This plank, showing plainly some carvings,
presumably done by a prisoner, is of the old gaol-house
bench in the early nineteenth century.
PRAY GOD GOOD PEOPLE remember THE POOR PRISONERS.'

There are these lines with crosses through them, someone crossing off the days. And this little drawing is carved into it: a stick man dangling from the gallows.

We're not allowed to touch of course. So I just stand there and this creepy feeling travels from my toes to the back of my neck and my skin prickles icy cold and then hot. I know without looking at my arms that the little hairs are all standing up on goose pimples.

In our school we all have names like Rutter, Crow, Harley, Martin, Gotobed, Lavender, nothing much changes round here. Fen people don't move away. So every one of us could claim it was their ancestor who carved the stick man, but I knew somehow with dread certainty that it was mine. Willie Beamiss.

A stick man dangling from a gallows. Looked like a child's drawing. But he was eighteen, older than me. It's the start of Year Ten by now and I'm fifteen. And I get Miss Lavender on her own in one of the funny little corridors off the museum rooms and I tell her this, I tell her that I feel sure this carving was done by my very own great-great-great-whatever-grandfather and I think I'm actually shaking as I say this, the feeling is so strong, I'm all wound up and certain, and I expect her to say, 'Don't be silly, Drew, don't you think every student in Year Ten thinks that?' but instead she smiles and looks at me sort of slowly, and carefully, and says: 'You might be right. Strange how strongly connected we sometimes feel to old things, isn't it?' I want to kiss her then. I almost do. We're close enough in the corridor to touch, but then another teacher, old Tansley, comes by and sort of gets in the way, and Jo looks worried and scuttles off.

I try and read some other stuff, notices and things. Stokey keeps coming up to me and saying, let's get outside in the Felons' Yard and smoke a fag? I shrug my shoulders, try and shake him off, jerk my head towards Tansley as if to say: he'd catch us. But the truth is, I want to look further at the piece of wood, think about this Willie Beamiss.

It was Dad who told me the story ages back. I always knew about the Littleport riots, like I said. And I knew that we had not one but two ancestors involved: Willie Beamiss the father, and Willie Beamiss the younger one, who was not much older than me and spent a year in this prison. But knowing it and feeling it are different. This is the first time I've *felt* it.

So now I read this notice that says that those stuck in here had to pay, they actually had to pay fees to their gaoler for beer or bread, their family had to bring the money in if they couldn't. That bit I didn't know. Any who couldn't pay were stripped of their clothes or belongings. I look around me. It's a tiny room. There's a tiny window. And guess who owned the place? The Bishop of Ely. Who also had the right to arrest and imprison people under this thing called the Liberty of Ely. The bishop actually made himself a nice little profit from the gaol.

I catch up with Jo again, say all of this to her. I'm angry, I'm actually panting, I don't know why. I can hardly get the words out.

'I know just what you mean,' she says. 'My Aunt Sarah was descended from another rioter who was hanged: Thomas South. Though of course names change when people get married.'

Weird how mad I am. So long ago.

'The Liberty of Ely Act was abolished some time in the 1830s, so his powers were reduced,' Jo says. She seems to be smiling again; I can't help thinking she's pleased that I've got all roiled up.

'Too late for Willie.'

'Was he one of those who was hanged? Or did he have his sentence commuted?' she asks.

'My Dad told me it was Willie's dad who they hanged. They didn't have much on him but they wanted to make a point.'

Jo nods. 'You know,' she says, 'look at the riots this summer and the heavy sentences . . . same thing really. Had to be clamped down on to prevent future ones.' Then she seems nervous again, looking from left to right, finding that we're alone again and the other kids have moved into a different room.

'Drew, we shouldn't—' she starts.

'What, we're *talking*. We're talking about history, about politics, about work! Mr Tansley would be well impressed.'

'I shouldn't even – I'm probably encouraging you just by talking to you on your own like this —'

She laughs. Then someone else is coming up the stairs and she moves away from me. Everyone in school knows I fancy her. But nothing *inappropriate* can happen, she says.

It's different now between us. It bothers me and it pleases me at the same time. It's part of my story, of who I am, and she admits, it's part of her story too. It's like a lid has come off something. I feel different. It adds to my all-around feeling that everything inside me is shifting, bubbling up, and Jo, only Jo can see this, and let me be like this, and not tell me off about it.

The next day I see her go into one of the empty labs and duck in after her. I feel sure she knew I was behind her: she must have heard the squeak of my trainers. Or maybe even smell me. I think I'm like an animal by now, tracking her.

'I – someone left this Bunsen burner on,' she says, wheeling around. She looks a bit caught out.

Did she hope I'd come in after her? She always eyes the doors and windows and then the shoulders come down, the smiley friendliness comes back.

'You made me jump,' she says.

151

I step towards her. I know she's crossed a boundary no teacher should cross by letting me. Letting me flirt with her. Smiling at me. Widening her eyes. Taking her glasses off. Joking. Tossing phrases back and forth. Letting me know I exist, I'm me, I'm real, I'm not just a boy, a schoolboy, one of her pupils, I'm me. I already tower over her. Sweat springs on me, whenever I look at her. The awesome feelings she produces – hard not to believe they're in here whenever we're together, they're so strong, they're in the room with us.

'Where do you think feelings *are*?' I ask her, suddenly.

'What on earth do you mean?' She looks startled, but then cracks another big smile. She likes my challenging questions, she's said, a while back, so here's another one.

'Well, are they, like, inside you? Do you produce them yourself? Or are they outside and they sort of get inside you from someone or somewhere else – like chemicals in the air or something? Or do you, like, inherit them, like genes or what?'

Jo takes a step back. It's as if she's trying to work out if this is dangerous or not. If she should answer as a teacher – I just asked her a question – or as something else. She stares at the tap in front of her, fiddles with it. When she looks up again her eyes are shiny, like she's trying not to cry. I wonder if I've made her think of her mum dying or her divorce or something, and I want to say sorry, but she carries on, ignoring that and trying to answer my question.

'Well, the romantics would say they're deep inside you, of course. In your heart. And these days I suppose it's more likely to be a chemical explanation . . . neuroscience. People probably locate feelings more in the brain, not the heart. But . . . there's a bit more to it than that, surely. I mean, there's Freud and the unconscious and a whole host of other explanations.'

She stops then. A noise outside the lab. She moves a little, puts a proper teacherly distance between us. She was explaining something to me after all. No crime in that.

No one comes. I put out my hand – I'm going to touch her cheek – but she shakes her head and this time we do definitely hear a door bang, and we both jump apart.

The next day I think about cooling off a bit. Give her a taste of her own medicine, see if she can stand it. So I stay off school for a few days, tell Mum I've got bellyache. And I'm right: when I come back, Jo can't wait to seek me out in the corridor.

'Oh. You well, Drew? Not like you, to miss school.'

Casual, oh so casual. I give her a big grin, I'm with mates, there's nothing she can say. I stride off with my kit over my shoulder, on my way to rugby practice. I'm learning.

'God, you've cheered me up,' she says, another time.

'Why, were you – like, depressed?'

'I – Yes. I suppose I must have been.'

And then it all pays off. It happens. Casual, but . . . One day, one day just like any other, she says I can come to the local history museum in St Ives, come 'do some work' with her there if I like. She says this easy, so easy, but I feel the room tremble and the walls of the school shine at me like a melting has begun.

'OK,' I say. 'See you Saturday then. But I'd need a lift. And people would see me. In your car, I mean.'

'You're very naughty,' she says, in a low, trembling voice, and I flood hot all over.

Awesome. She's flirting, no question. I could take her any time I like, I think. In my dreams she's always rearing over me, shaking out those blonde curls, riding me like a horse, bucking; arching. Grinding down. And sometimes, dirtier dreams, I'm a fountain – a fierce force of water shooting up – and she'd be trying to ride *that* and it keeps gushing at her, an endless fountain; keeps on filling her and pushing her up, up, she'd never be able to squash it down . . .

She arranges to pick me up out on the Great Fen road. I have to walk there.

In the car she says: 'It would be a terrible – it's not just about the – about my job. It's more than that. It would be wrong. You're so young, Drew. You're – handsome – lovely, you really are. You're—Any woman in her right mind would be – I certainly am – anyone would be – flattered.'

Oh, it's what you do to me, it's what you do to me . . . Is she in her right mind then? Who could expect me – at fifteen – to know?

In the car, she asks me to pass her a packet of Polos from the glove compartment. And in there is a scarf and I have to move it, and it's made of this silky stuff, it looks like underwear or something, and it gives off such a waft of her I want to pick it up and bury my face in it. She sees me touching it, rubbing the pale yellow and grey rose-spattered stuff between my finger and thumb. Looks at me. 'Want a Polo?' she says. But she saw.

She admitted later she was 'broken up in pieces' about Bob, about her ex. She felt the lowest she'd ever felt, she said. Strange, she said, most people have no idea how long it takes to get over a relationship, even a bad one. Two years, she says, since they first broke up and she still feels lonely for him sometimes.

But it's the talking like this that's whipping it up. She's having it both ways. She's saying no but she's talking about things, broaching it, making it possible, making it shine for me: making it *real*.

*   *   *

154

One time Jo puts that scarf on. Shakes out the fabric, rolls it a bit, circles it round her neck. She sees that I recognise the scarf – *I've been in your car, I've seen your things* – and she sees that I'm watching her and she doesn't stop, or move away. No other teacher would do that. No way. It's – out of order. The more she talks about how impossible it would be, the more possible it seems. To her as well as me, surely. Maybe I never really thought so until then. It was, like, a fantasy. A crush. That's all. They were my feelings, they didn't need to come out into the world and *be* anything else.

Mum would have gone ballistic if she knew about those conversations. Miss Lavender – Jo – didn't live near us then. Mum's nursing job meant she worked shifts, she often didn't see me in the mornings before school. Sometimes Mum would smile, running her fingers along my top lip and say: Look at that! Ah, Drew, you're getting a moustache . . . and she always had a go at me for spending too long in the shower. But that was it. She had no idea what went on at school. She was pleased I was doing well in History, that's all she knew.

Another time, a day in the school library, Jo goes: 'You're vulnerable, Drew, though you don't know it, you don't think so. And so am I. I'm not myself. I'm thirty this year. It's – well, I don't think I'm the only woman in the world thinking: Will I ever find anyone? Babies. Time running out, you know?'

'You want a baby, Miss?'

She looks startled. Embarrassed, shocked, even.

'Oh well, I don't know. I just meant—'

And I never heard what she meant, because that was the day. The day a pupil – Ellie Marsh – came to find me in the library and told me to come to the Head's office. And the day sort of stopped and all colour bled out of it and I knew, I just knew, before the Head spoke, before the English teacher, Mr Rutter, was asked to drive me home to see my mother, that something so bad had happened that the blood in my veins was flooding icy and my strange mind was saying: I must tell him. Watch out for the bales, Dad. I must tell him: Heavy fuckers, they are. Remember, don't let a bale fall on you.

This was daft – random. I heard what the Head said, I heard her go: 'I'm so sorry, Drew . . .' I wasn't bonkers, I hadn't gone mad; I just couldn't stop the other thoughts coming. He'd had a heart attack. Shock because of the bale falling; he wasn't crushed by it. He'd died at the hospital. Mum was there, a teacher would take me to join her.

It was too late for warnings but that was all I could think: must get home, and warn him. And I could see his docky on the table, cheese and Branston pickle sandwiches, wrapped in silver foil, and see so clearly his hand picking it up, and the fat belly with the checked shirt, the soft furry brown hair on his arms, car keys in his other hand, jingling. The sound of him, always keys and a big gruff laugh, and that smell – a smell like eddish, the first growth of grass after mowing – and hay and sun and tractor fuel and the radio in the tractor cab humming and me wanting to put out a hand and stop him, say to him: Don't go, Dad, don't go, I'm only young, I still need you, don't go yet; and him leaving the biggin (that word he always used for our house); great solid oak that he was – too big to fell, surely? – him leaving our little house for ever.

And Mr Rutter was kind, I remember that, he was nice enough. He seemed to be talking about birds, all the time he was driving, and mumbling something about *his* father and how sorry he was and even though I couldn't really hear him or listen another part of me was registering that he's OK, he's not bad, he's all right for a nervous tosser, is Mr Rutter. And I do remember this, we saw lapwings, we saw lapwings in the distant fen out towards Mildenhall, and the lapwings were dancing, with their wings spread and their perky little crests, their weird movements. There was a whole cloud of them in the field, lifting and reshaping from the grass, making signs. One minute an arrow, the next letters, a word. Shaping, forming, a message. Old and new, always the same. You can never miss a lapwing, can you, because of the weirdness of the tumbling flight they do. And I was saying in my head: *Are you still here then? Where are you?* And I looked and looked and the message came back: *Yes, here I am, this is where I am. I'm in your heart.*

That's was when I did it. I mean, not that day I didn't, but soon. I didn't tell anyone. I didn't tell Mum, or Jo. I went online and filled in a form and it said if you were under eighteen you could still register as a donor but someone else, a parent, would have to give their consent. Eyes. Liver, whatever. I just ticked *heart*.

The card came in the post with its big red heart on a shiny blue background, all lame and cheerful, you know, just to slip in your wallet, in your back pocket, until you flip it over and read that sentence: *I would like to help someone live after my death*. And I stared at it, and I still had no idea why I did it, why I registered; it made no sense at all. Because I didn't know who I would help. I wasn't stupid enough to believe Dad would have been saved if someone else's heart had been up for grabs; I understood that heart transplants are for people with, like, heart disease – not for sudden attacks caused by shock, by losing your job, or a bale nearly crushing you, or because someone you love died. No. Heart transplants aren't for what Dad suffered from, or me neither. That's something totally different; that needs something else.

He'd been laid off the week before by his boss, Farmer Martin. That was the point. And he was working out his notice. His heart attack came on him later because of a bale falling on him, caused, they said, possibly by a faulty gantry, by someone's sloppiness in Health and Safety, somebody not paying attention – but in my mind it was all about the job ending. All about the end of his life's work. *I would like to help someone live after my death.* Maybe I simply thought: Is this all there is? Is it going to be over soon, one day, and be like this, be so little, so short? What the fuck is a life – my life – *for*?

Everyone thinks getting the donor card was a good thing. Like a *really* good thing, sort of unselfish, or saintly or something, I know that. I'm not so sure. I think it was another kind of reason, more complicated. It was something spooky. I was angry, at that time, that's all I was, I was blazing. I signed up and I got this little blue card that says: *I would like to help someone live after my death.*

Nothing could have saved him. In Year Six, I might have thought there was a heaven somewhere with fluffy clouds in it and angels and all that stuff. But really, like, even if I try hard, even if I want to, I don't believe that any more.

I didn't cry. I didn't cry in school, we can't be soft. I wanted to turn over straw bales myself with my arms, my own bare strength. I went about turning over chairs, banging doors and windows instead. I got back to school and burned up the corridors with my swagger. And later, not long after the funeral but when I was still steaming, just for devilment, just for rage or fury or badness or fuck knows what, when we were on our own in the Design Tech room, she was trying to talk to me, trying to *console* me, I suppose, she was a bit too close, her face was close to mine, she was practically sitting on me; I got hold of Joanna Lavender and I tried to kiss her and I sort of grabbed her, shoved my hand a bit inside her shirt and got hold of something hot under the material, I managed to grab and squeeze just in this random way, before she slapped me across the face, slapped me so hard, and we broke apart and she burst into tears and that was that. That was Permanent Exclusion. That was Year Ten over for me.

I tell you one thing. Maybe she wouldn't want me to know. Her heart inside that shirt, inside that lace stuff, was beating *fast*.

Act first, think later: heat and blood and anger. If only, as Mum said, I'd engage my brain first. Maybe I got it wrong: the way Jo was breathing in my ear, the mix-up of what she was trying to say. There was mess and ugliness mashed together. Because another teacher, this one we all hate, the Geography teacher, Mr Tansley, goes and sees Joanna slap me. And Tansley marches us both off to the Head. And Joanna is crying, my face is red and mine is stung and we're in that office and the Head tells Tansley to leave, to allow her, please, to get to the bottom of things. And Tansley is furious, he is, like, five foot six, tops, and he sort of tries to tower over us and he doesn't want to leave and goes instead: 'I saw her! I saw a member of staff assaulting a boy! A – recently bereaved boy! This is no way to handle pupil discipline! This is an issue for the School Governors.'

And so the Head is closing the door, and saying to Joanna, 'Did you strike him, Miss Lavender?'

And Tansley goes: 'I saw her! I was passing the Design Tech room—'

'Yes,' whispers Miss Lavender, 'I did slap him.'

And I see Jo's career is about to slip down the pan and this Tansley the Pansy hates her and she's not going to expose me and it's going to be up to me to save her and what the fuck what do I have left anyway? I love her. I don't even care. I just say it.

'Miss. She did slap me. But I'd tried to – I done something first. I grabbed her. She whacked me in self-defence.'

159

Tansley is stunned. He stands there, huffing and puffing, and his glasses in his shirt pocket rising and falling, and Mrs Miller, the Head, says, 'I think I should perhaps get to the bottom of this, Mr Tansley, *on my own*, thank you. I'd appreciate it if you said nothing to anyone at this stage, please. Until I do. That will be all.'

Tansley doesn't want to leave. He's breathing hard. He must hate Joanna – maybe he fancies her and she – I don't know – turned him down or something and he must be thinking he's got her now. Assaulting a pupil. But you can see Tansley's mouth working, like the penny just dropped, and the fizzing feeling that it's something – disgusting, something unmentionable. That's the moment he backs out the door. Joanna is still crying, and Mrs Miller offers her a tissue.

'Dear me. I take that as a confession, Drew? You – assaulted Miss Lavender in some way? Is that right, Joanna? Can you confirm this? This might well be a matter for the police, Drew, if what you say is true.'

'Oh, don't, don't!' Jo says. 'He didn't mean it. He didn't know what he was doing. He's – he's not himself . . . I slapped him out of panic, I'm sorry, I'm sorry . . .'

And so it goes on. It's choking in that room. The shame, the shock, the feeling that no one can breathe. Jo wants to stick up for me; I want to protect her. And in the end it seems that Mrs Miller understands exactly what happened and that it was, as she puts it, 'sexual in nature. A sexual assault on a teacher. This is a very serious matter indeed, Andrew.'

And there's more blubbing, by Jo again; she's gone to pieces, it's like that day I saw her doubled up laughing, there's something wrong, something melting or breaking in her, like when the rivers burst their banks and the washes spread out, something gone all wrong and slippery, something losing its shape, flooding out.

I'm dry-eyed, though. No one's going to make me break my banks. Miller says I'm excluded for a week and that's not the end of it. She will have to see if Miss Lavender wants to pursue criminal charges, but she strongly suggests that as a course of action worth considering. A fourteen-year-old boy – no, newly fifteen – is old enough to be held responsible. She is going to talk to Mr Tansley about what he saw. I'm told to wait in the secretary's office while a letter is prepared for my parents. For my parents. *I'm sorry. I mean your mother.*

And Jo sobs all over again and the room just washes with shame, disaster, and ugliness.

That was the moment I knew I wouldn't be here for ever – I mean, here on this earth. It went something like this. *Just in case.* In case you think we're finished, we're nothing, we're nobody, Fen folk, from another era, people you can't imagine in your modern life with your train travel and your ebooks and your slick city stuff; we're the slype of the land at the back of Fen river banks – we're earth, we're bog oak, we're dirt, from long ago, invisible. Still, we're *not* finished, no way – you'll find out. We matter too, you know. We're the fucking Beamishes.

And so I looked at the organ donor card and somehow in the middle of everything bad and shit I thought: Well, it's not over. My life's not over, though Jo was acting like it was with all her tears and shock about the trouble I was in at school. A temporary exclusion turned into a permanent one when I showed no sign of calming down, when the minute I was back in school I was kicking over tables in class, picking fights with my mates, posting things to Tansley's Facebook account that amounted to 'criminal offences' . . . Yeah, they had to exclude me in the end. Regretfully, etc., etc. No other option, blah blah blah. *Result.*

I wasn't pleased for Mum – she's the only part of this that didn't feel good – but I was glad I made something happen, a dramatic thing that wasn't Dad's death but, just the same, was something. Sweet. Marked the end of things, or so I thought, at the time. The end of school. The end of seeing Miss Joanna Lavender every five minutes: popping up in classrooms and slipping through doors.

Only that's not it, for Jo. You'd think she'd be clever, being a teacher and all that, but no. She only goes and moves up the road from us. (She later tells me it couldn't be helped, the council allocated the place; she'd applied for a council house when she broke up with Bob, she had no idea the one they gave her would be so close to us in Black Drove, and she'd waited so long, she couldn't afford to buy, so she couldn't turn it down, but I ask you. Does that sound – believable? Or likely? Maybe she half believes it. People have a weird habit of deluding themselves about themselves, if you want to know what I think.) She's torturing me, is Jo. She's only about six houses up from me and while I'm lying here listening to my iPod she's taking off her blouse and lifting those epic tits out of that awesome bit of lace and she's snuggling down in her pink and cosy bed . . . Fucking hell. She's driving me insane, and at the first chance I get I tell her so.

Am I to blame here? She's a grown woman, and I'm a boy, as she keeps on telling me. If she was a man, she says, it would be commonplace. In fact her own teacher 'harassed' her in school and it's far more common than parents think. That's what she says. Double standards, she says, and gets herself all roiled up, with the unfairness of it all, because here she is, she says, being highly moral, and *resisting*, and men would just do it, take what they want, ruin lives, do whatever they like whatever the consequences because, you see, they're raised that way, to think that their feelings matter . . . Girls are raised to think endlessly about the feelings of others.

'Yeah,' I say when she goes on like this.

I know she wants me, whatever she says. I know the worst part of it for her was what I discovered – how fast her heart was beating. She wanted me. She's working herself up to it. She needs to screw her courage up. I keep replaying it. I remember that she was looking at me in a strange way. She even touched my cheek as if she was a blind person and feeling me; and told me how beautiful I was, how girls all over the world were going to melt at my feet one day. How much women know about boys, about young men, she said, once. How easy it would be. It's surprising it doesn't happen more often. But wrong of course. That's not feminism, she says. To take on men's values, to be as bad as a bloke.

The thing is, since my exclusion the Local Authority doesn't really know what to do with me. I'm supposed to have a tutor. I'm allocated one hour a day, four days a week, with Mr Rutter. They even say, as I'm clever, I can try for a couple of GCSEs a year early and take them on my own in the Pupil Referral Unit, which is actually just some rooms in Littleport. There's only twelve of us and most of the time we're on our own with the tutor. Rutter is the English tutor.

Rutter is OK. I like him. The days I see him are fine. He does this poet with us, John Clare, and his favourite novel of all time, he tells us: *Tess of the d'Urbervilles*. He reads us this bit he says is really chilling, when Tess suddenly wonders about the date of her own death, and he's droning in his boring teacherly voice: 'A day which lay sly and unseen among all the other days of the year, giving no sign or sound when she annually passed over it; but not the less surely there. When was it? Why did she not feel the chill of each yearly encounter with such a cold relation?'

Mr Rutter actually asks us: Has any of us ever had that thought? We all know our own birth-dates and we mark them every year, but what about the date we might die? Then he looks sort of horrified at what he's saying, I think he remembers about my dad or something, and he quickly goes red and shuts up. But I have this weird thought and what he says catches hold. What if the date is the same? The birthday and 'terminus in time' day, I mean. And actually, you've been marking it with cakes and candles every year, without knowing it.

I protest to Jo at the first opportunity. I see her out walking her dog Pippa along Twelve Mile Bank and chase after her. What about History? My best subject – why aren't they giving me some help with that?

She looks worried then. She tugs at her hair. She says that Mr Rutter would be able to put me in for the History exam and that maybe, just maybe, she could help me with the extra study. In her own time. But in deadly secret. I must on no account tell a soul.

'Would you be in trouble if I did?'

'We'd both be in trouble of course,' she says, and sharply. People often act sharp when they're in the wrong. I've noticed that. She knew – she must have known – but she puts it this way:

'I can't have you ruin your whole life, fail to get the History GCSE you so deserve, because of this – this *incident*, Drew.'

And I nod, like, really seriously, and we carry on and arrange a time to meet.

So on the way there, in the car, for the first time I mention it, this thing she calls the incident. 'I'm sorry. I really am. Did I, like – *assault* you?'

And she's driving so she just looks straight ahead and says, 'No, I don't think you did, really. It – you misjudged things, that's all.'

She tells me about this tutor she had at university, this bloke they used to call 'Peter the Wolf' who offers her a lift to a lecture and when she goes to his house of course he's there with the wineglasses out, and in his dressing gown.

'His dressing gown, Drew! Can you imagine?' She's laughing when she says this. I feel a blaze of horrible jealousy, picturing her all little and blonde and friendly, clutching her file to her chest, this wizened old yellow-toothed Wolf with his great hairy knob hiding inside his dressing gown, answering the door. God, jealousy. It's like a pain. It's like a snake, whipping up. I never knew until then. I try and hide it. I keep my face straight but that snake is twisting around inside me.

Jo gets bolder and bolder. She must be certain that everyone thinks the best of her and couldn't believe it otherwise. Or else – and this feels true – she just can't help herself. She gets me to call in at her house with her, during the day when she's sure Mum is on a shift at the hospital and won't be home. Pick up some paperwork for the museum which she's forgotten. I stand awkwardly just inside the door, smelling her, smelling her private teacher's life, her grown-up life away from me. She dashes in, I stand in the hall. She has this little dog, Pippa, and she's left it tied up in the garden and it's going berserk. She fetches something, she comes back, we walk to her car. Innocent enough. But . . .

'Do you think women are made of different stuff, then? Like, you're better than us?' I ask her.

'I think . . .'

She knows I like talking, I like philosophy and politics and all the things that Mum used to like too, but that now feel too dangerous, like they might unhinge her, pierce the bubble we've surrounded ourselves in at home. Bring on a random fit of sobbing and shrieks of: 'Oh I don't know, don't ask me – where is he, where's your dad when you need him?' Although if he was here I know he'd only say in his dry way: 'Talk's talk and changes nothing. Action's the thing.'

So we're at the museum in St Ives, quietly working along-side each other, and Jo goes: 'Well, you know, Drew, that there are far more criminal acts committed by men than women. Do you know how many men are in prison in Britain, compared to women?'

I don't know, of course.

'It's something like eighty-four thousand men, and around four thousand women. A tiny proportion.'

'Sick,' I say. Then, 'Maybe the women don't get caught. Might be better at not ending up in the nick?'

She smiles at this. But she goes:

'No, it's probably the reverse. Women are often imprisoned for quite trivial, non-violent offences – shoplifting, prostitu-tion, not being able to pay a fine. I think it's safe to assume, Drew, that violent offences, aggression or acting out, lack of impulse control, whatever you want to call it, is much more a man's problem than a woman's.'

'Is this about me getting excluded again? Not being funny but if you're going to have a go, don't bother. Mum's already been on this morning.'

'No, I think – I was just thinking. The people we're reading about. Burning things, rampaging. But it's – selfish, isn't it? Your heart's desire – might have an impact on others. Do damage even. We can't always . . . no matter how much we might want something.'

Oh, I don't know. And then I kiss her, and it's the first time, and she doesn't move away. My eyes are closed and I just feel her mouth, her lips, her tongue, the warmth of her and the smell of her and she's not moving away at all. The museum is dark dark with the tick-ticking of the clock and the dust and all those old Fen skates paused, those ones that will never skate again, and all those dusty green-glass bottles empty of Fen beer, that will never be drunk from again, and all those chain-suspended stuffed sea

166

creatures that will never swim or crawl on their bellies through the icy galls ever ever again: hovering, hovering: time just blasted in there, time cracked and smashed and suspended, just waiting for a boy to fall out of love with his teacher. *And it's not going to happen.* Not then. Not in this lifetime.

It doesn't matter what rules Jo sets, what 'boundaries' she tries to put around it. She finds me 'unusual'. I'm so unlike anyone she's ever met. She doesn't think boys like me come along that often. Couldn't we wait? Until I'm eighteen? Eighteen – fuck's sake! Sixteen then. Until it's legal. Sixteen, she thinks. Then she will feel she did nothing wrong, she took nothing from me, her conscience is clear.

She's running her tongue over her mouth. She's almost crying, she looks so sad, and tortured. I think this is a fucking mad idea. I storm out of the museum room. I rage and I bellow all the way down the street but then I reach her car and I have to wait for her, stand next to that stupid yellow Fiat; I can't drive it, I can't jump inside without her and her car keys to let me in. I'm a child here again. I'm almost in tears as she reaches me, running up to me.

'Drew! We can be friends. Until then. We can see each other if it's possible and – you should see girls. Try not to be so – you should – meet girls your own age. Go out with them. For you it's probably just a crush. Who knows what it is for me? I hardly know myself but I'm promising you, Drew, I'm promising to stick it out and – if you can wait until you're sixteen, it's barely a year, I'll wait too.'

I kiss her again. An angry kiss; she doesn't resist me. She lets me sort of push her into the car and I'm bigger than her and she's small and hot and fucking fucking hell I really am crying at last, in the passenger seat, leaning over towards her, tears smearing into her mohair jumper and kind of wailing in a muffled way into her longed-for chest:

I've got nothing and it's so unfair.

And, you know, there's only us parked there and it's a dark car park in the middle of a forgotten little town and tugging at that jumper she doesn't stop me, it's that one phrase, the thought of my dad dying and the sadness of that, and seeing my tears, my fury, seems to have done it for her: she's letting me, is how I think of it, she's pushing the chair back into the reclining position, letting me climb on top of her and unzip myself and she's even guiding me, it's quick, there's no light in here and I can't see her face, it's so dark and yet it's heat and fire, fire and heat like I've never known, she's holding me like I'm a burning stock of wheat in her hand, she's on her back in the awkward tight space on the seat and her skirt up and her jumper over her face and Oh God I love you, Joanna Lavender, I love you. Let me. Please.

Later, on the drive home, the car filled with the smell of sex, she's dry-eyed and smiles a little and says, 'Well, that's done now, I suppose.' Which makes me laugh.

I say, 'Not being funny but that's an understatement. You could maybe go to prison for messing with a minor!'

She smiles without opening her mouth, a little tight upcurl. She can see I'm not serious. We watch a muntjac deer lollop across the road, red eyes startled in our headlights. She's pulled down her skirt, tucked in her pink jumper. Its done it's done, she seems to be saying, as if she's crossed a terrible line (she has, for sure), as if that's the end of it. Like it's a sad thing, final. But for me, it's exciting. It's just the start.

Jo pulls over the car on a lay-by on the A10. She keeps the lights on and the engine running.

'Drew, I know you're sensible and you won't tell anyone. I know you understand the risks. Actually although the legal age is sixteen, it's *eighteen* when one of the – persons is a teacher or someone in a position of care over you . . . so you see. My position is – delicate. In a year's time it will be different because you're not in school any more; I'm not in that role. But I want you to fully know how much I tried to – how I tried not to take advantage—'

'I didn't rape you, though, did I?'

Having it both ways, like I say. Doing it, or letting me, but not somehow fully admitting she did. What I remember is her grip on me. Her fingers grasping, steering: helping me out. Like firmly shining a torch towards a dark point that might not be found, otherwise. And the salty wetness again. I'm not stupid. If girls don't want it they'd be tight, they'd be dry, they'd close their legs, they wouldn't widen them like that and help you get a better entry. They wouldn't moan and kiss your hair. They wouldn't let you pound away and whisper *Drew Drew* in your ear and kiss you and suddenly tighten and jerk and arch just as you went off like a firework inside them. It makes me grin, and she sees this, and takes the handbrake off and sighs, as she joins the road again.

'It can't happen again. That's all I'm saying. It's a one-off.'

'Yes, Miss.'

'Don't call me that.'

'Yes, Miss Lavender.'

She smacks my knee. I grab her left hand and hold it, only giving it back after the roundabout, which she whizzes over in fourth gear and then struggles to get up and running as normal again; to make a smooth drive home as if nothing, nothing at all has happened.

Part Five

They arrive with arms full of things. Helen has arranged to pick up Ben and give him a lift – another gesture of hers that strikes me as generous (why should she help me out, why should she help Lucy out?) – was she always like this; am I just noticing for the first time? They bring bottles wrapped in tissue, sliced turkey on a plate with a tea-towel over it; cheeses, a Christmas log (this from Alice, she made it herself, she says). Alice's boyfriend, Jake, shuffles in, shakes my hand, makes good eye contact. Promising. They fill the tiny bland place with noise and smells – of outdoors: pine needles, cigarettes, orange peel – screaming laughter. It's just the unaccustomed sound of girls, girlish voices, Alice and Helen, constantly bantering and giggling.

Ben is shy, and gives little away. He sits silently through the screeching and mayhem of the meal with us and shyly answers 'Yes' and 'No thanks' to questions about salt or bread sauce and 'Yeah, she's doing fine, I think' to Helen's polite questions about his mother. His mobile goes more than once during the meal and each time he leaps up as if scalded and answers it outside. We hear him say, 'Yeah, babe' and 'See you, babe'.

'Do you think he's going out with a pig?' I say.

Alice looks horrified: 'Dad! Don't be mean.'

'You know, I mean Babe. The pig in that film,' I hasten to explain. No one laughs. Ben rejoins us, a little flushed, and says nothing.

Alice spoons a giant forkful of risotto up to her mouth. 'I'm starving! I've been really good today.'

'Why – did you join Amnesty International? Rescue a child from drowning?' I ask her, eyes wide.

'Dad!' she says, speaking with her mouth full.

'You know perfectly well what she means, Patrick.' This is Helen. 'She probably ate only a lettuce leaf all day.'

'Ah. Being good. For women. So easy.'

In the kitchen Helen, flushed from the wine, moves close, says in my ear: 'Ben looks so like you at that age, Patrick, don't you think? It's unnerving.'

'Is that right?' I say, without turning round. She's too close. Her breath is hot. I'm loading the dishwasher while Helen pours herself another glass of wine.

'Although of course you're now much heavier and greyer.' She leans against the window, head on one side, narrowing her eyes, stroking the wineglass.

'Yes. Thank you, Helen. I *have* looked in the mirror.'

And then Helen does this extraordinary thing: puts her glass down, and kisses me. Stands on tiptoe (she's shoeless) and reaches up and pulls my face to hers, and holds my head, and kisses me. She's drunk, I taste the wine in her mouth, and feel the heat and sloppiness of her, her breasts pushing into my chest. A riot inside me: I've no idea what this is. I could push her off. Alice could walk in at any minute – the flat is tiny, after all, and they might even be able to see us, the kitchen door isn't properly closed. I don't know – I'm at a loss, for God's sake. The room just lit up and my head is floating like I stuck it in one of those Chinese paper lanterns and it took off, vacated my body and all things tethered and earth-bound.

This is the woman I've loved for most of my adult life. I say these words to myself. I don't know if it will help. It's hard to untangle a determined woman like Helen, and in mid-kiss, too.

I eventually get to take a breath. 'Helen. Do you think this is a good idea—'

'It's never a good idea. Never ever ever a good idea where you're concerned, Patrick . . .'

'No. So, shall we sober up? Shall I make us coffee?'

Then she is sobbing: 'I'm sorry! I'm sorry, I'm pissed—'

'Helen, darling, nothing to be sorry about—'

'I'm sorry!'

'Yes, yes, don't apologise, don't cry, come on, I'm surely to blame, as usual.'

'Yes. Actually, I was being mean. You do look very handsome . . . being grey suits you.' She sniffs into the piece of kitchen roll I offer her.

'Do I? Thank you. I think I was remarkably restrained, under the circumstances, don't you?'

I adjust myself inside my jeans and grin at her. 'But, Helen, I have to say, you're as gorgeous as ever.'

Helen can't resist smiling back. 'A leopard never changes its spots,' she says, sniffing.

I notice again how unsubtle the overhead kitchen lighting is, how we could indeed have done with candles or lamps. It is a ferocious yellow medical lighting, like being back in ICU at the hospital. Showing up every fault. Yes, no doubt Helen's right in her assessment of me, as in everything else. And yet. There is, after all, the small fact that I didn't go ahead. I didn't let her tongue get deeper into my mouth, I didn't press on, take advantage.

Later, when things are smooth again and we're back at the table, eating more food, Alice says shyly that she's been reading up about General Custer, the Boy General, that she thought she'd try and 'see what Dad was always on about' by trying to understand him, whether he was a hero or 'one big loser'.

'And what conclusion did you come to?' I ask.

'Well, like everything, I suppose it depends whose position you're seeing it from.'

'Yes. Of course. You, being a modern young woman, would no doubt take the part of the Native Americans and think he was utterly in the wrong in the first place, and wouldn't be interested in whether he was a hero or an idiot as far as his own countrymen were concerned.'

'Well, I'd want all the facts. You presumably have those, since you've studied it for so long? No offence, Dad, but how long can one book take?'

They laugh then. At least Alice and Helen do. Jake – the boyfriend – is a big bear of a youth, with a hearty manner and his best 'meet the parents' veneer. Probably wise not to risk a laugh at my expense. Ben is as mute as ever.

'Well, I did find a new detail the other day that I mean to add. A transcribed interview with a Cheyenne woman who said that on the battlefield – after his death, this is – she and another woman came across the body of Custer and managed to stop a Sioux warrior from desecrating it. She then filled Custer's ears with special cloth so that he might hear better – be wiser – in the afterlife. He'd broken a promise not to fight the Native Americans again.'

Alice gets up from the table, gathers up plates. She scrapes the risotto messily, as she does everything. Young, slapdash, all the time in the world to mop up mistakes.

'Yeah. That's a nice detail. You must get that in your book. Didn't they believe that an incomplete body could never get to heaven? Isn't that why they scalped their enemies?'

'God help *me* then, my body's a bit of a hotchpotch.'

'Or that poor boy!' Alice blurts out, taking the stack of plates into the kitchen.

'I haven't heard you talk about your book like that for years—' Helen begins to say to me and then looks embarrassed and rushes to join Alice in the kitchen, fetching the cheeseboard and clean plates, along with the great hunk of Stilton she brought.

We each raise a glass of port in a toast: 'To Patrick – to Dad!'

'To you! To all of you – and to Dr Burns! And modern medicine!'

'And to Drew Beamish,' I say, to myself. I'm not sure if I say it out loud or not; I'm drunk. *To you, lad*. And I raise my glass again.

Alice and this boy Jake leave in a cab, not long after midnight. Ben is staying over on the sofa in the living room; he's brought his own sleeping bag. That leaves Helen. She's in the kitchen, helping me unload the tiny dishwasher, so that we can load it again. She crouches in her tight jeans, flicks a strip of hair back behind her ear. She tries fitting a knife into the rack and out of the corner of my eye I see it jump out again, somehow manage to slice her, and then she's bleeding from one finger and I have to go and find tissues and plasters.

She holds out her hand like a child and I wind the plaster round her ring finger. 'I don't think you should drive, Helen. You're way over the limit.'

Helen nods. I tell her she can take my bed and I'll take the floor. I'll find some cushions from somewhere. I mean it. I honestly mean it, and I even offer her my pyjama top so that she can cover herself up and not tempt me with those fine, familiar breasts. Best intentions. She's been making eyes at me all evening.

She borrows my toothbrush and comes back into the room with her hair down and the pyjama shirt just skimming her thighs, and she sees me looking and gives me a drunken smile and a sort of shake of the head, mouthing: *Oh no you don't.*

'Just a cuddle, then,' I say, slipping into the narrow single bed with her and wrapping my arms around her and breathing in the smooth warm-cool fabric feel of her and trying to unbutton the pyjama top and she says, 'You! As if you could ever just *cuddle*,' and so I start kissing her neck and mouth and just testing, that's all, does anything melt, does she help me to undo any buttons, does anything seem to flow differently, or heat up, does she reach out and touch me, give me a sign and then suddenly yes, she does, she holds me in that unmistakable, resolute grip and I'm breathing in the Helenness of her – a smell that makes me dizzy with sadness, dizzy with the smell of blue hyacinths in a courtyard, in Oxford. She sighs and kisses me back and says, 'Your face is like sandpaper; when did you last have a shave?' and then, 'Do you think we'll regret this?' and all I say is: 'The new ticker seems to be holding up pretty well, it's hammering blue bloody murder!' and then we stop talking and the room contracts and all consciousness in me shifts gear, gathers in the one hot place. I dimly hear the shuddering squeak of the student bedsprings as I plunge myself into her, I dimly think of Ben in the front room and hope he's sleeping soundly. The sex – Helen's body – feels like going back to a house you grew up in as a child: everything indelible, you close your eyes and you get a jolt, remembering; but then – it's also not the same at all, it never will be. You're old. And someone else lives there now.

Later, she sits up in bed and wants the light on. She always loved to talk in bed, at night, while I lay dozing and pretending to be listening. This time she says: 'I hate being fifty. It's all about them now, isn't it, Alice and Ben, Jake. Their love affairs, the children they'll have, the marriages, the careers.

Their story. They're the protagonists. We're just the minor characters.'

God, thanks, Helen. I'm trying to fight these thoughts, not go under. To her I say:

'Are you fifty? Who'd have thought it,' clasping her buttock.

'So gallant . . . Be serious,' Helen says.

'Well, as I remember it you always had that notion. Even in the early days – what's that quote? You always had – a presentiment of loss.'

I close my eyes and lie back. Soon I can hear soft snoring; whether hers or mine, I'm not sure. I'm thinking, as I drift, about my mother and that poem I used to love: come back early or never come. *My mother wore a yellow dress. Gently, gently, gentleness.* And then vaguely conscious of the wet semen I'm lying in, my half-asleep, half-drifting thoughts turn to sperm, picturing, like a child, tadpoles swimming and that phrase of Alice's: I didn't ask to be born! And remembering that, as a very small boy, I asked Cushie once. Asked my mother how I was conceived. And, to her credit, she looked surprised, she laughed, I think, but she told me. A weekend. A weekend in Robin's Hood Bay, she said, hiding a smile behind her hand. It was lovely there. And then she slapped my behind gently and told me not to be daft. And I remember thinking: Are we called up then, from somewhere, called forward, asked to assume a form? Did I in fact *ask*?

Still later, in the early hours; Helen wakes me again, shoving me in the ribs and saying: 'This doesn't change a thing, you know that, don't you, Patrick? Nothing is different.' My bladder is full; I should go to the bathroom.

'Hmm?' For a moment I've lost my place, I think we are back in the other moment, the other conversation.

'I don't think I ever was much of a protagonist in my life,' I say. 'I think I was always just a subsidiary character.'

'Patrick, you do understand, don't you, that there's too much . . . It's taken me a long time to get over you. This can't mean anything.'

'I know that,' I reply.

She hasn't bothered to put the light on, or sit up this time. I hear her breathing. I feel her warm breath on my face in the darkness, smell the wine, the coffee, smell my own sweat on her, my molecules mixing with hers. I would kiss her again, but what's the point?

I think of that time when we lived in Camden, what was it, eighteen years ago? When I told Helen about Lucy, that Lucy was pregnant. Honesty the best policy, I thought. Actually what I'd been missing was my closeness to Helen, the horrible feeling that in deceiving her I'd made a fool of her, changed her into someone else: a betrayed wife, an idiot. And I wanted the old, competent, intelligent, *knowing* Helen back.

'How many weeks is she?' she asks. Two upward frown-lines – a central V – deepening between her eyes.

'She just had the twelve-week scan.'

'And she lives near here?'

'Stoke Newington. We met on a train.'

Helen seems calm at first. Reasonable questions. Practical concerns. Our own baby daughter sleeping in her cot with the blue terry-cloth teddy, Helen studying for her Bar exams by then; a little less skinny in her suits, worrying about breast-milk stains on her cream blouse. And she goes out of the room and it's summer, and she unlocks the door that leads to the roof garden, and goes up. After a pause, I follow her up the ladder, phrases forming. *I'm not going to leave you, if that's what you're worried about. Darling, it was nothing, she means nothing to me, but of course, I can't stop her having the baby if she wants it.*

And on the roof Helen, reasonable, sensible Helen, is climbing astride the black-painted rail that surrounds the concrete square of roof terrace. The red tail lights of an aeroplane slide by like fish in a black tank. We're on the fifth floor. Helen's hair is flapping around her face; it's windy. And she's near the edge.

'What's to stop me?' she says. 'Why should I bother with anything? With you, Alice, any of it? Why should I stay – when I could go so easily?'

'Helen—'

I take a step towards her and see her foot, in her black ballet slippers, making contact with the dirty concrete floor, but shifting, lifting slightly, as if she intends to push off, leap over there, launch herself. I reach forward and grab her by the shoulder. She twists away from me and in her silky blouse she feels soft, slippery, already not quite there. But I hold firm; my fingers grip.

'I'm sorry. Darling, it was nothing, she means nothing to me, but of course, I can't stop her having the baby if she wants to keep it . . .'

I try to pull her from her straddled position and succeed in an ugly toppling; she sort of crumples to the floor, but at least it's my side of the railing. And then she stays there, rolled over, holding her knees, her face down so that I can't see if she's crying or laughing or whether she's gone into some sort of spasm.

'Helen, darling. Come downstairs, please. Come and have – a cup of tea. Don't sit up here.'

There's nothing but hard surfaces below, and splattered pigeon shit.

She stands up and allows herself to be steered past the failing plants that she herself planted – hopeless little green things with their coating of city dust – down the ladder and onto the warm carpeted safety of our top-floor landing. I lock the door to the roof garden and pocket the key, breathing out. Make a mental note to throw it away, or, better still, move somewhere without a roof garden.

But I needn't have bothered. Helen went to the doctor after that, got herself antidepressants. Returned, if not to the woman I'd married, into a good impression of her. She asked quiet, reasonable questions about the progress of Lucy's pregnancy. She found out details of the hospital and sent a card when Ben was born. She refrained from asking if I visited and, as he grew older, when Lucy pestered me to ask if we could have Ben occasionally for the weekend, Helen always said yes, and put clean sheets with bunny rabbits on the camp bed in Alice's room.

Is it possible, like stepping into a freezer, to really face this deathly-cold blast? I carried on, seeing Lucy sometimes, and continuing to lie about it. I'm not proud of this. I'm thinking about it, is all. This is what I did. Lied to Helen, had phone conversations at work, slipped over to Lucy's flat in the afternoons, the excitement of that . . . Lied to Lucy too, carried on lying, until I moved on. Until Lucy grew tired of me and I found a replacement.

What did that feel like, to be a girl like Helen, unguarded, straightforward, who had allowed me to unpeel her like a mollusc from its shell, only to find that the exposure was devastating? That entrusting yourself entirely to someone can make you want to die? Helen, does it mean anything at all that I'm thinking these thoughts? That I'm able to remember and construct things differently? That for the first time I glimpsed it there from your point of view? Does it mean it's all over for me, for the old me?

*   *   *

In the morning Helen dresses quickly. She thanks me for a nice evening. She puts on no make-up and her face in that yellow kitchen light is all of her fifty years, with a dark crease under one eye that was never there before, her auburn hair now gathered up with clips, a dusting of grey at the parting. She kisses me on the cheek and I get a whiff of myself, I smell my own particular scent on her. I apologise. She says, 'Nothing to be sorry for, Patrick.'

We see when I open the door that it has snowed overnight, a thick white, like a coating of cake icing. The roads look bad. We note that no gritter has been out to make things better, or safer. 'It looks treacherous out there,' Helen says. She gets an ice-scraper from the boot of her car and I – still in pyjama bottoms and bare feet – go to fill a water jug to help clear the windscreen of ice. As I'm handing this to her in the doorway Helen says, suddenly: 'You do seem – different, somehow.'

'Performance not up to scratch?'

She smiles and bats my arm.

'Not that. I don't mean that. Something else. I don't know. You always kept a bit of yourself back.'

'And now?'

But she's unwilling to say more. We're interrupted then by a noise inside the flat. Ben rousing himself from his pupae on the sofa to call out 'See you Helen!' He falls instantly back to sleep.

The car windscreen cleared, there's no further excuse for delay. Helen and I say goodbye with a brief hug. Only after the door has softly closed do I want to call after her. I'm remembering her favourite insult for me and I want to say: Maybe I do now. Honestly, Helen. I do know I'm born.

I find myself glad I'm not on my own and wishing Ben would wake up. I make coffee, switching on the noisy bean grinder without closing the kitchen door, whistling. Eventually

I call out chirpily, 'How will you get back, Ben, do you need a lift to the station?' No reply.

I place the coffee mug next to his sleeping bag on the floor by the sofa, gently shaking his body inside the purple nylon, feeling his bony shoulders at the top of it and hearing his rattling, adenoidal breathing. He doesn't wake. I stare at him for a moment, trying to see what Helen meant, a genetic connection to me – but he just looks like any young man. Very young. He smells slightly smoky and unwashed. His brown hair doesn't seem at all familiar, doesn't look like *family*, I find myself thinking. Though perhaps it is the same colour mine was before I went grey, I can't now remember.

The coffee turns cold: mud-coloured. I gather up Christmas crackers from the carpet and abandoned paper hats, a tiny pair of silver scissors, a folded joke.

Ben wakes long after lunch. I'd been scrolling down Cambridge University PGCE courses, looking up retraining as a teacher. Popular among bankers apparently, searching for something more worthwhile. I glance up from my BlackBerry and Ben nods a greeting.

'Can I stay here?' he says in his unassertive voice. 'I don't want to go home.'

'Huh?'

He leans over, sips at the cold coffee, then sits up with the sleeping bag at his waist. He coughs, and I can see every rib defined in his hairless white chest. His phone slips out from under him and crashes to the floor; I see that he sleeps with it under his pillow, and leaves it on, too, the light must have been beeping at him all night long like a heart monitor.

'How long for?' I say, cautiously. I hardly know you, is what I'm thinking, but what I say is: 'This is just temporary. Hospital property. Now I'm better I've got to find somewhere myself, actually . . . start my life up again.'

'Can I find somewhere with you?' His voice is so quiet I have to get up and stand over him to hear it.

'Ben, I don't know . . .'

'Can't I live with you for a while? Please.'

And what the hell, I think. Everything else in my life is different, why not this?

'Yeah, OK,' I say. Ben smiles, and his pupils darken. He picks up his phone, which as usual is kicking off at him, buzzing and flashing and practically leaping from his hand.

A month later and I finally get my trip to Littleport. I'm driving along achingly empty Fen roads. The day is white, foggy still, frosted. Paused, somehow. Taking the turning from the A10 after Ely onto a wide road with a bank of iced white at one side, the river behind it, pylons that seem about to topple, and a long low electric wire on the other. I wind the window down; I can hear the electricity twanging in the empty landscape. The fog means there's nothing. The yellow eyes of other cars. Driving into clouds.

'What do you want to go to this next-life place for, anyway?' Ben asked. He's been staying with me since Christmas. The boy has nothing much to do, as far as I can see; no reason to go home, no friends, or interests. He is wedded to his phone; takes it in the bathrooom with him, never lets it out of his sight.

I'm expected to move out of here at the end of January and he says he's here to take care of me. I've been working on my Custer book and organising to rent a two-bedroomed flat in Cambridge. The city, of course, not the countryside. It might be nice to be close to Alice and . . . well, there seems to be no reason for Ben to be anywhere, in particular, since he seems to be – wilfully apathetic and incapable of making plans. He's practically a mute. I find myself wondering if Lucy ever had him tested for . . . I don't know what, deafness, or autism or something? We've been playing cards, drinking beer, playing Call of Duty together on his PlayStation. (Playing with my son: better late than never.) But today he's lying in bed and I slip out unnoticed, Ruth Beamish's letter in my pocket.

Well, I see what Maureen means: the landscape is bleak all right. Bare. It's hardly the Yorkshire Dales or the Lake District: no beautiful hills and dips, no sudden astonishing vistas of glorious colour. Utilitarian. Unlovely. Swept flatness, bent-over trees, the boringness of long straight roads. The middle of nowhere. But then again, there's something refreshing, calming about the emptiness: minimalist. Especially today. So white; fresh. A blank screen. No one knows I'm here.

I Googled it again, Littleport, after Maureen let slip about the funeral. There's a church – St George's. Perhaps that's where the funeral was held. I park next to the Co-Op on the main street for a look around. I feel self-conscious; this is hardly the place where a visitor would be inconspicuous. Especially a visitor with a newish BMW. I wouldn't be surprised if a ball of tumbleweed rolled down the high street. There's a bridal shop; a For Sale sign creaking back and forth. I hug my jacket close to my face, reassured by the scratching of the zip at my chin.

The church is in the centre of the village. *St George's Parish Church: Thieves Beware.* It's locked. There's a CCTV camera, a notice about the Christmas services; it's all closed up and sealed. *'It was here that the rioters were read the Riot Act by the Reverend Vachell whose vicarage was ransacked by the rioters although the church was left untouched.'*

A quick walk across the stiffened white grass. I find the headstone immediately, brush the frost from it: *'Here lye interred in one grave The Bodies of William Beamiss, George Crow, John Dennis, Isaac Harley, Thomas South . . .'*

Beamiss. That must be him. Drew Beamish's forefather.

'. . . executed at Ely on the 28th Day of June 1816, having been convicted at the Special Assizes holden there, of divers Robberies during the Riots at Ely and Littleport.'

Next to this there's a small green with a row of chestnuts. A high street with a library (closed for lunch), a bookies, a tattoo shop. A garage – Gulf – that looks abandoned but advertises on a chalkboard coach trips for pensioners to Hunstanton. I look for a café but aside from Rumbles Chip Shop, which looks more like a takeaway, I can't find one. The only person I could ask seems deaf: an old woman bent nearly double, wearing a grey hoodie, trundling a shopping trolley, ignoring my feeble 'Excuse me, my dear.' She pushes the trolley down a side alley towards the Ex-Servicemen's Club. The pedestrian crossing beeps long after she's crossed the road and yet the van driver still waits, frozen, hypnotised by his windscreen wipers.

Across from the church there's a piece of public art, a metal motorbike. A silver Harley-Davidson larger than life, on a metal plinth with the inscripton: *Littleport Harley Society 2003. William S. Harley of Littleport co-founded the Harley-Davidson Motor Company . . .*

I find a café eventually, the white-bread-bacon-sandwiches sort, and drink a weak cappuccino in the warm fug, before heading back to the car. Move along now; nothing to see here: for some reason this phrase rattles through my head. As if there's been a disaster of sorts, an accident. There was, I suppose. A motorbike accident. But that was nearly three months ago, and all that remains of it is not here, not to be seen or found in Littleport, but is *literally* – as Alice would say – deep inside me.

You're made of somebody else's dead parts, so what are you then?

Black Drove. I'll just take a quick look, and then it's fine, I'm done, I'll take myself home. Twelve Mile Bank is scarcely more than an unfinished track chasing the river; it looks as if someone laid out a grey ribbon atop a field and forgot about it. This is what they mean then by a drove, a sort of bank, higher than the road, blocking all sight of the water. There must be a river there, because two cormorants hunch on the telegraph wire, beaks trained on the water.

The fog here is deeper, massing in front of me. The grasses, the twigs, the telegraph wires: everything crusted with white. When the little row of council bungalows appear it surprises me: I'd thought this place was empty. I check the address on the letter in my pocket. Yes, this is it. I switch the engine off. Somehow, I've no desire to put my jacket back on; to get out of the car.

The bungalows are curious: each the same, dinky, and somehow with no context: it's as if they were just plonked down on this flat landscape with nothing behind or in front of them. The fog only adds to this feeling. Jubilee Close. So a street constructed in the seventies. In front of the row is a children's playpark, again with the sense of Toy Town, of being recently placed there. A solitary blue elephant, wet, unappealing; an inert merry-go-round. Beyond that, in the mist I make out a spindly fringe of trees in the field – the fen – and all of them leaning, like a row of old men pulled by some invisible string. The open fen behind it looks vulnerable.

And then I see it. One of the trees has flowers tied to it, drooping in cellophane. At the base is a toy of some kind, perhaps a teddy bear. I don't want to get close enough to see what kind: Winnie the Pooh, Paddington, whatever. I don't need to read the inscription to know. This must be the place. I step out of the car and wrap my arms around myself to warm up. Enough.

This next-life place. Ben's phrase; horribly apt. I've seen it now, the spot.

A huge bird is flying there, over the blank landscape. A soft, ghostly bird, the golden colour of a baked loaf, with wings so long they could be ears, the body of a fat bumble-bee. Its flight is swooping, low: it's hunting. I watch it for a while, knowing that soon it will come and sweep right past me, wings making only the softest of silent beats. There's no avoiding the hunt in the eyes, that heart-shaped face. I know it is the barn owl from my dream.

On the horizon is a windmill. Or rather – must be a wind-pump, a redundant one. The heart as a pump. The historian in me is suddenly certain that people could understand the heart as a pump only once theories of circulating blood became known, but, more importantly, once the pump had been invented, once it had become a familar mechanical object to them. Once they saw it for themselves. Before that, the heart must have been understood differently, using other avail-able metaphors.

Seeing the squat black shape against that white landscape, the empty page, I'm thinking: the Fens. Not so bleak as I thought at first but more stripped, exposed. The ditches and droves are the arteries, the marshy lands the muscle. The aorta? The River Ouse. Yes, all right, I can see: they might be lovely in their way. A strange idea to think of the land being underwater at one time, and then suddenly revealed: the underbelly. What Lies Beneath – (what is that from? Some movie that Alice loves). And all this fog and cloud and wispi-ness. Something unreal about it. Insubstantial, dreamy. Like those thoughts that float up from somewhere you know must exist but can't be trusted; that can't always be seen, but then suddenly here they are, in all their glaring plainness. Things dredged up. *Endless possibilities.*

I make my way back to the car. Only when I'm driving away do I remember: 'endless possibilities', that corny phrase from the sample letter that Maureen showed me.

That night I dream of the barn owl again. One minute I'm the bird, the next I'm a vole, being chased. Then I'm a heart, but a heart with legs: a shrew. My tiny shrew-form runs this way and that, then in a panic skitters over the bank and dives down into the river, disappearing with a red splash.

The dinner with Maureen takes a while to set up. She says at first that she regretted saying yes, that she wonders if that was unprofessional. She explains that there's something slightly problematic about it for her, so we decide to wait for a little while, until her role in working with me is officially over. We decide after some discussion that it would be nicer to go out rather than for her to come to me. I'm moving into the new apartment near Cambridge station with Ben and it's all at sixes and sevens; I haven't even got chairs yet. (It's just dinner, for God's sake, not a marriage proposal, I find myself wanting to say, but I can tell that, for Maureen, these things are taken rather seriously.)

Maybe it's this awareness of the significance that *she* attributes to it, but I'm uncharacteristically nervous about something so unimportant, something that doesn't matter at all. I shave more carefully than usual. I actually find myself thinking of her, of Maureen of the tufty hair and dancer's slender body, and picturing her, while I'm showering. Daisy, whom I haven't thought of in months, slides into view. (Always one woman blends with another; hard to keep them separate.) I lose track of the argument in the *Today* programme; some vicar outside the Occupy camp at St Paul's. Talk of the riots last summer. The huge discrepancy between rich and poor. Blah blah. The one per cent they keep going on about. Who are they? I can't remember which minister they're even interviewing.

'Are you religious, Maureen? Do you mind me asking, but I have wondered. Is it why you do this job, this ministering to the . . . sick or the – *spiritually impoverished*, is that how you think of me?'

'No, I wouldn't say I'm religious.'

Now, that's unexpected. We're at a restaurant in Ely, near the river. It seems there aren't too many choices and Maureen is worried that, being a Londoner, I'll find it all a bit, 'you know. Small fry.'

'I'm actually not a Londoner,' I tell her, dipping bread in olive oil. 'I'm from the North-East. I know you'd never tell by the accent. My mother used to have an accent, a Geordie one, I mean. Dad didn't. School soon knocks that out of you.'

'Does it? My kids seem to be going the opposite way. Cassie, in particular, drives me mad. It's all "sick" and "minging". She says sick means nice or something. I'm so confused.'

We talk then of the idea of me becoming a teacher. At a local school round here, not a posh one, as she admits she imagined when I spoke of it. Like the kind of school I went to. No, a state school. More than that, I'm quite interested in disenchanted children. The ones who have got a bit . . . over-looked. Maybe I'm barmy to be considering it? Of course Maureen thinks it's a marvellous idea.

'They're crying out for male teachers in secondary schools. More role models for boys. Give something back,' she beams.

'Well, I wouldn't go that far. It's actually more selfish than that – it's about the challenge. I think many kids, maybe boys in particular, are turned off by education. And when I was a lad – well, learning. After my mother died. I have been thinking that in some ways, though it didn't seem like it at the time, I was particularly lucky. My father was very busy and for me, doing well in school, succeeding, reading, I found it very—'

'Comforting,' she says, nodding. Finishing my sentences already. And comforting was not the word I was looking for.

Maureen takes a sip of her fizzy water. 'You were just eleven, you said? That's sad. Awful. The worst age.'

'Is there a best age? For one's mother to die?'

'Well, oh—'

The waitress appears. A sultry blonde in a tight blouse. Thank God. Somehow Maureen's platitudes, vocabulary: tonight I'm finding them irksome. I'm being a snob, I know, but I long for the bracing intelligence of the kinds of things Helen might say; the ways she was never afraid to challenge me. Thankfully, Maureen looks good at least, I can tell she's made an effort. Maybe she's done something to her hair, or is it that colour she's wearing – a vivid red? Clinging to her neat shape. It suits her.

'You look very pretty,' I venture. 'Have you – changed your hair?'

She flashes me a look, which I pretend not to understand. Her hand goes up to her elfin crop and she laughs.

'My ex used to say I had hair like a Jack Russell. You know, the little terrier dog?'

Ha!

'He was like that. He used to tease me about being short. You probably don't realise this but I'm only four foot eleven: I tend to wear heels. His nickname for me was Midget Gem.'

'I'm sure he meant it affectionately.'

'Trust me, he didn't. But you're lucky. Your ex-wife. You seem to be on good terms. There's no way I'd do all that *helping*. I can't imagine it. I'm not sure I'd even visit any ex of mine!'

'Yes, Helen. She probably didn't know what she was letting herself in for when she met me.'

Are we flirting? In my experience, when women ask about your past relationships, they're digging. Women like to flag up for you what's possible, whether they're up for it. They're always pretending they can handle whatever you can throw at them. I ought to feel excited, encouraged.

'So, the specials look good. I might have the sea-bass or the bream. What about you? What do you fancy?' I say.

She orders the steak. (Funny that, I had her pegged as a vegetarian.) Maureen asks me if I've read the book she left me. The one about the heart transplant woman and the changes she goes through. I have read it. Very carefully. To Maureen I say:

'The changes she's talking about are so . . . trivial, though, in the end. I mean, she didn't like a certain vegetable – green peppers, was it? – and now she finds she does—'

'And beer! And chicken nuggets—'

'And she dreams of her donor a lot. And she, um, what was the other change, she starts to feel more like a man, walking differently, because her donor was a young man?'

'She dreams the donor's name! She dreams his name is Tim and no one has told her this!'

'She could have heard one of the doctors mention this, during surgery. I mean, you did let slip to me my donor's name, eventually, didn't you, after that newspaper article.'

'When she meets the family she feels a huge connection. As if their stories, the family histories and background, a very different one to hers, are forever joined.'

'Could all be explained by her *imagining* herself to be different, couldn't they? I do concede you end up *thinking* about your donor quite a lot.'

The main course is brought then: a welcome interruption. Maureen is growing animated in her defence of this idea and I belligerent in my desire to fend her off.

'Perhaps, yes, there may be some truth in the idea that one's internal . . . something has shifted,' I start. 'The story you tell yourself about your own life, how you got to be who you are, because now you're a person with a transplanted heart and that's . . . different. But I don't think I'm convinced by the idea that the heart itself carries memories in its cells.'

'Lots of scientific ideas were not accepted at first. People thought electricity was magic, didn't they.'

'Yes, but—'

'Anyway, I don't believe you. You don't want to give it a chance, this new thing inside you,' Maureen says, peevishly. 'You might feel differently if you met the mother.'

A wrinkled party balloon from another table seems to be drifting our way. 'I think you're – if you don't mind me saying – in denial about the ways in which your life has changed.'

I sigh, as loudly as I dare. *In denial.* A little knowledge is a dangerous thing. It turns out Maureen is a bereavement counsellor, when she is not being a transplant co-ordinator.

'Sometimes I think you're . . . afraid of me, in some way,' she says now.

I put down my knife and fork, wipe my mouth with my napkin. I wait for her to look up at me again. 'Perhaps a glass of wine?' I suggest. 'After all, you're not driving.'

She shakes away my offer of the wine menu. I put it carefully back down on the table between us.

'What would I be scared of?' I'm trying to keep my voice playful.

'Well. Because you know I know the donor's story. That I sat with Drew's mother, helped her fill out the forms while he – passed away. As if I'm some sort of go-between, you know, someone who can travel to the Underworld and back or something.'

Like Eurydice, you mean, whom Orpheus brought back from the Underworld but couldn't have because he didn't show faith, he didn't hold his nerve, he wasn't willing to die for her? I don't say this, of course. I murmur: 'You must have to listen to a lot of sad things. It's not a job I'd relish.'

'Actually the things people say at the end are – ordinary. Those dying usually have the same regrets. Simple things. They wish they'd counted their blessings; told someone they loved them. That's about it, really.'

Suddenly I feel exhausted. The slowly deflating party balloon brushes my hair and lands on our table. I bat it away and it dribbles to the floor. I look across at Maureen with her hopeful dress and pink lipstick and rather nicely shaped hands, and I reach for one of them. 'I've wanted to say: you really have helped me through this. The weirdest time in my whole life.'

Her lip trembles.

'You look – lovely this evening. You couldn't look more lovely,' I add.

She smiles, and the coffees are brought, and we fall silent while the pouty blonde pours the milk and offers us sugar.

'I don't normally take sugar. I suddenly fancy some—'

I spoon in three big lumps. I'm thinking: Great that I picked Maureen up from her house, that I'm the designated driver. Even better that she has to go back via Cambridge, arranged for her girls to stay there with a friend. I've wrangled the new flat all to myself tonight; I gave Ben money to go to some gig. I've even bought myself a double bed. Easiest thing in the world to suggest that we call in for coffee at mine before picking up her girls and then dropping her back to Ely.

'I should text Cassie. Tell her I won't be late,' she says now, reading my mind.

And that's when it happens, when I snap out of it. A picture of her life with the girls. I see them both – I even remember their names, Cassie and Chloe, and I think of them, around at some friend's, sitting with laptops on their knees, or watching TV, or curling up on sofas, giggling together, as girls do. Two girls I've never met. A rather sweet, mini-sized mother who perhaps makes a habit of throwing herself at losers. I have no good intentions towards this family, I realise.

And I do something I don't believe I've ever done. I pass up a chance for a random shag in favour of something odder, something awkward and unfamiliar. A second coffee, and a short conversation about the ways in which Maureen has helped me. A chaste drive home, a peck on the cheek at the door to her friend's house, where she's decided she'll stay too, for tonight. A mumbled goodnight as she pauses, finger hovering at the doorbell, her face inscrutable.

'I will always be grateful to you,' I say. It's a formal phrase, but it will have to do.

Part Six

Late spring. Dad died the autumn before. Tried shagging Poppy for a few weeks, with her smiley face big as a satellite dish, but it was no good. Nothing scrubs out Joanna for me. Mr Rutter, he's all right, though he makes us laugh with his stammer, and I like the things he's teaching us about poetry. John Clare, the poet from round here. How he isn't as famous as Keats but he should be.

All the people I know who were in the year above me and left school last year are still on the dole. Dole. Dad used to use that word to mean an allotment. Your dole. You know, a share, a portion, of land. I think of that meaning, whenever Stokey says he's off to the dole office. That's your lot.

I see Jo now and then, here and there. I always try and talk to her and she always looks shifty, looks from side to side, wondering who might see us talking.

Once, she's standing over by the playground in a cagoule with her little dog, Pippa, off the lead and it's raining and I come in close, close enough to touch her, and Jo says – under her breath – not to mention what happened. It can't happen again. She says I'll get over her. She has her hood up, this orange cagoule, and her face inside it looks all teary and wet and she says: 'I'm trying not to bump into you!'

'Bit hard when you moved in six doors down,' I say, and walk back to my house.

I think of her telling me not to keep mooning around after her, to see some other girls. I text her sometimes and sometimes she answers. I tell her about Poppy. *Good. I'm glad. XX* she texts, and then seconds later: *Hope it's not too serious? Don't forget me. X*

There's a lot of people on the dole out here. You sleep a lot. Your life gets smaller, you don't feel like going out. You've never got any money. Every day is sleeping, watching telly, playing on your PlayStation in your dark room, eking out your fags until your mum will buy you some more.

I think to myself if Dad hadn't been hit by a bale this TV and PlayStation world would have been his life, too. Indoors when he wanted to be out. Dark when he needed sun. Silent when he needed the sound of wind trembling through the sedge, the voices from Heart Radio in his warm and fuggy tractor cab, the birds chattering behind him. That life – his life – washed up at the age of forty-five because work meant everything to him. Well, it's not every fucking thing to me. I've got Jo.

I come up with a plan. When Dad's life insurance money comes through, I put it to Mum. A motorbike. I'm not old enough but Stokey's mate is selling one. There won't be another cracking bargain like this, I say. Mum says surely a car makes more sense, but Stokey has already taken me to his shed to see it, his brother's Kawasaki Ninja 250R, and I'm in love.

Mum says it's bonkers. 'Why buy a motorbike you're not even legal on?'

And I say, 'For the future.' (I know that phrase will get her juices flowing.) And I promise I won't take it on the road, not until I've passed my test, until we can afford the insurance, I'll just practise in the fields near our house and get the feel of it. 'I can always resell it,' I tell her. A Ninja will keep its price, it's awesome.

Because we both know how bad my job application form is going to look. In the place of education: Permanently

Excluded. In the space for 'Qualifications': two GCSEs from the Pupil Referral Unit, if I'm lucky – Mr Rutter says I can try. He's letting me sit for them on my own, a year early, in a little room with a laptop he's lent me and him to invigilate. A bit random, if you ask me. But I'm indulging him, he's all right.

I'm only at the PRU for about an hour a day at most. I don't really want to hang out with the fat preggies smoking their heads off. The rest of the time is at home, it's dark, you don't see much sunlight somehow. Mum coming in from shift work at the hospital at strange hours and nagging you; every day just the same. Mum saying she's worried I haven't been grieving for Dad, no, not properly. I tell her to shut it. Then I say I'm sorry and she cries and we're back to the same old same old.

Mum folds in the end. She feels sorry for me, that's what it is, what it always is with her. Gives me plenty of leverage. She's seen me mooning around, listening to the Plain White T's ('Hey there, Delilah' . . .) and she probably thinks it's Poppy Martin I've gone daft over. Dad's money amounts to a grand and she says it won't last five minutes but she lets me take out half of it, and when she sees how excited I am, how I actually get up off the sofa and drum my fingers on table tops and just perk up and come alive again, attack my beans on toast in the old way, take a shower, stop this slow, half-dead, depressed lying about, slobbing around; I think she's pleased. Or maybe just relieved. I start sitting in our front room in daylight and staring out at the fen, all keen again, watching the crows work the field, pecking at seeds in lines that always look so organised, that always make me think of rows of volunteers searching for a body.

That bike is joy to me.

It's so beautiful, I've no complaints. It handles well, can take a beating, and can hit about a hundred if you're willing to redline it. It's easy to go eighty on that bike, and ninety is just a bit more twist. I don't care that I can't take it on the road yet because I've nowhere to go anyway and I'll take my test soon enough – just as soon as I can afford the insurance – and I'm sure to pass. I love the purr of it under my arse, like a big cat. I love the wind tearing at my face, the smell of fuel and speed and dirt flying up (mostly I don't bother with the helmet; I mean, I'm not on the road, am I). I park the bike outside my house and I try not to notice the curtains flicker six doors down as I stand there running my hand over it, over the red paint, covering it with a tarp, or polishing it with a duster. If I didn't know for sure Jo was watching me I'd lie down on the driveway and kiss it.

I know she's watching me all right. Sometimes in the night, as I'm dozing off, the little beep and the flash that means she's thinking of me. *U haven't told anyone have u Drew?* she texts. *U must stop texting me like that.* But if she really meant it, she'd be silent now, wouldn't she. Wouldn't text back at all.

I'm counting the months until I'm sixteen. They drag past like snails. I take my exams on my own in a room just as Mr Rutter suggested and I'm doing it before everyone else – special dispensation or something – and it's fun in the end, I probably did OK, I end up thinking. Harvest time comes along at last and I apply for some work picking beets but it seems that's all sewn up. Polish, Eastern European, working in great gangs, living together. They do it every year and the farmers round here don't want to take on a skinny lad like me when they can get hulking workers with sunburned skin the colour of toast who go at twice my speed.

This one guy, Poppy Martin's father. He was Dad's boss. I go and see him.

He's this great big obese guy, got a little dog and he also does falconry, all dressed up, squeezed into his khaki. I don't know if it's a hobby or what but I think to myself: He owes me. He owes Dad. So one day, the day I go to ask him, I see him standing on his land beside an old tree that's lost its head, you know, been recently pollarded. And he has this huge falcon on his arm – this awesome bird with a wingspan bigger than his shoulders and an evil-looking beak, and he sort of gives a toss of his arm as if a signal of some kind and the bird streaks up.

I just wait. I watch it, in the sky. There's a red paper kite attached to some food, some kind of tripwire thing, and I watch the bird go for it. Swoop. Fast. Snatch. He's dead on, like an arrow to a bull's eye. And then he sweeps down again and onto Farmer Martin's arm. Falconry. It's three thousand years old, you know, people have been training birds like that, to take out songbirds. To kill beautiful things in mid-air. You know what it makes me think, watching this little scene? Farmer Martin has all the power. Like he has a weapon that really proves he's the boss round here. That bird, it's really horrible. It's got the nastiest of watchful eyes and a sort of black moustache that makes me think of Hitler. I think it's a peregrine falcon. Its beak gets so close to his sunburned face, it could peck Tom Martin's eyes out. But it doesn't. Instead, dangerous birds do Tom's bidding, keep their talons in and land on his leather glove. I hate that man.

'You got anything?' I shout. 'Fieldwork? Picking, whatever?'

He shakes his head.

'I'm a Beamish. Bill's lad.'

He shakes his head again.

You wanker, I think. You owe me. Blood money, for Dad. You're such a shit. You made no effort whatsoever to argue for him, to say he'd been a good worker, twenty-five years on this land, instant redundancy the minute the farm got new management: you said nothing. When Dad was my age he worked like a navvy in the drownings (that's Dad's old word for the Fens). He said his face was scratched to buggery: every time he leaned over, his face got stabbed by the bents of the cut grass, and the soil is grumpy, another old Fen word, means it's hard, it doesn't work easy.

I walk away. Give Martin the finger. Pass the fields full of tented stands and dark blokes with their old-fashioned jackets and their cheap mobiles and Tesco carrier bags of docky and their strange language. Bastard, that Martin. Couldn't even be arsed to answer me.

The woman at the job centre takes one look at my muddy jeans from where I tramped across the fen and and asks did I do any farm labouring work? Then it's all stupid questions about further courses you can attend and what kind of work you'd like to do – I mean, the answer is *yeah, brain surgeon, please.* She finds out I'm only fifteen. I'm not entitled to job seeker's allowance anyway, she says.

I start counting the weeks, not the months, until my birthday. Then the days. Like a prison sentence. Like Willie Beamiss, sad about his pa, drawing that little hangman, but forcing himself to think of the future. Go forward, not back. Scratching out the days with a knife, until none at all are left and the longed-for day is here.

Part Seven

Alice predicts that I won't last one day in a modern school and filling out the application, reading up on this SCITT idea – School-Centred Initial Teacher Training, starting in September – I begin to fear she's right. But I'm buoyed up by my recent success with Ben. He and I go to visit the Head of an independent sixth form college in Cambridge and I explain that my son has been having a 'year out' and would now like to continue his education by 'taking a few A levels – he has AS photography (apparently) so probably it would be good to go for an A level in that, and we thought – oh, I don't know – maybe Politics and Business Studies?'

The sixth form centre is in a large bay-windowed old house, near the rail station. We're shown into the Head's office. After a brief chat about fees and the fact that Ben would be joining so late in the term, the Head – an avuncular type with a beard (I imagine him with a pipe too, though none is visible) – gets up and shakes Ben's hand, the deal done. Ben looks up, startled, and the Head offers to 'show us around'.

We step into rooms with leather sofas, rooms that have paintings on the walls and fireplaces and the sense of being in someone's front room. They smell of coffee beans, and new wool carpets, and shoe polish. Each room contains a smiley teacher and four or five black-haired boys in suits, bent over laptops.

'We have a lot of Chinese students. It's mostly a crammer for them to get into Oxbridge,' the Head explains.

Ben is as quiet as only Ben can be; but I'm comforting myself with the fact that he hasn't said no and he's managed to go the full hour without pulling his phone out of his pocket, biting his nails or smoking. It seems to help that it would take him exactly ten minutes for him to get from his bed to this homely classroom and that it being spring now the windows are full of green-budded trees and this place doesn't, as Ben said as we walked up the gravel-filled drive, 'seem like any school on this planet'. Result.

Outside on the street he rolls a cigarette, licking the paper, shaking the tobacco into it. He offers it to me.

'When are you going to give that up?' I say.

His phone starts trilling and he turns away, cupping one hand over his ear, to answer it. I can hear the tinny sounds of a female voice; it seems to be shrieking. It's the same voice I've heard constantly. Ben doesn't reply, he doesn't call her 'Babe'. And then suddenly, he shoves the phone at me.

'She wants to talk to you.'

'To me? Who?'

'Mum. She says you've kidnapped me. You deal with it.'

'Lucy?' Why now? Has she only just noticed he's gone?

'Patrick!' She's sobbing. All conversations between us for years have been tight, controlled. It's a long time since I've heard Lucy cry. And now I remember, she used to do it all the time.

'What the bloody hell is Ben doing? Why is he staying with you for so long and refusing to come home? Now he's saying he's doing some – I don't know – some fucking sixth-form course or something! How much is that costing? Fucking hell, Patrick. Has he left me, or what?'

'*Left* you? He's – we've decided it would make sense for him to resume his education. I thought you'd be pleased.'

'Oh, he's decided, has he? Or have *you* decided – because you want him now, you need him to keep you company, because you're lonely now you've had a fucking operation and you can't find anyone to shag and so you think it's *your* turn—'

'Lucy, I don't know what you're on about. Please. Calm down. I can barely understand you—'

'Put him on! I WANT TO TALK TO MY SON!'

I interrupt her with my gentlest voice, and after a moment she stops shouting and I hear her taking a deep breath. 'Lucy,' I persist. 'It's short term. You can visit us here at any time. I'm sorry, I should have told you. I should have *asked* you.'

I've got her attention at last. I hold the phone close to my mouth.

'But, you know, Lucy, you've done a great job with Ben. I'd like to say – well. All credit to you. He's great, isn't he? He's funny, he's smart, he's good company. Well done. I like him!'

Silence. The phone seems to give off some kind of fizz.

'Lucy? Are you there?'

Then: 'Whoah. What's up with *you*?' she says, in a tone of astonishment.

Ben comes wheeling back and snatches the phone from my hand and yells into it: 'Give me a fucking break, will you!' and stabs at the phone to switch it off, and whisks it back into his pocket. We stop in the street and stare at one another.

'I feel obliged to say – that's no way to talk to your mother,' I mumble.

I'm conscious that passers-by are looking at us oddly, that perhaps a net curtain in one of those cosy rooms in the sixth-form college we're still beside will be twitching. I'm struggling not to think about Ben and Lucy, not to wonder if it was Lucy he kept calling Babe and, if it was, what does that say about the relationship they've got themselves into?

There's a strange moment when I think Ben is going to walk off, or punch me, or burst into tears. His brown eyes are huge, surprised at his own behaviour. Clearly, if I've never been grown-up before, then Ben's never before been childish. I just released us both.

He takes the roll-up from where he's parked it above his ear, puts it back in his mouth and lights it again. When he's taken a drag he says softly: 'You know what she's like. You must know.' And I think: Yes, I do. And poor Ben. Of course I know. He's been the man of the house, shouldering things I should have taken on, or rather: shouldering Lucy.

I met Lucy on a train. She was working on a manuscript, and told me she was an editor. I rang her publisher to get her phone number; told them I was her cousin. Anyway, bizarrely, at some point when I was trying to seduce her, Lucy read the Tarot cards for me. I can't remember if she proposed it or if I asked. I know she said she made money at music festivals reading cards; she had hennaed hair and a tattoo. I indulged her. She turned over card after card, all hilariously serious, cross-legged on her bedroom floor – she lived in a squat in Stoke Newington – and then all I had to do when she turned over that one – The Devil, it was, I remember it vividly – was stare at her and say: 'Never mind that, I've been wanting to do this all night.' A corny line. (There was something false from the start.) She went to get a tissue to wipe her lipstick off.

She had an open, smiley mouth – nice to kiss, she tasted like aniseed – and she laughed easily, and told you every last thing she was thinking as if there was no edit of her internal monologue going on at all (I soon learned there wasn't). She could be entertaining, she was loud and giddy, energetic in bed. But she could barely finish a coherent thought. She would veer off mid-sentence and trying to pin her down on a discussion, or a date, or a plan, soon drove me insane. It was exhilarating, distracting – her sudden exuberance, her bursts of dancing in the middle of a conversation, her unembarrassed way of telling you exactly what she felt about everyone and everything.

One morning in Lucy's poky kitchen, standing in my boxers about to cook us some breakfast, it occurred to me how sensible I'd been, what a success I'd made. I was taking eggs out of a cardboard box; there were four, one in my hand, three in the box. And I thought of the phrase, 'Don't put all your eggs in the same basket,' and I was glad, reassured, because Lucy and I had a child, and we'd been together in secret ways on and off for a couple of years now, and there were others, too: a student with a mature outlook called Sandy, also the young wife of my Head of Department, a dark beauty called Therese. So – though admittedly the egg metaphor is all wrong – I hadn't. Put them all in the same basket, I mean.

I poured oil happily into a pan, whistling; cracked the egg into it, tried to pick out a fleck of shell by pressing it with the flat of my finger. The other three eggs sat perkily in their cone-shaped cardboard nests. A safety net might have been a better metaphor. Never mind, all I knew was that even if Helen died or left me I would be all right because there were others. I hadn't put all my feelings in one place.

But three, four years later, the mayhem of being in Lucy's world was exhausting, and the calm order of Helen's offered itself with renewed charms. Helen knew me, thought of that side of me as, well, a sort of a sickness, I think; something to do with me being a motherless boy. We even laughed – during the divorce, which was one of our chummiest times – about the day she caught me struggling into my trousers in our living room, with the window open and a blonde girl crouching on our patio outside. 'The smell!' Helen said, tears streaming. 'I thought a fox had got in! I thought that's why the window was open.' (I still maintained I'd been interviewing the girl – we needed an au pair for Alice.)

I never believed that Helen might eventually, and not even in a unkind way, call time. And just say one day, rather gently: 'Enough. Sorry, Patrick, I don't think I can stand it any more.'

Now I'm thinking: Ben is more like Helen than me. He could have been Helen's child, not Lucy's. The sensible one, the one always washing the glasses the morning after a devastating party. How could I have left him to be the sole keeper of Lucy, for so long?

'Ashok dumped her,' Ben says mildly, on the walk back to our flat.

'Ah.'

She wants me home so she can sit me in the kitchen and tell me what a bastard he is. All of them. Him. Me. You. Especially you.'

'Yes. I can imagine.'

We walk in silence after that. It's not that Ben says *nothing*, I've learned. If you listen, and don't interrupt him, he will offer information eventually. In his own time. Perhaps all those years with Lucy have taught him the merits of continence. To say something you mean, quietly, once, and without embellishment. Not to spill.

Later, Alice asks me, 'Why secondary schools? Why not go back to being an academic – no offence, Dad, but what do you know about *kids*?'

'I was once a kid, you know.' We're walking along the Backs, Alice wheeling her bike over wet leaves, an ancient college presiding.

'Like – hundreds of years ago, Dad. They're not all bonny lads in boarding schools in Geordie-land who want to be successful, all eager to learn, you know. Like in your day.'

'What a charming, hilarious version of my life you have!'

'I'm just saying. It might be tough.'

'I can deal with *tough*. Actually I'd really like to get stuck into something.'

'But what about . . . you know, the harassment case? Won't any new school do, like, some kind of police check?'

A squirrel races out in front of us, stops dead at our feet, twirls theatrically, casts its tail around it like a seasoned actress whisking up her feather boa, and races away again. I stop and put my hand on the handle of Alice's bike to make her stop too.

'I'm not a bloody sex offender. Actually – apparently – Daisy withdrew her complaint.'

'Oh. That's good. I'm glad for you. I mean. Mum said . . . I had wondered if *that* was why you didn't want to go back to London, if you were . . . you know. Good. That's good then. Isn't it?'

'Yes.'

'And you can work on your book, can't you.'

I can, yes. I'd even been writing a little of it, today, thinking with some small pleasure about the idea of changing the title of my Custer book to *Great Big Cock-ups and the Stupid Men Who Make Them*. Or, more likely: *Wisdom after Death – General Custer: A Re-Evaluation of his Legacy*. I offer you whatever comfort I've come by honestly.

(Would I be allowed to teach the kids about the Battle of Little Bighorn? Fights, battles: I know enough to know that's how you draw in teenage boys, having spent these last few weeks on the Xbox and PlayStation with Ben. Helen has long pointed out the irony of all those loud voices deploring knife crime in London but saying nothing over posters everywhere to advertise *Inglourious Basterds* with Brad Pitt practically *licking* a sabre. There's always an outcry when it's girls and anorexia, she says, but no one protests when it's boys' weak spots being exploited. Still, perhaps I can exploit them in the interests of re-engaging them in education? But maybe it has to be an entirely British history curriculum, one of the reasons I needed to do the course – I have no idea what they're taught in schools these days. Not that I'd concede this to Alice, of course.)

At last, I am going to get to meet Ruth Beamish. Maureen brings me the letter. We're having dinner in a Vietnamese restaurant in Cambridge and I'm drinking glass after glass of water to quell the chilli I just accidentally bit into, and in between gulps I'm telling her about my course, the other people on it, mostly much younger than me, but one guy, a banker, about my age, with the same idea. Maureen waits for me to stop coughing and talking and then she produces the letter from her handbag as if it was casual, the most casual thing, not sizzling with portent, with longed-for meaning. As if she'd almost forgotten about it.

'Oh. I meant to give you this.'

Dear Professor Robson,

I'm the mother of your donor. You mentioned in the letter you sent me at the end of last year that you would be willing to help me. There is something you could do for me, if you are still willing. And if you would like to meet me, I think I'm ready now. As long as you don't mind if we keep it short.

Yours sincerely,

Mrs Ruth Beamish, Jubilee Close, Black Drove, Littleport.

Interesting, that line: 'I'm the mother of your donor.' As if I could have forgotten who she was. I protest to Maureen that I didn't mention I would *help* Ruth Beamish, and then understanding dawns.

'You didn't give her *my* letter, did you? Did you give her that load of old Hallmark card bollocks you wanted me to write instead?'

The sweet-faced Vietnamese restaurateur glances worriedly towards me; is that man going to make a scene? Maureen has the grace to look embarrassed, and to mumble sorry.

I'm not mollified. 'Hugs and tomorrows. I ask you. What's wrong with a bit of plain-speaking?'

'I'm sorry, I know, you're right. It's just that – in my job – it's just that, I didn't want her to be *upset*. Your letter was . . . unfeeling.'

'You're confusing feeling with clichéd shit! And now she wants me to do something for her and presumably I promised, and what the hell can it be?'

Maureen stabs at a piece of chicken with her chopstick, starts to speak, but I interrupt her.

'Ruth Beamish is bound to be upset, no matter how I sugar-coated it.'

My voice is sharper than I intend and I see from Maureen's quick glance down at her plate, her stumble as she goes to pick up a prawn with her chopsticks and fails, that she is stung.

'Sorry,' I say, hastily.

The chopsticks pause at her mouth. 'You know,' Maureen says, bouncing back as usual, 'I was once counselling this woman – over at Downham Market. And she just couldn't talk about the really ghastly way her daughter died. She couldn't tell me. And then one day, in the room with us, I felt it. Like I couldn't breathe. I was coughing. It was a choking attack, my lungs burning. And so I said it. I said it nicely of course. Did her daughter die from an asthma attack? And this woman bursts into tears and it was like – the whole room felt freed up – and she goes at once, yes.'

I consider this; what am I supposed to deduce?

'Well, you know of course that's easily explained,' I suggest. 'A kind of body transference – her transferring something unconscious or that can't be acknowledged to you, and you "receiving" it, intuiting it. Surely your training taught you that?'

She chews on her prawn. 'Yes, OK. Not the spirit from her dead child speaking the unspeakable to us? No. But in the end, aren't they the same thing? Just different explanations, different words used. Transference, counter–transference. OK. I mean, years ago, in the past, a heart that could live in the body of another would have been – freakish, wouldn't it? Spooky and unreal. It still is for many people, not ordinary, not modern medicine or science. And it's just the words in the end, isn't it, just the words people are comfortable using.'

Our relationship these days, now that it's clear we're not going to have a sexual one, is one of easy banter and friendship. Argument, yes, irritation – on my part, at least, I can't speak for her – but also ease. I'm myself with Maureen, I realise, whatever that means. It's what Helen used to say about the midwife who brought Alice into this world, a woman called Janet, who, to my great surprise, became close friends with Helen when they met again at some hospital fund-raiser years later.

'God, Janet's seen me at my most vulnerable; I feel myself with her,' Helen would say.

So now that I'm going to Littleport again Maureen offers to come with me, 'keep me company'. Once, I might have welcomed this. But no.

If Ruth Beamish is brave enough, I can be. And I have another reason to go to Littleport. The course again. We've been encouraged to check out as many educational establishments as possible, including facilities for those children who had been permanently or temporarily excluded from school or are being educated 'other than at school'. The Fenland Pupil Referral Unit. The place that Maureen let slip that Drew attended. I'm surprised to find myself excited. Maybe I'm not cut out for that kind of thing. Bleeding-heart liberal and all that – maybe it's too late, not me. But I won't know unless I give it a go.

The landscape is no less surprising this time for being more familiar. It's something to do with the gap between the word 'rural' and what it conjures in my head, and this. Giant pylons straddling the flats; houses dropped down any old where, like an American backwater. The forlorn pieces of abandoned farm machinery nesting in backyards; houses with their black-eyed windows, their gardens full of tyres or piles of beets for farm feed. I ask myself what it is about this unlovely landscape that still manages to charm me, that keeps making my mood lift, that makes me feel – what do I feel, staring at it? Calm and energised. Yes. I could even imagine, I've begun to imagine, I admit, living here. Houses here would be a fraction of the price of Cambridge. I would love the space, and the plainness. A fresh start. A clean-swept floor.

A train keeps pace with the car; I wait at various railway crossings, suddenly filled with a strange longing for a cigarette, when I spot a rail worker in his high-vis coat, skulking near the tracks, smoking. The past might well be another country but it seems you can get there quite easily from King's Cross.

'This area of Cambridgeshire has a high proportion of five-to fourteen-year-olds. Residents tend to have fewer higher educational qualifications than the national average. A high

proportion work in manufacturing, retail, or construction. Littleport has some of the highest scores for deprivation compared to other areas in the district . . .'

So, first I call in at this Pupil Referral place. Actually, it's not a school, as I imagined, not even one central building. It's a service, and one I'm told is in danger of being cut. I meet the bloke who is supposed to be explaining it to me, in a damp, coffee-smelling community building in Littleport. Next to the Ex-Servicemen's Club. A converted church hall with hastily added plastic chairs, colourful posters advertising events at 'Ely Beet Club' and second-hand computers.

'Is it definitely going to be cut? What does that mean? What happens to kids who are expelled, then?' I ask.

'Quite,' says this chap.

An English teacher himself, he's already told me that he found the noise and chaos of large classrooms in the local school he taught in for years 'a bit much' and that this one-to-one tutoring work, and visiting pupils in their own homes, and getting them through exams, suits him much better. He has a stammer, I notice, but he's intense, determined to say what he needs to, despite it.

'It's not all – misbehaving or – or – excluded children, you know. Sometimes it's girls – it's girls who get pregnant. There are three of those at the – at the moment. And I also tutor a boy with Asperger's Syndrome who needs the – who needs the calmness and routine that only one-to-one tutoring can provide.'

The contrast with the school Ben and I visited could not be more stark. But although it's shabby the atmosphere is cosy, comfortable. And from what he says, even if the service is to be cut, there will still be work of one kind or another with these children. I try to imagine myself here. Standing here. Facing the kind of children he's describing. Is Alice right? Would they be too threatening for me, too foreign?

I consider whether I dare ask this teacher about Drew Beamish. I haven't told him why I'm here, or who I am exactly (whatever that means), but it occurs to me that he must have taught him?

'Was it – was he one of your kids? The boy who died in a motorcycle accident at Black Drove last year?'

It's a small place. I won't need to say more, I know that.

'Drew Beamish,' the man says, simply, and nods. Then, 'I used to teach him at his old – at his old school too.' A pause. I get the definite impression he is deciding what to tell me. His stammer intensifies. 'He lost his – his father the year before. Very sad.' Then, from nowhere he adds, rather breathlessly: 'He loved birds. He was good at History, and Art. In Year Seven, he did an art project called – it was called "Birds of the Fenlands". A kingfisher and a reed bunting and. And a – a greylag goose. The beak is – a – it's a – salmon pink, you know.'

'You grow fond of them,' this man says, shaking my hand as I leave. 'It's good to be – to be useful.'

He's young, I notice, barely thirty himself, and he's clearly local from his accent. He doesn't seem the least suprised that I would consider a piecemeal job like this, one with such an uncertain future and remit, rather than a big school or a new academy.

His parting words are barely audible: 'The Fens. Most people find them – boring. Most people think they're – a – a bit flat.'

As I start the long drive to Black Drove, the scar, the wound at my chest, draws tight. I expected this, there's nothing I can do about it. Ruth Beamish has the door open, and is waiting for me, on the dot of four-thirty. This, she tells me later, is the time of day that Drew died.

*   *   *

The first small shock is that I was right: she does have big dark eyes, she *is* a woman of uncommon beauty. I put this down to how much time I have spent imagining. Many is the hour I have dreaded this encounter, that's all. She isn't *exactly* as I imagined her, but there is a shimmer, a shudder, some kind of recognition when she opens the door. She's wearing a baggy shirt over jeans and she is slim, I can see, underneath it, and vulnerable, like a child herself. She has these extraordinary dark eyes, and long lashes, and young skin, skin with that bloom still on it, like Alice's skin; that of a lovely young girl, not a woman of, what is she? Late thirties maybe. Her dark hair is gathered up from her neck in a ponytail, caught in an elastic band.

She launches in with no preamble. It was me who telephoned the hospital, she says, sopping the blood that poured from her son's ears and nose with his T-shirt; rummaging in his pockets until she found his mobile, miraculously still working. As was his heart, she thought at first, when she buried her face close to Drew's chest, breathing in the washed cotton of his favourite T-shirt, her own fanatical laundering, only the day before.

'I'm mad for washing things,' she says, 'I love it.' Then: 'You don't mind me telling you this? No one else lets me talk about him. But I want to.'

She settles down on her sofa with a cigarette. There are two cups of tea on the low coffee table in front of us. A cat on a cushion. And photographs everywhere.

She'd made calm replies to the questions of the Emergency Services – 'Well, I'm a nurse, see, you'd expect me to, wouldn't you?' (No, he had not been wearing a helmet, no, he was only messing on the bike in a field, no, he wasn't on a public road). They assured her they were on their way, and she hadn't wanted to look, she couldn't bear to, no, it's true, she didn't see the strange angle of Drew's head, the fact that he didn't open his eyes, and didn't make a sound and seemed in all respects – apart from that one fact she clung to, 'Just that, you know, that steady tick' – to have slipped under the gate in the field and away from her.

'Well, I've seen it before, you know, lots of times, being a nurse. I was with my husband at the end, too. You know when they're there, and you know when they've gone. But I kept thinking, look, there's tiny shoots of stubble on his chin, things still growing and living and moving . . . you know, that's alive, surely?'

She draws on her cigarette. Doesn't bother to offer me one. The craving hits me again, more powerfully. Did he smoke, I wonder, suddenly? Of course he smoked. The room smells of cigarettes, and cats, and also some menthol-type thing, some cold cure. I'm feeling quite choked, unable to breathe out, but I don't like to say so. I'm trying to be quiet, and do as she asked, and let her talk.

'He had sort of broad shoulders, but he was skinny, you know. You want to see a photograph of him?'

I grunt something. I try to make it sound like yes.

She reaches for one of the many photographs in frames on top of her TV screen. A child wearing a fake moustache and brandishing a gun. He stares hard at me; points the gun. Then another one, a boy and a man, fishing by a river. The man looks into the river, the boy examines me. He looks unconvinced; I clearly fall short in some way. Then a third, more recent, a teenage boy, brown eyes, dark lashes, as if he's wearing eyeliner. Looking straight at me. An accusing look, challenging: What are you going to *do* with it, then, now you've got it? A prominent Adam's apple.

(When he was eight, first hearing the phrase, Drew had cried: I don't want Adam's apple! I want my own apple! she says. She tells me he was funny. People liked him, he was so clever. He had a funny way of looking at things.)

The sudden hot stink of him: smoke and leather and motorbike oil, warm and tall and laughing, a rucksack over his shoulder, saying *wot's up, Doc?* like Bugs Bunny, the old cartoon, like she says he often did, and grinning. In a frame, she hands me his History GCSE certificate. Grade A*.

'They let him take his History and English GCSEs early. I don't know if you know about the PRU? Did the exams on his own in a little room in the summer.'

'He must have been clever,' I manage to say. I know this is the right thing, because she smiles then. For the first time. Then she unfolds a piece of paper and shoves that towards me too.

'This is his – I kept this. The order of service.'

I stare at the paper she puts in my hand. Another photograph of this handsome brown-eyed boy, on a photocopied sheet.

A Service for the Much Loved Andrew Beamish,
fondly known to his friends as Drew
24 October 1995 – 24 October 2011

Inside it states the hymns and the prayers and a poem.

Happy the man, and happy he alone,
He who can call today his own:
He who, secure within, can say,
Tomorrow do thy worst, for I have lived today.
Be fair or foul or rain or shine
The joys I have possessed, in spite of fate, are mine.
Nor Heaven itself upon the past has power,
But what has been, has been, and I have had my hour.

'And we had Amy Winehouse. It had just come out, this duet she did just before . . . with Tony Bennett. 'Body and Soul'. Do you know that one?' she says, taking the paper back from me and smoothing it out.

I'm all for you, body and soul. I do. I nod. In my head I hear the Ella Fitzgerald version, but I know it all right.

'I just expect him to walk in, you know? And I can show him it, and say did we pick the right music? Did we pick the right poem?' she tells me.

I nod again. I swallow. The tea in front of us has gone cold.

'Could I make us another cup of tea?' I suggest. 'Is it through there? Why don't I do that? You sit down, don't worry. I'll find everything.'

In the kitchen I breathe deeply, lean back against the cold hum of the fridge. Close my eyes. On opening them I'm greeted by another photograph of Drew, younger, a school photograph with recently cropped fringe and best smile. This one is innocent. In this one he thinks he will live for ever and never lose anyone he loves. Me too, lad. I thought so too, back then, I want to say. Maybe you knew better than me, Dryden surely did: *the joys I have possessed, in spite of fate, are mine.* Even the tea bags, once I find them, seem vulnerable, tender – small and crumpled – in a jar with a chipped lid. I stand there for a very long time, holding the tea bag and thinking: This is his house. This is his mother. This is where he stood.

Something tugs at me. Small fingers. Snatching at the fabric of my shirt. Tugging. Insistent. *Hey.* I shake them off, stare at a Mother's Day card stuck to the fridge with a magnet. Childish writing. '*To the best ever Mum – I mean it.*'

'I'm a bit out of my depth here, Mrs Beamish,' I say, carrying the mugs. My voice comes out like the husk of a voice, with its centre missing. I feel it is a lie.

Here you are: this is it. Come on, Patrick. Square up. Be a man, look again, look deeper.

Drew, she calls him. Never Andrew. She prattles away. She didn't approve of the donor card at first, she says. But she understood. It was about his father. His father had died from a heart attack and Drew believed – wrongly, of course, since only a few people with, like, certain illnesses can benefit from heart transplants – that a heart transplant would have saved him.

'There was some trouble. That's why he wasn't in school. You probably know about that? He had this crush – this woman. This is a small place; Maureen must have told you. He really was crazy about her, that's just the kind of boy he was. Nothing happened. It was just to do with – it was because he was upset about Billy, his dad, you know. And afterwards, after the accident, the police came round afterwards, asking. About the barn. But there was nothing there either. They had to let it drop.'

Now she's lost me. It feels best to let her do the talking. She cries a few times, of course, but she pulls herself together pretty quickly. She's tough, admirable. Her accent, I notice, is not quite the one I expected either. Yes, there's a rural aspect to it but it's more of a mixture. She doesn't quite pronounce the 'oo' sound that I've been led to expect – 'bootiful' like the ad for Norfolk Turkey, but there is a suggestion of that, yes, now I'm listening hard.

'He was stubborn, you know?' she continues. 'About the card, I mean. You could never change his mind once it was made up. He was always like that. Everyone said he was happy-go-lucky, sunny, that kind of thing. The vicar even said "sunny" at his – at the – but . . . they didn't know him. He was like his father. Like all the Beamishes. Like his grandfather. Bloody stubborn.'

She has gone to the kitchen to get sugar, and I've followed her, standing in this tiny room backed up against the fridge, hugging my mug of tea. She crouches to the washing machine, opens the door and pulls out a sock. 'Look,' she says.

I don't understand what I'm looking at.

'I can't bring myself to use this: I take myself off to the laundry in Littleport. He used to hide things in his socks,' she says. She shows me a lumpy blue sock. Something stuffed down in the toe. She pulls it out. A boiled sweet. Yellow. A pear drop. She puts it back in; shakes the sock at me.

'I think he meant me to find this. Drew. He liked his jokes.'

I stare at the sock in her hand, at the lump in the toe from the sweet. Like he just put it there yesterday.

'People said, people say this thing: You're still young. You could have another baby. Why do people say that? It's horrible. It's a horrible thing to say. As if Drew wasn't special. Like one person can be just swapped for another.'

This isn't the flipping exchange department in Marks and Spencer.

Back in the living room there's the sound of the cat purring. A thrumming sound, machine-like. I glance at the window, at my car, silver and real, on her driveway. My cup is quickly empty. I reach forward and put it on the coaster on the table. She seems at last to focus on me. A glassiness lifts.

'It's his motorbike,' she's saying. 'That fucking Ninja. It's in my garage where the police put it – where they put it that day – and – there's not much damage, in the end. Hardly a scratch. I want rid of it and I need the money. I thought you could – put it on eBay or Auto Trader or whatever people do. Or just take it away for me. I don't want to look at it. I don't want to go in there. You said in your letter I could ask you—'

'Yes, yes, of course,' I say, relieved to find that the request after all – the offer I purportedly made – is something tangible, something within my capabilities. She nods to where the garage is, alongside the house, produces a key. I pocket it, ask if she minds if I come back for the motorbike tomorrow, today makes no sense as I can't ride it, I can't exactly fit it in the boot. (I'm thinking, though it would be tactless to mention it to her, that Ben would love to help me.)

'Did Drew like broccoli?' I ask her, politely, as if I had only just thought of it; as if it has no importance at all.

'Broccoli. No. Why?'

'No reason.'

'You're well, are you?' she asks, suddenly seeming to remember that she should ask. Remembering that I must have been ill. 'It's worked, has it, the operation?'

'Yes. I had – it was severe. If a donor hadn't come along last year I would have. Died—'

There's murmuring all around us, the vibration after a tuning fork has been struck. The cat purrs, louder than ever. In fact the whole room seems to be vibrating, thrumming wildly. I abandon myself to it, to the shaking. I feel I should move now, leave perhaps, but my legs won't shift. A sluice of sadness. A sweeping feeling, so unlike anything I've ever felt. A memory of my own mother, sitting on a sofa beside me like this, and an envelope between us, unopened, a letter I was scared to open: a school entry letter. And Cushie saying, 'Away, pet, I don't even mind about any of this stuff, that's just your father. There's more to life than winning things, you know. Just be a good man, that's all I ask.' Oh *Mam*. Why did you set the bar so high?

My shoulders are shaking. I don't know if this Ruth is looking at me but suddenly she's moved around the table between us and is close to me. I smell her, a smell like cloves or something medical, and a whiff of warm breath.

'I know this is a bit funny, but could I—' she says.

And before I know it, before I can say yes (would I have said yes?), she has her ear squashed to my chest, and her warm cheek there, and she's listening. She's nestling against my shirt. She seems to suffer no embarrassment at all. I would undo the buttons on my shirt to help her get closer but her cheek is pressed there, I can't push her face away to do it. I seem to be holding my breath. She's crying again – I feel the spread of warmth, of wetness, against the fabric. A soft ticking sound like a watch enveloped in cotton.

She's listening to her son's heart.

It pounds away: I think of mobile phones, their steady flickering light. Stars. A motorbike engine, throbbing. A yo-yo with no string, but still bouncing. Hospital machinery. That frown-line between Helen's eyebrows.

We separate after a while, we return to polite behaviour; we're both embarrassed now. Once, she looks out of the window and asks how come I haven't moved away and when I mutter something non-committal about liking the Fens, she says, as if she's been thinking this for a while, 'I suppose we're connected now, aren't we? Like – if someone did a family tree they could include both of us.' I am about to disagree – there's no logic to this – but something stops me.

I agree to take the motorbike off her hands, to come again on Friday. The irony is not lost on me – the completeness of handling this boy's bike, the temptation to ride it. Full circle: possession of something my new heart once loved, my heart's desire. I'm so preoccupied – choked – that I don't remember the one thing that Maureen insisted on before I came. I forget to thank her.

Stepping out onto the little close, I have the strong feeling of being watched. It's early evening now, the sky darkening to lavender. I move further away from the Beamish drive, walk a few yards from the car, stare out towards the field.

Are you here again? I whisper. *Are you here, lad?*

My heart beats fast, in reply.

Above the tree, the tree with the cellophane flowers still bedraggled and hanging from it, though now reduced to scraps, in the whiteness of the air is a shape, a soft brown bird. A kestrel, hunting. It must have spied something on the ground, a shrew or mouse, somewhere near that cuddly toy. It skitters in the wind, its wings beating fast in order to hover there, seeming to gutter like a candle flame, and then rally. I watch it for a moment, noting how hard those wings beat, in order to stay poised like that. And then it dives and misses, and buggers off.

The kestrel I saw the night of my surgery.

As I'm standing there a thought forms then like a blown seed. Helen. It's not too late in the evening. The drive to London, straight down the M11. I could be there by – what, eight o'clock? There's still time. Is there still time? She might have someone with her, a voice murmurs. Take the risk: she might not. I feel the need to shake something off, shake off the stupor, the sadness that the visit steeped me in. Rinse out all the tea in me. Let this thing, this new thing in me, if it exists, if Maureen is right, let it take shape. Spread out a bit. Get comfortable at last. Whichever way you look at it, I did – as I said back there – nearly die. Funny how I don't think I've said that before. That I've been gifted some unexpected extra time when the game should have been over: I've gone into injury time.

Turning towards the A11, passing signs for Newmarket, I replay the conversation I just had. While she was talking, before the moment when she wanted to listen to her son's heart, the title of a children's story kept popping into my head. Something my mother used to read me: *The Prince and the Pauper*. And I think it was a film too, a Disney film I watched with Cushie. About these two boys who swap places. And the pauper gets the chance to be prince and all the courtiers are amazed by him; it's clear he's the one who is truly good: he's compassionate, he makes all the right decisions. He's the one with the real values, the true prince among men, or something. When things work out and the actual prince – the spoiled type who didn't know his own luck – comes back, he has to eat humble pie and realise his own wrongness, change his ways. Anyway, that story kept knocking round my head in there. Like I've just swapped places, swapped my life with this strange Fen boy's life in some way. Only I haven't, that's bloody ridiculous, he's not a pauper; I'm not a prince! He's a boy of sixteen who got expelled, who made some pretty crap decisions by the sound of things, so – that's not right at all, what can a boy like that possibly have to teach *me*?

I muse over this, because the story won't budge and the things Ruth Beamish had said about her son have stuck. *The joys I have possessed, in spite of fate, are mine.* Stubborn, she said. A positive spin on that might be: devoted, decisive. Fixed, faithful. Full-on. Constant – a constant heart. Passionate? Risking all. I turn on the radio in the car and a rich tenor consumes all the oxygen. I can't breathe, I open the windows to let more in; coldness blasts my face. I fly past a speed camera. A curious sensation that I'm suddenly taking up too much room in my own car; that I'm growing bigger. Or that I might even have left the car, left that engine behind and be outside myself as I am so often in dreams: flying, sweeping along, watching, thinking, seeing everything.

And then I see. Look: there's my lovely young daughter wheeling her bike, wet leaves stuck to the tyres. My son: a fat caterpillar in his sleeping bag, sliding his slim white body out like some kind of unearthly worm, like an unknown creature, a new insect forming. The animal aliveness of both of them. A heart beating in my chest, blood pumping through my veins. So many tiny cars: tyres on the road splashing up spray; a gathering violet dusk, birds, the blue dizzy smells of flowers. And maybe. Is it possible? Something unfinished with Helen.

Part Eight

So. The day of my sixteenth birthday I go after Jo.

It's after school. About quarter to four. I know she'll be home, she didn't stay late for a meeting; her car's in the drive. I'm carrying a bottle of rosé which I know girls go mad for and a Tesco carrier with three beers in it. I walk up, as game as Ned Kelly. Actually I'm quaking inside. I feel all hot and cold and hot again, with sweat trickling inside the arms of my grey hoodie. But never mind, she won't see that. She'll see me, all six foot four of me, *holy bootiful* as Dad would say. You're holy beautiful, you are – awesome, it means. Ultimate.

So, I'm striding up, towards the back door, the one we always use and I see Jo in the window of her kitchen. And she glances up, and makes a darting movement, and I catch sight – a sort of sense really more than a sight – of someone with her. Fuck. Hadn't reckoned on that. But here I am walking up to her kitchen door in bald daylight and I can't back-pedal now, can I? It would look lame. It would look like I'm ashamed. It would look like the whole point – *now I'm sixteen and no one here can say there's anything wrong with this* – isn't true.

She answers the door before my knock. She looks worried. She looks holy beautiful herself. She's wearing her glasses and her hair is a little longer and less curly and she has a sort of short wool dress that looks a bit like a long jumper. And woolly tights. And she's standing on her kitchen tiles with no shoes. I stare at her feet. The shape of her toes all private and cute under the wool – God, they look so sweet I could cry. Her house smells just like she does, like she always did: that faint, tickling smell, feathery, and the smell of her dog, Pippa, a shaggy little terrier.

I can barely look at her face. I don't know what I'll see there. This isn't going how I thought. I'm grinning and then I'm not grinning and my body doesn't feel quite right, like my legs might not hold me much longer, and I want to jiggle about and I even want to say Hello, Miss and I know I mustn't, that I'd blow it if I said that; that would be more daft, more lame, more stupid than I could ever dream. Instead I say: 'Hi, Jo. It's my birthday,' and she glances over her shoulder as if someone is right behind her in her hallway and she says: 'I've got a – visitor.'

She doesn't invite me in. I stand there like a dickhead, drinking her in, and breathing in the smell of her and her house and the sight of her and all those nights I've waited for this, all those days and nights. I can't wait for her to say *come in.* I step over. I close the door behind me. The dog – Pippa – whizzes over and licks and leaps at me in just exactly the way I hoped that Jo would do. I crouch down to ruffle her behind the ears.

'Hello, baby, hello, Pippa, how you doing?' and then I straighten up, watching Jo watch us. I'm squeezed between the fridge and the yapping Pippa and I reach for Jo. She leaps away as if I trod on her toe and puts her hands up to fend me off.

'Let me – just a minute,' she squeaks.

Her house is small, like ours. The distance between the kitchen and the front room, the only downstairs room, is tiny. Obviously this visitor is in the front room and she doesn't want her – whoever – to hear us. I'm starting to lose my nerve because when I dreamed it, when I planned it, it wasn't like this. Jo just fell into my arms.

I go, 'Aren't you gonna say something nice to me?' I lean in. 'Aren't you gonna say: woah, Drew, you've grown . . .'

Now I can't stop myself grinning and she does at last give a worried little smile back. I can see this is awkward. She'll have to get rid of whoever she's got in there and then come back to me. I can wait. I've waited this long. Pippa twirls between me and then the door and noses in her red bowl, finding one little bow-shaped snack, and then hurls herself at my legs again.

'Shush, shush, Pippa.' Jo clutches the dog by the ears and, opening the kitchen door, shoos her into the backyard. 'Drew, can you close the gate, so she won't get out?'

I do this for her and I have a sad and muddled thought all about how familiar her gate is; the way it closes, the latch fitting neatly over that silver knob, how masculine and manly and familiar of me now to do this, and for her to ask me. All sorts of weird thoughts. And then I come back.

'Why so funny with me? Who you got in there? Can we go out? Didn't you hear me – it's my birthday. My *sixteenth*.'

'That's nice. Happy Birthday—'

'And I've got wine. I've got – we can celebrate.'

The door to the front room opens. A man comes out from in there and into the kitchen. Mr Rutter. He looks at me, recognises me. Glances at Jo.

'Should be going, I think . . .'

'Oh, John, yes, here – where's – didn't you have a jacket?'

God, she's awkward now. And I'm stunned. I feel as if she hit me. Him. That twat. That tosser. That lame-o. Mr nervous pathetic Rutter. I can't breathe. I can't think straight. *Him*. My heart has just gone ballistic. I feel as if blood is pumping into my head. My eyes are black. Something is exploding. I can't even think what I'm saying or doing, I just sort of push past both of them, maybe I slam the carrier bag down with the wine and beer in it, I don't look back, I hear Jo say: 'Drew, wait – come here, don't be silly—' and the dog, the mad-eyed bitch, is barking like crazy but I'm off, I'm back to our house, getting my motorbike out, I've never felt so fucking humiliated; my face is burning, Oh God, head to toe I'm just one big wash of shame, of embarrassment. I see her, but I don't see her. I hear her and I have some kind of impression of him, too, and I'm in my own yard, my own shed, and dragging out the Ninja, starting her up and the gleaming red and the roar is taking over, at least there's that at least there's that – I just want to go, escape, let the cold wind blow through me, cool me down at last, sting my eyes.

All this time. It never occurred to me. I never thought.

'Drew! Wait—' Jo goes, in full view of the neighbourhood, standing at her back door, a pale shape, a ghost, with her mad Fen dog, and I've got the wrong idea, she says; she shouts it, but I'm not an idiot. I've got eyes in my head.

I set off over the fields and ride further than usual, I use the old track, follow the railway, out towards Martin's barn. I don't have my helmet, and I'm cold, I'm freezing now in fact, but I've got matches and fags in my hoodie pocket, when I can stop crying, when I can calm down, I'll light one. I'm ill. My heart is pounding in my ears one minute, the next trying to scarper, right out of my chest. I'm shivering. I'm scared. And I'm sobbing, like I've never sobbed, and I know it's not just about Jo, but about everything, all the things she meant to me and now I'll never have. Who am I to think for one minute that someone beautiful and clever – a teacher – someone like Jo would want someone like me? I'm just some little shit with no future, no father, no education, no job, no hope. Is that what she thinks of me? Is that all anyone thinks, you know, your Asbo boys, your nobodies, *the white working classes, the rural poor, the Permanently Excludeds*, what are we – all of us boys – the *dregs*?

And, you see, it's when I'm thinking like this that I get a bit blind-sided. I get so I don't care; I can't see straight. Strange things seem true. Mad things are reasonable. I leave the bike. I prop it against the side of the barn.

I take the matches out of my pocket and strike a flame and stare at it. I get close enough to feel the heat wafting onto my nose. To smell the sulphur. To stare at that glow until my eyes ache, until when I close them the flame is still there, on the black-pink inside of my eyelids. A barn full of haystacks. You know. All piled up, dead neat. Not covered in their black plastic, like wrapped-up giant Babybel cheeses. No, they smell warm and fresh and sweet. They scratch, when you climb on them. They smell like your father, like your childhood. They smell like all that's gone and done and all that will never come again. They smell like fucking Farmer Martin and all his money and all the things he holds in his hand – the old ways, the power. But if you hold a lit match to them, it's awesome. It's instant – wow. Crackling. A stick of hay – black and done. Awesome.

I chuck the match on the floor. I light another piece of hay, crouching near the bottom of the bale. I watch as that goes up too, and the flames lick the base of the haystack, blackening it. Dirty flakes fall away on the barn floor: smell of sweet autumn green. I scuff them with my foot. The thing is. A barn is one thing. Hay is one thing. But outside in the field there's much bigger bales. *Straw*, straw bales, stacked up ready for transport to the straw power station. It's an awesome sight. We've got the largest straw-burning power station in the world out here in the Fens these days. Money should be good, should have been good, for people like my dad if German businesses hadn't decided to buy out the company. If Farmer Martin hadn't decided to say yes to their offer and lay off his loyal, long-term manager with the slightly dicky heart.

All those bales stacked up, ready to go. Mow, Dad used to call straw. Mow, or sometimes a rucking, as in rucking-stack. Mowfen was his name for any field that had straw bales in it. So many words he had, that no one else knew, and now they won't ever know them, will they?

The sky over the Mowfen is turning pink. There's a rushing, heady, crackling sound. Did I mean it? Am I just messing? What would I say if it had ever come to it, you know, if anyone asked? Andrew Beamish of Black Drove near Littleport in the Cambridgeshire Fens, did you deliberately and with intent cause damage to property via an act of arson and did you act recklessly without due regard as to whether you endangered the life of others . . .

Once, long ago, I'd have swung for it.

I don't look back. I just get back on the Ninja, peel away. Can't even remember what I'm thinking. Whether burning down Farmer Martin's straw bales is enough. There's smoke pinching the back of my throat, my nose; I can taste it. This is for you, Dad. Jo can wait. Because – I tell you this. I am alive. I *am*.

I didn't mean anything more than that, I wasn't thinking beyond that. I did a bad thing. I was proud, I mean, it was sweet, it had symmetry. Burning stacks as a way for farm labourers to avenge themselves – the Swing Riots: I did an essay on that too. Another history lesson.

I saw Dad one last time, that morning he took off for work. He had worked on that fucking farm his entire adult life. A week before the straw bale hit him, he had been given notice. The farm was being sold to a German buyer and Dad's services as manager were no longer needed. He told us this, told Mum and me, calmly at breakfast, and when she burst into tears he just stood up, and put the kettle on. Mum's crying washed over him: he paid no mind to it. He had a plan, he said, and said no more. The farm was huge by then, all that land owned now by one enormous conglomerate. Dad's services no longer needed. I believed I knew what his plan was, rightly or wrongly, I was sure I understood. That morning, he went out the door in his usual way – clean-shaven, a peck on Mum's cheek, docky in his bag, shirt tucked neatly round his spreading belly. I never saw him again.

But then I kept thinking, where is he? And I'd be walking into the kitchen, about to ask him for a fag, expecting to see his checked shoulders through the bars of the wooden chair, him there glancing up from where he's eating his toast and dunking it in his tea and reading the *Express* at the same time and expecting to hear that creak of the chair as he looks up and to get told off for asking – fags at your age! – and maybe a clip round the ear and then I remember. Oh yeah. He's dead. But it feels like he's still here, so alive, so big and funny and familiar and so loudly *talking* to me, in my head. Where is he then? Not deep in that black ridged soil, slicked by the plough, not in the clouds.

By now I'm calming down. The black smoke appears, massing over the fields. I feel – scared. I try to think more clearly about Jo. What was it she said? I had the wrong idea. Maybe that Mr Rutter, he could have just been – like, discussing something. Some pupil referral problem. Nothing more than that. She was just embarrassed because I'd marched in, full of myself.

Weird but I'm thinking about Willie Beamish again. Not much older than me, losing his dad like me. Getting into trouble, sentenced to death, then at the very last minute – he escapes. *Escapes!* What have I done? Is it too late? I swing my leg over the bike. I turn her round, I'm rolling at a speed right away and running up the gears and the bike's screaming like she's doing a zillion miles per hour. Put distance between me and the barn. Head for home.

And then. What happens next. That's just my return journey. Near our house. The tree, the smoky landscape hurtling towards my face, the speed of it. Yeah: sly all right, but not unseen. Didn't I think of it once, get a hint, just for a second, in that class with old Rutter, not so long ago? That's just my luck. Black Shuck catching up with me, having his little joke. You know who Black Shuck is, the dog you sometimes see on a late-night foggy walk in the Fens – a black dog, an inky hound with red eyes, this is the third who walks always beside you, along the drove. Me, Dad and it. That means death. The end for you. And I never saw it, but now I come to think of it, the last thing I saw at Jo's was that yapping little Pippa, shadowed small and black against the sky and yes, maybe, at a stretch you might have said it could have been the red glitter from a fag end. But there again. It could have been the red eye of Black Shuck, come to tell me: OK, Drew – calling you in. Come on, boy, this is all for you, your portion, your dole. Sorry, lad. Your time's up.

And I thought: did I think? – I saw, rather than thought – I saw them. Down the road I looked, and there stood Jo. Blonde hair hanging in curls like little question marks at her chin, and she's running and calling after me and trying to stop me; and there's Dad, all warm and real and big and kind and the sound of his singing in the smoky fug of his tractor, drowning everything; and there's a kestrel, hunting, right overhead, trembling on the wind; and there's Mum, in the kitchen, an apron over her nurse's uniform, and I want to call out to her and say, Mum, Mum, here I am I'm still here I'm sorry I didn't mean it

I tried to beat harder and stay, I tried, I tried – I really did – and I see what she's doing now: she's slotting candles into little plastic flower holders, for a birthday cake she's made me. I have to tell you: you'd better hope this is your lot, your hour too. I'm not even complaining: when you come to think of it, isn't it enough? Isn't it holy beautiful, isn't it fucking *ultimate*.

'Here I am between Earth and Sky – so help me, God.' Words of William Dawson, another rioter, from Upwell; friend of Pa. Shipped off to Botany Bay, he was, and never saw his beloved Fens again. Between Earth and Sky. That's where we are, here: the fog hanging over the marsh and the dykes and you're nowhere but everywhere, betwixt and between.

'I would sooner lose my life than go home as I am. Bread I want and Bread I will have.' William Dawson again. Plain enough. Fen Tigers, that's us. *The Law of the land will always be too strong for its assailants*. Maybe . . . maybe. Not wholly convinced, myself. I never more celebrated obedience; I learned a bitter lesson. The riots – the 'daring act of outrage' as the newspapers had it – taught me that the law was made not by God but by men and by powerful wealthy men at that, who would not share the wealth of God's green land with us. If you have money you throw it at any hardship. No hand that life deals you is so cruel that money can't amend it. Susie's father had sympathy with our plight, but no sympathy with our anger, our mischief. There was only one farmer who had any sympathy with the rioters. His name was Henry Benson, but they put him down for a madman and he was given notice to quit his farm by the Earl of Hardwicke.

Afterwards, after coming home, I could never speak of Pa to a soul. Grief kept us company in the first years of our marriage and I knew that my Susie understood, and did all in her power to make our life lively and keep turf burning in the stove; to be a helper to me when I took up shoemaking again. Once our first-born Walter arrived the low-ceilinged cottage at Wicken Fen trembled with his lusty cries and I no longer had the queer thought that Pa was just behind me, rushing through the sedge like the wind.

That was my daytimes. Night-times was another story. As I closed my eyes next to Susie's warm and snoring form, words overheard in gaol the day of the hanging would come back to me:

'His heart continued alive for a full four hours, expanding and contracting after the body was cut down . . .'

'Its powers was visible past one o'clock . . .'

And I would dream, night after night, of Pa's heart soaring through the Fens with powers all its own, a heart travelling alone, flying along the drove like a bird.

Acknowledgements

This is a work of fiction. Any resemblance to real people is unintentional except for Part Two, which tells the story of Willie Beamiss pretty much as I discovered it. The Littleport Riots took place in 1816 in Cambridgeshire. The names and situation of the five men who were hanged and others involved in those events are as I give them here. (I apologise in advance to any descendants of the Beamisses who feel I have taken liberties with their story.) I used the excellent *Bread or Blood* by A. J. Peacock (first published in 1965 with a foreword by E. P. Thompson), *Report of the Trials for Rioting in Ely and Littleport* edited and revised by Philip Warren (Fieldfare Publications, 1997) and Sabine Baring Gould's novel *Cheap Jack Zita* (Methuen and Co, 1893) for the context as well as the facts, along with original documents from Cambridge University Library, newspaper reports, letters and writings about the Fens from a variety of sources. I'd like to thank Frank Bowles for his help in uncovering this material; also Louise and Robert Topping, and the brilliant staff at Topping Books in Ely.

Fay Bound Alberti's book *Matters of the Heart* (Oxford University Press, 2010) and many first-hand accounts from heart transplant patients have been tremendously instructive. I'd also like thank Dr Leonard Shapiro (Consultant Cardiologist MD FRCP FACC) for his kindness in reading the manuscript and offering his comments on the details of the surgery; also Dr Tim McFarlane for his generosity and patience in answering my probably foolish queries. Any remaining errors are mine.

The lines 'Come back early or never come' and 'My mother wore a yellow dress; Gently, gently, gentleness' are from Louis MacNeice's poem 'Autobiography' published by Faber and Faber.

The lines 'Happy the man and happy he alone, he who can call today his own. . . .' are John Dryden's translation (or paraphrasing) of Horace, *Odes*, III, 29.

Lines from Dusty Springfield's 'Yesterday When I Was Young', written in 1965 by Charles Aznavour and Herbert Kretsmer. Used by permission: Editions Musicales Charles Aznavour, France, assigned to TRO Essex Music Ltd, London SW10 OS2 International copyright secured. All rights reserved. Released by Dusty in 1972.

'Out of the tree of life I just picked me a plum' is from the song 'Best is Yet to Come' sung by Frank Sinatra. Lyrics written by Kurtis Henneberry, Michael Nadeau, Leif Christensen, Anton Yurack and John O'Leary. Permission to use that line has been sought from Universal Publishing Group, EMI Publishing Group.

The lines 'Oh it's what you do to me' are from 'Hey There Delilah' by the Plain White T's, words and music by Tom Higgenson © 2005 WB Music Corp. (ASCAP), Fear More Music (ASCAP) and So Happy Publishing (ASCAP). All rights administered by WB Music Corp.

My thanks are also due to the best agent and editor a writer could have: Caroline Dawnay and Carole Welch respectively. Also to their assistants Sophie Scard and Lucy Foster and to the copy-editor, Celia Levett. Most of all, I'd like to thank the friends who sustain me during the writing of my novels: Sally Cline, Louise Doughty, Kathryn Heyman, Suzanne Howlett and Geraldine Maxwell.